THE HIKE

Sunday Times bestseller Lucy Clarke was inspired to write *The Hike* after trekking through the wild, rugged beauty of Norway with a tent on her back. She is the author of seven other destination thrillers, which include Waterstones Thriller of the Month selection, *The Castaways*, and Richard and Judy Book Club pick, *One of the Girls*.

Lucy's novels have sold over a million copies worldwide. *The Blue/No Escape* has been filmed as a major international TV series for Paramount+, and two further novels are currently in development for screen. When Lucy isn't away on research trips (her favourite part of the job!), she can be found writing from a beach hut on the south coast of England. She lives with her husband and their two children.

Keep in touch with Lucy –
www.lucy-clarke.com
@lucyclarke_author
/lucyclarkeauthor

Also by Lucy Clarke

The Sea Sisters
A Single Breath
No Escape (previously published as *The Blue*)
Last Seen
You Let Me In
The Castaways
One of the Girls

THE
HIKE

LUCY CLARKE

HarperCollins*Publishers*

HarperCollins*Publishers* Ltd
1 London Bridge Street,
London SE1 9GF

www.harpercollins.co.uk

HarperCollins*Publishers*
Macken House, 39/40 Mayor Street Upper,
Dublin 1, D01 C9W8, Ireland

First published by HarperCollins*Publishers* 2023
2

A catalogue record for this book is available from the British Library

ISBN: 978-0-00-846242-0 (HB)
ISBN: 978-0-00-846243-7 (TPB)

Typeset in Sabon by Palimpsest Book Production Ltd, Falkirk, Stirlingshire

Printed and bound in the UK using 100% Renewable
Electricity by CPI Group (UK) Ltd

This book is produced from independently certified FSC™ paper to ensure
responsible forest management.

For more information visit: www.harpercollins.co.uk/green

For Matt Clarke

PROLOGUE

Her body lies broken on the mountainside. It rests on a bed of dark rock, a thin pillow of green lichen beneath her cracked skull.

Her irises hold the reflection of the sky, clouds travelling across unseeing pupils. Her face is undamaged – almost unnervingly so – her skin pale and clear. The breeze carries the scent of earth, salt, blood. It toys with a wisp of hair at her temple, then worries the collar of her top. Other than that, she is still.

Blafjell mountain towers above her, an impassive, brute witness. It saw everything but tells nothing.

In a few hours' time, the first person on the scene will check her pulse. Radio in.

They will speculate about what went wrong. Question why her pack is missing. Why there are crescents of dried blood beneath her fingernails. Why four heart-like bruises kiss the top of her left arm.

Police will want to speak with the witness who last saw this young woman alive.

Locals will ask why a female hiker was found on the mountain alone.

Loved ones will pilgrimage to the spot, feet pounding the trails in their search for answers.

For now, her body lies alone, undiscovered.

The mountains give away none of their secrets. Yet out there, hidden within their granite folds, someone knows exactly how this woman died.

And why.

ARRIVAL DAY

1

LIZ

Liz knotted the laces of her hiking boots, then eyed herself in the hallway mirror. Her friends would tease her for wearing them to the airport, but there was no space in her backpack. She'd been scrupulous with her packing. She enjoyed the efficiency of it, the paring back, whittling down, every gram counting. It was pleasing to be able to step out with everything she needed on her back. There was an autonomy about it that she liked – maybe a little too much.

She checked her watch. If she left now, she'd arrive at Helena's fifteen minutes ahead of schedule. Her backpack was waiting in the car. The tank was filled with petrol. Her checklist was ticked. There was nothing left for her to do except say goodbye.

Hard to believe that, by this evening, she, Helena and Maggie would be in Norway. It had been her turn to choose the holiday destination. In previous years she'd picked Corfu, Madeira, the south of France. She'd loved those beach holidays – the kiss of the sun, the buzz of being with girlfriends, the languid days poolside – but recently she'd been thirsting for something different. She was thirty-three, a wife, a mother, a GP. Her everyday life was organised, buttoned down, scheduled. What she needed was an adventure.

'You're serious?' Helena baulked when Liz pitched the idea of four days wild hiking and camping in Norway.

Liz was. 'I've always wanted to see the fjords and mountains.'

'So book a cruise.'

A few months earlier, thanks to a broken fan belt that the garage took an age to repair, Liz had been forced to walk into the surgery. As she'd walked, something magical seemed to happen; with each step, it was as if she were shaking off the chaos of lost homework, packed lunches and missing uniform items. She noticed birdsong, learned the names of the trees she passed, took the time to wave good morning to neighbours. By the time she arrived at work, her thoughts felt more spacious, her body grateful for the movement. She had been out in the weather and felt the day. The action of moving her feet, step after step, meant she arrived fresh and energised.

Liz being Liz, she wanted to understand the physiological benefits of walking, so she'd dived into the research. She discovered that regular walking improved the immune system, lowered cholesterol, and strengthened feelings of wellbeing. She shared these findings with her patients. 'I'm prescribing you a daily walk.' It was simple, free, do-able for most. Life-changing in some cases.

Right now, Liz needed *life-changing*.

She glanced towards the kitchen. She could hear the morning symphony of breakfast: the clink of bowls set on the table, the gush of the tap, the scrape of a stool, Evie's voice pitched above Daniel's, the calming tone of Patrick mellowing them both.

She moved towards the noise and warmth of her family. The thick-soled tread of her boots made her gait feel unfamiliar. She found herself standing in the kitchen doorway unnoticed and – for a few disconcerting moments – it was as if she were watching someone else's life. How much would they miss her, she wondered? Patrick knew the routines of family life so well:

he was the one who made the packed lunches, did the school run, and helped with homework.

Evie, hair mussed from sleep, was the first to spot her. 'Mummy! Are you leaving now?'

'Yes,' she said, feeling tears lodged at the back of her throat. She'd never liked protracted goodbyes. Out the door and get on with it. That was best.

Patrick turned, warm brown eyes sliding over her face, but not meeting her gaze. 'So, you're picking up Helena first? Then Maggie?'

'Then Norway here we come.' She tried for upbeat, but her tone fell flat.

'Please get a photo of Helena in hiking gear!' He grinned.

Liz moved towards her son, who was sitting at the breakfast bar, shovelling cornflakes into his mouth. She pressed a kiss on his cheek, feeling the machinations of his jaw.

Evie put down her spoon to wobble a front tooth, asking, 'Will this have fallen out by the time you're back?'

Liz nodded. She would probably return to find her daughter with a new gap in her perfect line of baby teeth. She would miss that sweet moment of slipping into a dark room to swap a tissue-wrapped tooth for a shiny pound coin.

She was used to missing things: Evie's first word (Dan-dan); Daniel's first steps across the lounge floor – caught in Patrick's arms; watching the twins in their first swimming lesson. But there were many more things that she had been there for, and Liz knew that tallying up the misses and the been-there-fors only led to a scorecard etched in guilt.

'Look after each other while I'm away,' she said, breathing them in. She kissed their heads; told them she loved them.

She followed Patrick to the front door. He opened it onto a sun-bright September morning and there was something about the gesture that made Liz feel like a guest.

'Excited?' he asked.

She forced a smile, nodding. 'I'll see you when . . .' she faltered. She wouldn't see him when she got back. The arrangement was a month apart. A trial separation, taking it in turns to be out of the house so it wouldn't affect the children: a week in Norway for her, then a week for him visiting his brother, and then more switching and organising on her return. A month apart to give them time to decide what they wanted.

What do you want? she wondered, looking briefly at Patrick.

'Bye, Liz,' he said, leaning down to press a kiss against her cheek. He smelled of toast and coffee and the fabric of their home.

She had a strange vertiginous feeling – as if she needed to reach out, grip onto his solidity, as the rest of the world spun away from her.

She blinked quickly, looking down at her neatly laced hiking boots. She took a deep breath, then turned and stepped out of her life.

2

HELENA

Helena eyed her backpack. It leaned with jaunty arrogance against her front door, blocking her exit. Buckles and straps strained against the bulk of its contents. She'd cut the price tag from it this morning, nicking her thumb with the nail scissors. A single bead of blood had dripped onto the front of the pack, leaving a tiny dark stain. If Maggie noticed it, she'd believe it was a bad omen. But Helena didn't believe in omens. She believed she needed to be more careful with scissors.

She sipped her coffee, luxuriating in the deep, velvety flavour, knowing it would be her last Aero-Pressed coffee for a while. Four sachets of instant coffee were sealed in a pocket of her backpack – one for each morning of the hike. She'd Googled travel-sized coffee makers, picturing the romance of one perched on a hissing camp stove, framed by a beautiful Norwegian backdrop. She'd liked the image enough to press *Buy*, but once the coffee maker had arrived and she'd laid it out on the spare bed alongside the other packages that landed almost daily – dry bags, waterproof over-trousers, merino wool socks, two-man tent, down sleeping bag, lightweight roll mat, camping stove, gas canister – she knew she couldn't justify the extra weight.

She moved cautiously towards the backpack, the way you

might approach a wary horse, slowly placing a palm to its flank. Was she really going to lug this through the wilderness for four days?

She laughed at the absurdity of it. Her, Helena Hall, going wild camping in Norway!

Bloody Liz. It was her year to choose the destination. When it had been Helena's turn three years earlier, she'd picked Ibiza. Even Joni had shown up, flying in for two nights in the middle of her tour schedule, hooking them up with VIP club passes. The four of them had spent a week lazing in the sunshine, swimming in rocky coves, and partying until sundown. That was a holiday.

Hiking in Norway? *It'll be an adventure*, Liz had assured them, her lips working a bit too hard to stretch into a smile. Still. She wasn't going to stick here alone in her flat while the others went off together. When you're single in your thirties, you jump at the chance to go anywhere with your girlfriends.

Earlier in the week she'd messaged Liz at midnight: *Toilets! Where do I go for a crap?* And Liz had sent back an emoji of a poo and a forest – and then sent a link to a trowel.

Fine. It was going to be absolutely fine.

She finished her coffee, rinsed and dried the mug, then returned it to the cupboard, handle pointing outward. She smoothed her hands against her thighs. Looked around. The granite surfaces were empty. The downlights switched off.

She glanced at her watch. Liz would be here in fifteen minutes.

Moving into her bedroom, she looked wistfully through the open window onto the city. Outside, the early September light held a golden warmth to it – the last breath of summer. Her city – Bristol – smelled of diesel and concrete and warm bins. She filled her lungs with it. Oh, the beauty of pavements, and buildings, and traffic, and the clip of heeled footwear. Not a hiking boot or fleece in sight. She pulled the window closed reluctantly.

She caught sight of a package resting on her dressing table, still in a carrier bag. She eyed it for a moment, lips pressed together, heart rate picking up speed, deliberating. Then she snatched it up, tore free the bag, and stared at the pregnancy test.

A hot flush of dread swam through her. She didn't want to take the test. She didn't want to even *look* at it. But she needed to get it done. Then she could put it behind her and enjoy the trip. It would be a good anecdote for the plane. Liz and Maggie could poke fun at her feckless single lifestyle.

She ripped open the box and scanned the instructions without reading a word. She knew the drill. Pee on a stick. Wait for three minutes, sweating.

She carried it to the en suite, irked to notice her hands were trembling.

Do I even need a wee? she wondered, slipping down her knickers and crouching over the toilet.

She held the pregnancy test between her legs. Closed her eyes. Tried to concentrate on relaxing.

She'd been poised for only a moment when the door buzzer blared. 'Christ!' she cried, leaping from the seat.

She snapped up her knickers, then strode into the hallway, zipping up her trousers.

'It's me!' Liz's voice beamed through the intercom. 'I'm outside.'

Course Liz would be early.

'You ready?' she trilled.

Glancing at the unused pregnancy test, she felt a bolt of irritation at Liz for arriving early – but, beneath that, Helena felt a sense of reprieve, of a bullet dodged.

She pressed her mouth to the speaker. 'Ready.'

11

3

MAGGIE

Maggie studied her daughter, watching her tiny fist gripping the crayon, the tip of her tongue poking from the corner of her mouth as she concentrated.

Outside, gravel crunched beneath tyres. Phoebe looked up, eyes large and round. A crease appeared on her otherwise smooth brow. 'Daddy?'

Maggie made sure her voice came out warm and bright. 'Yes.' She glanced at the kitchen clock: he was an hour late. *Arsehole.*

'Don't want to go.'

'I know,' Maggie said, opening her arms to the warmth and weight of Phoebe's body as she climbed into them. She pressed her face into her daughter's neck, inhaling the sweetness of her skin.

Phoebe had never stayed at Aidan's. Maggie had put it off, citing the need for breastfeeding, and later co-sleeping, but now that Phoebe was three, Aidan had insisted that he finally have her overnight. It was fair, she knew that. She did. And Maggie wanted him and Phoebe to have a relationship – yet the thought of being apart from her was a physical, wrenching pain. There was something instinctive and primal about the need for her

12

daughter's flesh to be pressed to hers, to feel her heartbeat each night through her cotton pyjamas.

That's why Norway had come at the right time. Maggie couldn't stay at home without Phoebe. Every corner of their rented cottage was lined with reminders of Phoebe: the farmhouse door covered with curling paintings; the pine table where they had milk and biscuits in the afternoons; the giant beanbag they flopped in for story time; the windowsill where they'd planted cress in tiny pots made from newspapers.

She heard the exhale of brakes as the car pulled to a stop in front of the house. The engine quietened. A door opened and closed. Footsteps on gravel.

Maggie pasted on a big smile as she carried Phoebe to the door, saying, 'You'll have such a fun week.'

The doorbell rang.

Maggie wrapped her fingers around the handle and steeled herself.

'Auntie Helena!' Phoebe beamed, wriggling out of Maggie's arms.

Helena was standing in the doorway, in cropped black trousers, red lipstick, her dark bob sleek. She crouched low, opening her arms as Phoebe barrelled into them.

'We thought you were Daddy!' Phoebe cried.

'Oh no. I'm much better-looking than Daddy.'

Behind her, Liz, dressed in full hiking gear, stepped forward and gave Maggie a huge hug.

Helena glanced up, eyebrow cocked. 'Not here yet?'

Late, Maggie mouthed.

Helena rolled her eyes.

'I'm scared,' Phoebe said, sidling even closer to Helena, fingers reaching for the gold horseshoe that hung from a delicate chain on her neck. 'Are you a pony?'

'Not today, because ponies can't pass through airport security. But sometimes I am.'

Phoebe nodded sincerely.

'Now, tell me: why are you scared?'

Phoebe pointed at the bright purple case and folded duvet that waited in the hallway. A cuddly leopard was sitting guard on top. 'I'm going to Daddy's house. I might want to go home.'

Maggie felt her heart squeeze tight. She had to stop herself from reaching for Phoebe, telling her, *You don't have to go. We'll stay here! Mummy won't leave!*

'Ah,' Helena said, her expression matching Phoebe's seriousness. 'Yes, I have that feeling sometimes. In fact,' she lowered her voice, 'I have that feeling right now.'

'In true life?'

'Yes, in true life. You see, Liz is making me go to Norway and camp in the mountains – and I've not done that before, and I'm a bit scared that I might want to go home.'

Phoebe tilted her head, considering Liz.

'I'm not exactly *making* her . . .' Liz added.

Phoebe looked unconvinced. After a moment, she strode to her case, plucked the stuffed leopard from its perch, and held it out to Helena. 'You can borrow Leopold.'

Maggie bit down on her bottom lip. Leopold was Phoebe's favourite toy. She slept with him tucked beneath her chin, the fur on his collar worn thin from loving him so hard.

'Oh, sweetheart,' Helena said, 'you are the kindest. But Leopold might be nervous about staying somewhere new, too, so you need to look after him, okay?'

Through the open door, they all turned to see Aidan's red sports car crawling down the narrow lane. The paintwork. He'd hate to scratch the paintwork.

He parked behind Liz's Ford and cut the engine. A moment later he stepped out with expansive arms, beaming. 'Phoebe!'

Phoebe pressed herself against Maggie's legs, tiny fingers bunching around the skirt of her lemon dress.

'Hello, Aidan,' Maggie said, trying her hardest to smile and mean it.

'Maggie.' He nodded. 'Liz. Helena.'

Helena was watching him with the disdainful expression reserved just for him. It was something to do with the poise of her jaw line, her chin lifted just a few degrees higher than most people's, giving the impression that she was literally looking down her nose at him. And in Aidan's case, she was.

He scanned the exterior of Maggie's terrace, and she could guess he'd be noticing the peeling paint where the render showed, or the overgrown window box she'd not had the chance to weed. What he couldn't see was the fun she and Phoebe had had planting those flowers together, tucking seeds into secret earthy beds in the spring, and afterwards soaking their hands in a sink of warm water, popping soap bubbles with crescents of earth still pressed beneath their fingernails. Aidan had always seen mess where Maggie saw joy.

'You all ready, trooper?' he said, stepping forward and ruffling Phoebe's hair. 'I've got a treat for you in the car!'

Already with the counterfeit love, Maggie thought.

'Let's get you buckled in,' Maggie said bravely, scooping up Phoebe. She carried her to the car, pressing her love into her daughter, ingraining it, their bodies stamped with each other.

She fastened the belt as she told her, 'I love you so much, baby. I'll miss you. Look after Leopold, okay?'

Phoebe nodded. Then she whispered, 'Look after Auntie Helena. She's scared of the mountains.'

'I will,' Maggie said, smiling. She kissed her and kissed her and kissed her, and then she forced herself to step back, close the car door, mouthing, 'I love you.'

15

Behind her, Aidan was remarking to her friends, '*Maggie's* climbing this mountain?'

With a smile, Helena replied, 'She was married to you for two years, so scaling a mountain should feel like a walk in the park.'

Maggie had a thousand things she wanted to say to him – *If Phoebe wakes in the night, sing her 'Twinkle Twinkle Little Star'. She crashes after eating too much sugar. Don't plonk her in front of the television when you get bored. Don't drink too much when you're with her* – but all she said was, 'Please, keep her safe.'

Phoebe's face was turned to the car window, eyes glistening with tears, Leopold squeezed to her chest.

No, she couldn't do this. Couldn't let her go. As she stepped forward, she felt Helena catch her hand. Liz linked her arm through Maggie's other, her friends holding her up from each side.

Aidan started the engine. Phoebe's palm was flattened to the window as if she were trying to break free.

'The dance,' Helena said, kicking out her left leg like a show-girl. 'Do the dance.'

Maggie's throat constricted. A sob was heaving up from her chest.

'Do the dance. Right now, Maggie. Do it!'

It was a dance from a musical they'd watched one afternoon last winter, and Phoebe had thought it was the funniest thing when Auntie Helena and her mummy copied the moves, can-canning their legs, while making jazz hands.

Helena kicked her other leg, Liz joining in. 'Come on!'

Maggie forced herself to kick out her right leg, then her left, falling into rhythm with her friends, the breeze filling her dress.

Making jazz hands, Helena said, 'There we go! We're dancing! We're moving! We're waving!'

Phoebe's little mouth lifted into a smile, her fingers peeling away from the glass as she gave her own little jazz-fingered wave.

They carried on dancing as the car crawled down the lane, until it had disappeared altogether, and Phoebe was gone.

'It's okay, Mags,' Helena said, 'you can stop dancing now.'

Maggie felt her body collapse into her friends, who held on tight.

'That's the hardest bit – the leaving. And you've done it.' Liz squeezed her as she said, 'Now you get to look forward to the coming home, okay?'

Maggie sat in the back seat on the way to the airport. She'd stopped crying about twenty miles ago, but a tension headache still viced her temples.

In the seat pocket, she spotted an age-worn book from their schooldays. N-O-R-W-A-Y was spelled on the front in bubble writing, coloured in the red, white and blue of the Norwegian flag. Liz and Joni's names were written beneath.

'Your Geography project!' Maggie said, pulling it onto her lap. 'You found it!'

'It was in the attic,' Liz said.

Beneath the title was a picture of a woman standing on a pinnacle that jutted from a sheer-sided mountain, arms spread wide to a clear sky, an arctic-blue sea stretching west, and below her, the trace of a silver river, cutting through a landscape made of undulating hills and valleys.

'So this is the mountain we're going to climb?' Maggie asked.

Liz nodded. 'That's the one. Blafjell.'

Maggie remembered that, as teens, Liz and Joni had made a pact during Geography class that, one day, they'd hike to that spot together. It had been February. A relentless grey sky. A world of school bells, damp satchels and wet concrete. The mountains had looked like a different world – one they wanted to explore. She'd seen them pinky-promise, little fingers hooked together across their school desks.

'Still no word from Joni?' Maggie asked.

'Nothing,' Liz said.

Maggie caught the arch of Helena's brow in the rear-view mirror.

It would be the second year running that Joni hadn't shown up for their holiday. She'd been silent on the group chat for weeks.

'She's touring,' Liz said, loyally, but Maggie knew how disappointed Liz must have been. Joni was always good company: game for anything, happy to strap on a backpack, or laugh when she needed to shit in the woods. She'd have made everything golden and more fun because she was Joni.

'Let's send her a photo,' Maggie said, passing her phone up front to Helena.

Helena leaned in so all their faces were in shot. Liz took a hand briefly from the wheel to salute. Helena pushed out her red lips in an exaggerated duck pout. Maggie gave the peace sign. The shutter clicked.

Taking back the phone, Maggie stared at the image. Then she typed: *There's still time* – and pressed *Send*.

4

JONI

Naked except for a black thong, Joni staggered across the hotel suite in search of her leather jacket. She passed a mirrored table covered with empty champagne bottles, lipstick-kissed glasses, and a powder-trail of coke. A girl she'd never seen before was sprawled on the chaise-longue, a false eyelash dusting her cheek.

Through the open door to the bedroom, she could hear Kai's ragged snores, and beyond that the drone of traffic mixed with music pulsing from a speaker somewhere.

She screwed up her eyes. *What city is this? What country am I in?*

Two solid knots of pain were lodged at her temples. Her throat felt like bark. She hadn't warmed up last night. She'd been running late because—

Berlin! she recalled with a surge of relief. That's right! They'd played at Huxley's. A packed crowd, a girl bursting onto stage during the final song, T-shirt soaked with sweat . . .

The thought broke free as she spotted her jacket slumped on the floor. She crouched, bare knees pressing into the thick carpet, patting down the pockets. Her short nails were polished black, a lightning bolt striking her left thumb. Joni hadn't asked for the lightning – Rhianne, her make-up artist, couldn't

19

have known Joni was terrified of thunderstorms. As she'd snatched her hand away, Rhianne had protested, 'But I've only done one bolt!'

Joni had glanced down at her still-wet nails and shrugged. 'Lightning never strikes twice.'

She wanted the polish off. Wanted the hairspray cleaned from her waves of dark hair. Wanted last night's sweat and sex washed from her body. Wanted to stand under a steaming shower and scrub away every trace of herself.

There! She pulled the bag of coke from the breast pocket, her phone tumbling out, too. Only enough for a couple of bumps. She'd always claimed she only did party drugs. A hit of coke and a couple of shots before a gig to get her sparkly, then afterwards champagne and more coke to keep the vibe high, and then a bit of weed and a couple of pills to take the tempo down and help her sleep. So what was this, then? A hit to get her going in the morning? She'd seen others on this path. Wasn't going to follow it.

I'm slipping.

A child's laughter drifted through the open window, and she glanced towards the sound, squinting into the stream of light. She wanted to catch a glimpse of them and the parent they were walking with. Were they holding hands? Were they going for breakfast? Going shopping? She wanted to know, watch. She couldn't say why. Maybe she just needed to know there were good things out there.

Her phone beeped with a notification. She glanced at the screen and her heart contracted: a photo of Liz, Helena and Maggie, squeezed into Liz's car. They were grinning, faces clean and wide-eyed and fresh. And so damn beautiful! Liz, one hand on the wheel, another saluting. Helena, glossy black bob cut blunt to her chin, pouting. Maggie leaning forward, cheeks kissed with freckles, hazel eyes crinkling with warmth as she gave the peace sign. They were there, right now, together, hurtling towards an adventure.

A strange, uneasy sensation washed through Joni, as if she were looking at them from a distance, watching something that had already happened, and she could never reach.

The message read: *There's still time.*

Joni shook her head, teeth clenched. *You're wrong.* She could taste her own breath, foul and craggy, feel the greasy layers of last night's stage make-up. She was filled with disgust and shame and a seething self-hatred, violent enough to feel as if she were ripping open. Yet there was nothing left inside her to spill out, and the emptiness felt terrifying.

She dropped the phone and staggered towards the low table, swiping aside bottles and glasses. She tapped out some coke on its mirrored surface, peaks of a snowcapped mountain waiting to carry her away from herself, fill that space with a brief, golden light.

As she leaned down, a fingertip pressed to a nostril, she caught her reflection. She looked bleak, like someone she didn't recognise. She emptied the whole bag of cocaine over her reflection. She needed to obliterate herself. She wanted to die.

To die.

The thought made her lurch back, shocked at herself.

She clutched her hands to her mouth, as if she were scared she'd say those words aloud and then it'd mean something.

She was shaking.

She rushed across the suite into the main bedroom, foot connecting with an empty bottle, which she sent spinning, clattering into the bed leg. She heard Kai shift, grunt, saw a tattooed calf hanging off the bed.

She pulled on an oversized jumper and pair of denim shorts, grabbed her leather jacket and bag.

Shoes! Where are my shoes?

She scanned the bedroom. Then the main lounge. Her gaze caught on the line of coke still dusting the table – and she felt the pull in her body, something tidal dragging her out to sea.

Leave. Leave right now. The voice was there, deep inside her.

She left the hotel room, took the lift, then hurried across the polished lobby floor and emerged into the Berlin morning, barefoot.

She raised a hand for a taxi. The other she kept in her pocket, fingertips resting against the smooth screen of her phone: *There's still time.*

5

LIZ

Liz stared from the plane window. The landscape glimmered with rivers, lakes and fjords. Thrusting mountains rose from the earth, the tallest crowned white with snow. There were so few towns or buildings or roads, just earth and water and sky.

A flutter of fear brushed her chest: they were going to be hiking out there.

'Another?' Helena asked from the aisle seat, holding up a mini bottle of wine.

Liz shook her head. 'I'll be driving soon.' Once they landed in Bergen, a long drive north awaited them. She'd booked them into a lodge in the foothills of the Svelle mountain range, where they'd spend their first night before setting out the following morning.

Maggie, who was wedged between them, a book face down on her tray table, asked, 'How many hours a day do you think we'll walk?'

'Seven, maybe eight,' Liz answered. Seeing Maggie's expression, she added, 'You'll be fine. All the training will pay off.'

Maggie picked up her plastic wine glass and took a drink.

'How are you feeling about being disconnected from the office?' Liz asked Helena.

Helena turned over her phone and looked at the screen. 'I feel like my phone and I could use some distance.'

Helena owned an events company and ran huge corporate days for clients like BMW and Hilton. She was sharply organised, brilliant at negotiating, and charged a premium for it – but it meant her clients expected her to be accessible all hours.

'You've been working so hard,' Liz said. 'You deserve a holiday.'

'Now that we're on the plane,' Helena said, 'I think we can stop pretending this is a holiday.'

Liz grinned. 'You agreed to it!'

'It's our annual trip. You could've suggested shark diving in South Africa, and I'd have been there. Always going to show up.'

Liz felt a warm burst of love for Helena.

Helena poured the remains of the wine into her plastic glass and said, 'Good to catch up with Patrick last month.'

'He talked about that steak place for days.'

'He's my favourite vegetarian,' Helena said with a smile. 'He seemed well. Great that he's getting commissions from the Clifton shop.'

'It is.' Patrick serviced and repaired grandfather clocks, and if he had a delivery in Bristol, he'd sometimes meet Helena for dinner or a drink.

'You guys good?'

Her alert signals went up. Had Patrick said something? She was sure he wouldn't.

Sharing any complaint about their marriage felt disloyal. Patrick was Helena, Maggie and Joni's friend, too. He'd been two years above them at school – best friends with Liz's older brother – so they'd known him as the teenager who skated to class, smoked in the woods, and wore the same Nirvana *Unplugged* T-shirt for two straight years. Liz had had a crush

on him since she was thirteen, finally kissing him at their leavers'
ball, while Helena, Maggie and Joni cheered from the wings of
the dance floor.

Liz had never kissed anyone else since. It had once been a
point of pride – but more recently, it had begun to trouble her.
She'd never moved away from her hometown, either. Never had
any job but medicine. Never dated anyone but Patrick. The
others had all done so much with their lives. Maggie had been
a waitress, a flower arranger, a reflexologist, and now made
bespoke name prints using pressed flowers. Helena had moved
from the council-owned flat where she'd grown up, working
her way up the career ladder, and now ran her own business
and owned three properties. Joni's music had taken her all over
the world, touring in major cities and recording albums in some
of the most famous studios.

What had Liz done? Moved two streets down from the house
where she grew up. Married her childhood sweetheart. Worked
in the surgery where she used to be a patient.

'Y'okay?' Helena asked.

Liz blinked. She realised she'd been wringing her hands. She
separated them, flattening her palms against her thighs.

Maggie and Helena were watching her with puzzled expressions.

'I'm fine,' she said. 'We're fine. Patrick's great.'

Maybe she was having a mid-life crisis. That could be it.
Some people embarked on an affair or bought a sports car –
while she bullied her friends into going wild camping in the
wilderness.

She glanced out of the window. God, she hated flying. Too
much sitting still. She'd be fine once they were hiking. That's
what she needed. To get out on the trail. *Walk.*

6

MAGGIE

'Almost there,' Liz said, putting the rental vehicle into a lower gear as they bumped down a single-track lane.

The mountain range to the west was cloaked in cloud, so all Maggie could see was forest-lined foothills rising into billowing white mist. Late summer colours had darkened with the coming season shift. They rounded a bend, and a wide lake was revealed, its dark, still surface like the back of a shining beetle. At its foot crouched a timber mountain lodge.

Liz pulled up on a gravel lot beside a pick-up truck loaded with logs. She cut the ignition, unclipped her seat belt, then threw open the door.

A sharp breeze, scored with the scent of rock, blasted into the car. Maggie shivered.

Liz stood with her hands planted on her hips, staring at the mountains. She'd travelled in her hiking gear – boots, technical trousers, and a navy fleece – and looked ready to stride out. 'This really is wilderness,' she said, and Maggie wondered if there was a hint of fear in her voice.

Helena turned in her seat. 'You coming, Mags?'

She swallowed. Her legs were stiff as she climbed out. The wind lifted the hem of her dress, and she pulled her cardigan around her shoulders. Tension fizzed down the left side of her spine, her emotions showing themselves in her body.

Maggie had always considered her home on the outskirts of Bath as living in the sticks. She saw herself as someone who loved nature and the wild outdoors. But as she stood here, drinking in a landscape carved from rock and ice, strewn with lakes and forest, thrumming beneath a wind-blasted sky, she understood her previous scale of wild had been annihilated. On the long drive here, they'd been drawn through dense forests of unbroken green. Mountains had risen from the earth, their peaks swallowed by cloud. They'd passed rivers so deep and muscular they seemed to tear through the landscape.

Apart from the lodge, she couldn't see a single other building. *This* wild was dizzying. It was too much. Too big. She felt suddenly panicky, like she'd made a terrible mistake. She was beginning to sweat. The scenery looked rugged, beautiful even, something to be marvelled at through a window, but hiking through it? Climbing mountain paths? Sleeping out *there*?

Liz had heaved their backpacks from the car and was wrestling hers onto her shoulders. 'I'll check us in.'

Maggie didn't move.

Helena said to Liz, 'We'll follow.'

Liz locked the car, then strode towards the lodge entrance, her top half obscured by her backpack.

Helena bumped her shoulder against Maggie's, asking, 'Y'okay?'

She shook her head. 'There's so much . . . space. It's too big. Too much of everything . . . I feel so far from home . . . from Phoebe.' She pulled her phone from her dress pocket, blinking at the screen. 'I've only got one bar of signal. What if I can't call Phoebe? I need to be able to speak to her. What if there's a problem? If she needs me?'

Maggie knew she shouldn't be complaining to Helena – she

was the one who'd paid for her flights as Maggie couldn't afford to come – yet all her anxieties were suddenly spooling out, unstoppable. 'Remember that exercise regime Liz sent through? The one I said I did? I lied. I printed it off. Stuck it to the fridge. Planned to follow it . . . but . . .' She shook her head. 'I know I sound like one of those mothers who make excuses because they have children – but honestly, there was no time to go on training hikes. Phoebe is too heavy to carry now, and the only time I have to myself are the two mornings she's in pre-school, but that's when I do my Etsy orders.'

She glanced towards the lodge as Liz disappeared inside. 'Liz told me to do Joe Wicks's workouts in the evenings instead.' She grimaced. 'I did three. Well. Two. And the final one, I only managed three burpees, before collapsing on the sofa and watching Joe doing squats and lunges while I ate biscuits. And now I'm out here, completely unfit, and I'm going to let you all down and . . . it would be better if I just left. That's what I should do. Yes. I should go. I know you paid for my trip – and God, you're so generous and good to me, and I feel terrible that now I'm saying I want to go home – but I do. I want to go home.' She was nodding feverishly. 'I'm a shit friend, but I need to leave. I'll go back – use the time to get some jobs done. Paint the window frames. Clear out the shed. Reseed the bare patches in the lawn . . .' She trailed off, finally running out of words.

Helena was looking at her steadily. She arched a single, dark brow as she said, 'You'd like to go home and reseed your lawn?'

Maggie lifted her shoulders.

Helena pressed her red lips together. 'You know that you always do this, right?'

'What?'

'Get scared. Want to leave. Remember the holiday to Barcelona when you wanted to turn back at the airport?'

Maggie thought for a moment, recalling how she hadn't liked

the high-rise buildings, or the smell of tar from the roadworks, and that everything felt unfamiliar and out of balance. 'I always do this?'

'The long weekend in France?'

She thought back. 'I got heat rash and worried it was an infectious disease and decided I should go home to be in the care of the NHS.'

'That's right. By tomorrow you'll be fine. You'll be raring to climb these mountains.'

'Raring?'

'Maybe not raring. But you'll have made peace with it.'

Maggie sighed, feeling a sense of relief. 'It's true though, about watching Joe Wicks working out while I ate biscuits.'

'I watch him while taking a bath.'

Maggie grinned.

'Maybe don't mention the lack of exercise thing to Liz. She keeps doing her thousand-megawatt-smile, which means she's secretly crapping herself, too.'

'Do you think I can do this? The hike?'

Helena eyed her. 'Y'know why I paid for your trip?'

'For my charming monologues and emotional intelligence?'

'Because I wanted to hike with someone who'd hate it even more than me.' She toed Maggie's backpack, then her own. 'Come on. Let's see if we can lift these bastards.'

7

LIZ

With thumbs hooked beneath the straps of her backpack, Liz gazed up as she entered the lodge. She breathed in the pine scent of new wood. Traditional timber walls met a huge glass expanse that stretched across the south-facing wall. The glass framed the jaw-dropping view of the lake and surrounding mountains. A large woodstove was positioned in one corner of the lodge; low seating surrounded it, draped with furs.

Near the entrance, a tall man in his late fifties was sitting alone at a wooden bench, wearing a faded plaid shirt buttoned to the collar. A dark peaked cap cast his eyes in shadow. At his feet, a wire-haired dog was licking its paw.

'Hello,' Liz beamed, elated to have arrived.

He responded with a nod, eyes following her as she moved towards reception.

The reception desk, carved from a single trunk sanded smooth, housed a slim laptop, red folder, and no staff.

An open door led into a small office, where Liz could see the profile of a broad-shouldered man dressed in shorts, socks and hiking boots. His thick, sandy-brown hair was pulled into a topknot, revealing a square jaw and neatly trimmed beard.

He stood with a hand slung in a pocket, face set as he listened to someone speaking rapid Norwegian out of sight.

Not wanting to interrupt, Liz pulled off her backpack, glad to be free of its weight, and propped it against the desk. She stepped towards a hiking map pinned to a noticeboard. She loved maps. It was the combination of precise organisation married to the promise of adventure.

Using a fingertip, she orientated herself from the lodge, noting the array of day hikes circling the lake, or cutting deep into woodland. Her gaze travelled beyond those to a longer, red-dashed route that marked the four-day Svelle trail.

She felt the creases of the map as she traced the path west of the lake, passing through a valley, then alongside a river, near which she planned for the group to spend their first night wild camping. After that, they'd cross the foothills of a mountain that would deliver them to a remote stretch of coastline where they'd camp on the beach. She let her gaze swim out across the Norwegian Sea, where nothing lay on the horizon as it swept north towards the Arctic.

She swallowed as she tracked the final – and hardest – leg of the hike: a steep ascent up the north face of Blafjell, followed by a ridge-top crossing connecting to a second peak. They would need to make the ascent in a single day to ensure they were safely off the ridge and camping lower down the mountain on their final night. After that, it should be a straightforward return to the lodge.

Hearing raised voices from the office, Liz turned. The broad-shouldered man with the topknot was still listening, palms opening. There was a long silence. Then he exhaled, pushed his hands deep into his pockets, and gave a firm nod, eyes lowered.

A moment later, a second man with white-blond hair cropped close to his head exited the office. His skin was even and deeply tanned, setting off ice-blue eyes as he smiled at Liz. He crossed the atrium – the wire-haired dog leaping to its feet to receive a pat – before he disappeared through a doorway leading into a dining hall. Liz glimpsed a group of people gathered around long tables, the boom of voices and laughter competing against the scrape and clink of cutlery. She caught the warming smell of potatoes, meat, and something salted, before the door swung shut.

'Sorry to keep you waiting,' the man with the topknot said, stepping out from the office. He was her sort of age – early thirties – but with the tanned skin of someone who spent their days outdoors. He looked preoccupied, running a hand over his jawline as he said, 'I am Leif. Welcome to the Svelle Lodge. How can I help you?'

She took in his full height and the muscular curvature of his body. He had strong, generous features – a heavy brow, a straight nose, square jawline.

She found herself standing a little taller as she said, 'I have a booking under the name Liz Wallace. There are three of us.' The entrance door swung open, and she turned to see Helena striding in, lipstick on, pack riding high on her shoulders, polished boots clicking across the wooden floor.

Maggie trudged behind, her yellow dress creased by the straps of her backpack, her spine curved beneath its weight. When she reached the reception desk, she flung down her pack and peeled off her cardigan.

Liz saw Leif staring at Maggie wide-eyed. His brow was stretched in surprise as he stood rooted to the spot, as if he recognised her.

Maggie, seemingly unaware of his reaction, pulled out a bottle of water from the side of her pack and took a drink, the skin of her throat flushed.

'You have the booking?' Liz prompted.

Leif blinked quickly, gave a sharp shake of his head, and cleared his throat. 'Yes. Your rooms are ready.'

'Is this us?' Maggie asked, stepping closer to the hiking map. 'The Svelle trail?'

Liz nodded.

Maggie bit down on her lip. 'Looks like a long way.'

'It is a beautiful hike, but challenging in places,' Leif told them in perfect English.

'Do you think we can manage it? It looks so far,' Maggie said, glancing up at him, hands worrying the pockets of her dress.

It irritated Liz that Maggie was always ready to hand over her autonomy to any person with so much as a whiff of authority.

Leif considered his response. 'It is not the distance that causes problems. It is the elevation. The challenging terrain. The possibility of poor weather. The river crossings. People's fitness. You're setting off tomorrow, *ja*?'

They nodded.

'Check the weather. It is changeable in the mountains. And sign the logbook, too,' he said, placing a palm flat against the red folder. 'We like to know when to expect hikers back. The route is meant to be well marked,' Leif went on, 'but the markers aren't always reliable by the end of season, and it's walked so infrequently that I've not had any recent reports about the state of the tracks. You have a map and compass, yes?'

'Yes,' Liz answered.

Maggie asked, 'Will there be mobile coverage out there?'

Leif shook his head. 'The mountains are problematic for coverage. Expect to be out of range most of the time.'

When Maggie's face fell, Leif added, 'You might be in good luck and find reception on a peak – but only if the weather is clear.'

'It'll be fine, Mags,' Liz said with a reassuring smile. 'It's just a few days.'

Outside, a group of young, athletic-looking men passed the lodge, arms laden with firewood and crates of beer. One splintered from the others, shouldering open the lodge door. He was wearing a black sleeveless T-shirt, a thick leather cuff around his wrist, and dragging an amp by its handle. He loped towards Leif, high-fiving him, before shouldering through to the dining hall, where a crowd of voices rose in greeting.

'It is our end-of-season party tonight,' Leif explained. 'It'll be busy. Climbers, hikers, seasoners. Plus, the locals will come up from the village. We are setting up for some music later. If you will like to eat, the kitchen shuts in half an hour.'

As Leif handed them their room keys, an older couple entered the lodge, arm in arm. The woman had deep shadows beneath her eyes, her shoulders rounded.

The man in the peaked cap hadn't moved from his watch on the bench, the dog still sitting obediently by his side, and he greeted the couple as they passed. 'Bjørn. Brit,' he said, nodding at each in turn.

Then Leif came forward to welcome the couple. The woman smiled warmly, placing a hand on his bare forearm. He dipped his head a little, face solemn. They were speaking Norwegian, but Liz could sense an intensity in the greeting. Leif shook the older man's hand, clasping it between both of his. After a few more words, Leif indicated to the dining hall and began to lead them towards it.

As the woman followed, her gaze skirted over their group – and then froze, gaze on Maggie. Her eyes widened. The colour seemed to drain from her face.

Maggie looked back at her, uncertain.

Noticing, Leif began to speak to the older woman in a low voice, placing a hand on her arm and gently steering her towards the dining hall. But even as she walked away, the woman kept glancing back over her shoulder, sad eyes on Maggie.

'What was that?' Maggie whispered as the dining-hall door swung shut behind them. 'Did you see the way she stared at me?'

'Leif did exactly the same when you walked in,' Liz said.

'You look like their daughter,' a voice said from behind them – and they looked up to see the man in the peaked cap rising from the bench, followed by his dog. 'I'm Vilhelm.' Then he looked at Maggie with a thoughtful, considered expression. 'It is your hair,' he said slowly. 'And your eyes, too, I think.'

Maggie blinked. 'Oh. Right . . .'

'But it was like they'd seen a ghost,' Liz said.

Vilhelm nodded sadly. 'Last year Karin disappeared.'

'Disappeared?' Liz repeated, voice hushed.

'She was hiking in the mountains.' He glanced toward the line of dark peaks, his gaze turning distant. 'Never found her way back.'

Liz shivered, as if a cold breeze had just travelled over her skin.

8

HELENA

In the dining hall they were served huge portions of steaming meatballs with creamy potatoes, which they ate from chipped canteen plates. It was no-frills – but Helena gamely scraped the final flecks of potato onto her fork, knowing it would be the last proper meal for the next four days.

When she was finished, she stood. 'My round.'

She slipped through the crowd, making her way to the busy bar. A group of young men swung in, fist-bumping a guy with a carabiner hanging from a loop on his shorts. Central tables were being pushed against the walls to make space for a make-shift stage, where a man with a flaming red mountain logo on his T-shirt was plugging his guitar into an amp.

The barmaid, a middle-aged woman in a thick woollen cardigan, her hair in a single plait, was serving a crowd of hikers wearing Patagonia clothing.

Helena drummed her fingertips on the bar top, waiting. Glancing around the room, she decided that everything in the lodge was so wholesome – the wooden floors, the storm lanterns hanging from the walls, even the people, she thought, looking around at their vital, windblown complexions and healthy smile lines. Their fit, muscular bodies spoke of lives lived outdoors. She doubted there was a Starbucks loyalty card between them.

These were not her people. Helena's people were too busy texting while slurping takeaway coffees to notice a view. Her people wore footwear that inhibited their natural gait and underwear that restricted their breathing. Her people stayed late at the office, and even later at the bars, and only dragged themselves outdoors on a Saturday to forage for a place that served a killer brunch.

She tried – and failed – to catch the barmaid's attention. She sighed, folding her arms across her chest – then winced, dropping her arms. Her breasts felt tender. She eyed her cleavage with suspicion, a flicker of anxiety pricking at her skin. An image of the unused pregnancy test sprang unbidden into her thoughts. She had shoved the test into her backpack before climbing into Liz's car. So now it was out here in Norway, a cloud lurking above the trip.

A man, her own age, with shaved white-blond hair, approached the bar. He wore a fisherman-knit jumper, sleeves pushed up. He rested his forearms on the bar as he waited, a silver watch caught in the weave of golden arm hair.

'Austin!' the barmaid greeted him with a smile. 'How's the boat?' she asked in English.

'All good. All good.'

'What are you drinking?'

He indicated Helena. 'This lady was first.' His gaze travelled across Helena's face, slipping briefly over her body.

Helena leaned across the bar as she said, 'Bottle of merlot and three glasses, please.'

While the barmaid fetched the wine, the man turned his ice-blue eyes squarely onto her. His smile was boyish. 'Are you here to climb or hike?'

'Never been asked that question at a bar before,' she said,

turning more fully towards him. 'Hike. We're supposed to be doing the Svelle trail.'

He raised an eyebrow. 'Supposed?'

'It's a little ambitious.'

'All the best plans are. You are from England?'

She nodded.

'I've always wanted to visit. So much history. Buckingham Palace. The Houses of Parliament. Big Ben.' He listed the names of landmarks like he'd just finished a school project on the capital. 'I want to travel one day,' he told her.

'What's stopping you?'

He blinked as if he'd never considered his answer before. 'Work. Money.' He looked over his shoulder. 'My father.'

The barmaid returned with the bottle of merlot and uncorked it gracelessly. She set it in front of Helena.

The man pulled out a thick wad of notes. 'I will buy this.' He was handsome; something confident, yet boyish, in the wide set of his features, the piercing blue of his eyes.

She tipped her head to one side. 'I don't accept drinks from strangers.'

He hesitated, then – realising his cue – reached out his hand. 'I'm Austin.'

'Helena,' she said, shaking it. 'Now we're not strangers.'

He grinned at her, his palm warm and dry around hers.

She thanked him for the wine, then picked up the bottle and slipped through the crowd back to her friends.

9

MAGGIE

Maggie was only half listening to Liz, who'd spread her hiking map across their table, and was pointing to a steeply contoured section that she'd circled in red. 'We should be able to reach the foot of Blafjell on our second night.'

Maggie was aware of a prickling across the back of her neck and had the sensation that someone was watching her. She waited a few beats, then turned.

In the far corner of the bar, the older couple, Bjørn and Brit, were glancing in her direction. When she looked up, they averted their eyes.

Maggie felt uneasy, her cheeks growing warm. No one wanted to be a doppelgänger of a girl who had disappeared.

Helena returned with the wine, setting down the bottle on the centre of the map and pouring three glasses. 'So, Brown Owl. What's cooking?'

Liz slid the wine to the edge of the map. 'We're talking camping spots. Once we reach Blafjell, there won't be much flat ground at that elevation to pitch our tents, so we need to make sure—'

Maggie felt something brush against her legs and looked down to see the dog from the lobby beneath their table. It had a cracked leather collar that looked too tight, and she leaned down, rubbing his ears affectionately. The dog lifted its head towards her touch.

'Runa, *kom!*' called Vilhelm, its owner.

As the dog loped towards him, its lead caught around the table base, sending a slosh of wine spilling across the map.

'Runa!' Vilhelm growled, freeing the dog's lead. 'I am sorry,' he said, taking a napkin from his pocket.

'It's fine,' Maggie said, stroking the dog.

As Vilhelm blotted the map, Liz's red marking smudged. 'Blafjell,' Vilhelm remarked, peering more closely. 'That is where you are hiking?'

'Yes,' Liz answered.

Vilhelm's gaze remained on the spot, something wary in his expression. 'It is a challenging peak.'

Maggie looked at him closely, sensing that there was more he wanted to say. She waited, but after a moment, he carefully folded the napkin and returned it to his pocket. He tugged on the dog's lead and went to leave.

'Wait,' Maggie said, a strange, cool feeling spreading in her gut. 'Earlier, you said a girl disappeared in these mountains.'

Vilhelm paused. Then slowly, he nodded. 'Karin.'

'Where was she hiking?'

He pressed his lips together, as if he didn't want to say any more – but Maggie could sense his answer in his silence.

'It was Blafjell, wasn't it?'

Vilhelm's gaze lowered. 'That's where she was last seen, yes.'

'Is Blafjell . . . dangerous?' Maggie asked.

'All mountains can be,' Liz said crisply.

Vilhelm nodded at Liz, then made to move away, as if dismissed.

'But there's something about Blafjell, isn't there?' Maggie called after him.

Vilhelm hesitated. Quietly, he said, 'Some locals think that there is . . . an energy about the place. A sense of something larger than us.' He spoke only to Maggie. 'A vibration, if you will. This one knows it. Hackles go up. Ears pinned right back. Starts to whine. Dogs can sense the other.'

Maggie's skin grew cool. 'The other?'

Vilhelm looked directly at her, his gaze clear and intense. 'Something beyond the limit of our understanding. That feeling of unease, of not being alone, that isn't immediately explicable. It's where the mist hangs. Chills you to the bone. Not the temperature. It's a feeling. Like something pressing on your chest.'

Maggie shuddered.

He lowered his voice. 'Blafjell is said to be a . . . *thin* place. You know what that means?'

Slowly, Maggie nodded. She'd read about thin places before. 'It's where the distance between our world and the next is thinner, more permeable.'

'Correct. Where order meets chaos. Where life meets death. Where you see things you'd rather you hadn't, *ja?* I don't go up the mountain. Stick to the forest, the river, the other peaks. Not Blafjell.'

'Thanks for the warning,' Liz said, tone clipped, 'but we'll be fine.'

Vilhelm straightened. Nodded once. Then he tugged lightly on his dog's lead, and the two of them slunk away.

'Think he works for Visit Norway?' Helena asked.

Maggie leaned forward until she could feel the table edge pressing against her lower ribs. 'What if he's right? What if Blafjell is a *thin* place?'

'He's winding us up,' Helena said. 'He probably saw the price tag still on Liz's fleece.'

Maggie looked at the map, tracing the tightening contour

41

lines as the green rush of forest turned pale brown, rock rising out of earth. 'It's over a thousand metres! It looks terrifying.'

'It's a map,' Liz said.

Maggie found herself saying, 'I don't think we should climb it.'

'Because of Vilhelm?' Liz said, incredulous.

'Perhaps we should just do the first part of the trail.'

'It's a circular walk,' Liz said. 'You can't just do a part of it!'

'Blafjell is too high. Too challenging.'

'It won't be if you've done the training,' Liz said shortly.

There was silence.

Maggie felt heat spreading up her neck.

'We're not backing out now,' Liz persisted. 'We've come all this way to hike to Blafjell.'

'I haven't,' Maggie said, shaking her head. 'I'm here because I didn't want to be in the house without Phoebe. And Helena's here because she needs a break from work. The only reason we're in Norway, in this lodge, is because it was your turn to choose, Liz, and we wanted to support you – but why did you have to choose something so hard? So inaccessible for the rest of us?'

'We've done the poolside holiday again and again. I'm over it! I need a change! An adventure. A reset.'

Maggie caught the strained, reedy quality to Liz's voice, as if it was set to crack.

Helena picked up the wine bottle. 'Let's have another drink. Relax. Shake off the day's travelling. We'll feel differently in the morning.'

10

LIZ

Liz needed air. She exited the dining hall, striding through the reception area and out into the cool bite of the evening. The night was pricked with stars and colder than she'd expected. She zipped her fleece to her chin and pushed her hands into her pockets. Took a deep breath.

She shouldn't have been surprised that Maggie was having doubts. That was vintage Maggie. Liz had tried to help her prepare for the hike: she'd sent a training schedule, forwarded links to fitness videos, said she'd look after Phoebe on weekends if she wanted to train – but with Maggie there was always an excuse.

She rolled back her shoulders, trying to shake off the tension. Then she remembered the cigarettes zipped into her fleece pocket. She'd bought them en route to Helena's. Too risky to buy cigarettes in the village where her patients lived. You couldn't be a GP and smoke. It was like being a vegetarian butcher.

She turned the pack in her hand, flicked open the cardboard lid, and lifted them to her nose. Her eyes closed, the honeyed, malted smell of tobacco drew her back to her teenage years when she'd smoke out of Joni's bedroom window while Joni's gran watched *Countdown* in the living room.

Pressing a cigarette between her lips, she thumbed the lighter.

The flare of flame was dazzling in the darkness. She inhaled, the hot sting of smoke filling her throat.

Smoking felt illicit, a little kick of rebellion. Habitually, Liz was a rule-follower, a law-abider, a reviser-for-exams, a seeing-things-through-till-the-end sort of person – and that was exactly why she needed the occasional cigarette.

She took another drag, glancing back through the glass wall of the lodge into the dining hall. The place had filled up, a three-deep queue to reach the bar. Music thrummed at the glass. She could just make out Maggie and Helena at their table, heads together. She knew they would be talking about her; she'd always been on the outside of their unit. It didn't affect her when Joni was with them – everything was in balance then – but as a three the dynamic was off.

Liz took another draw of her cigarette, studying the peaks of the mountains which cut black shadows against the charcoal night. They looked foreboding, impervious to her small worries. Tomorrow they should be hiking out into all that wilderness. She wanted it. Wanted the burn in her thighs, the exhaustion, the physical toil and endurance. Walking had saved her over the past few months. Emotions that felt stuck and stagnant released as she moved, energy shifting.

Homo sapiens had always walked – even before there was language, they'd walked. It was a simple, fundamental need of their species: walk. So why did everyone outsource it: cars, electric bikes, escalators, lifts? She liked reminding her patients of the incredible mechanics of the human foot: twenty-six bones, thirty-three joints, and over a hundred muscles, tendons and ligaments – all working in structural harmony to enable us to walk.

Tomorrow morning, that was what she, Helena and Maggie should be doing. She couldn't let Maggie derail this. She needed it.

Liz ground out her cigarette, the smoke tasting acrid, as a flare of headlights crested the hill above the lodge. She squinted into the glare, wondering who would be arriving at this hour.

A taxi ground to a stop outside the lodge. The rear passenger door opened, and a backpack was tossed from it. Then a pair of slender, tanned legs stepped out. They were stuffed into black DMs. Liz's gaze lifted, seeing the back of a woman leaning into the cab to pay her driver. She slammed the door shut, and the taxi took off.

The red taillights illuminated the figure in a cloud of dust as she turned. Denim shorts, the loose slouch of a leather jacket, dark hair piled on top of her head, kohl smoked around huge eyes.

Liz blinked. Her hands rose to her mouth.

She shook her head, not believing what she was seeing.

Then her face broke into a grin. 'Joni!'

11

JONI

Liz. Liz. Liz.

There she was! Looking exactly as she always did: skin clean of make-up, eyes bright, hair tied neatly back, smiling.

They rushed at each other, hugging hard, cheekbones clashing, arms locked, laughing and kissing.

'You came!' Liz squealed.

'I did! And you've been smoking!' Joni said, breathing in cigarettes and washing powder. 'Don't tell me I missed Doctor Liz Wallace having a cigarette?' She drew back, patting down Liz's pockets until she found a slim carton of cigarettes. 'Busted!'

Liz laughed, head tipped back.

Joni flicked open the carton, plucked out two cigarettes, tucked one behind Liz's ear, and another behind her own. 'You know you're not allowed to smoke without me.'

'What are you doing here?' Liz cried. 'What about the tour?'

'Over.'

'You had one more show.'

She loved how Liz kept up with her schedule, remembering which countries and arenas she was playing. She'd text, asking, *How's Helsinki? There's an amazing portrait gallery on the waterfront if you've time to visit? Or, I saw you had sold out in Paris!*

'I'm done. I needed out.'

Liz's brow furrowed. 'Why?'

How could she explain what her life looked like to Liz – or any of them? She thought of the photo of them driving to the airport – *There's still time* – and how she'd wanted to believe that there was. She needed to pull herself free of the life she was living. She wanted the clear, fresh beauty of the wilderness. A place to lose herself.

When she had stepped out onto the cold Berlin pavement, barefoot, a passing mother had recoiled, tightening her grip on her child's hand – and Joni felt as if she'd been slapped. She didn't want to be the sort of person who made parents draw their children closer. She took a taxi to the airport, stopping only to buy a pair of boots. She'd washed her face in a sink with cold water and cheap hand soap, then walked to a check-in desk and booked the first flight to Bergen.

Waiting in the boarding lounge, hands shaking, head spinning with exhaustion, she'd texted Kai, her boyfriend and manager, telling him she was out.

She knew the explosion she was leaving behind. The band wouldn't forgive her. You don't bail. She was letting everyone down. She couldn't even think about the fans who'd bought tickets months earlier, made plans to watch her perform. But it was done. Over. She had nothing left in the tank. Not a single piece of herself remaining that she could recognise.

'I need to decompress. I want to be here, Liz. I need my friends. I need you.' She reached forward and took Liz's hands. 'Can you sign me off? Write a doctor's note? I'm still registered at your surgery. Say I'm exhausted, stressed. It's all true.'

Liz looked concerned. 'Of course.'

'Thank you,' Joni said, pulling Liz into a quick, tight hug, before releasing her. Then Joni grabbed the strap of her backpack and heaved it on her shoulders. 'Take me inside. I want to surprise the others!'

Liz interlaced her fingers with Joni's, her wedding ring clashing against the silver skull Joni wore on her middle finger as Joni was drawn through the crowd. The dining hall smelled of food and wood-smoke. People were dancing in front of a makeshift stage where a guy was strumming a guitar. Joni apologised as the heft of her backpack forced the crowd to part.

Ahead, she spotted the others. Maggie, wearing a lemon dress, waves of auburn hair loose around her face, had her chin resting on her hand as she talked. Helena was opposite, leaning back in her chair, one leg crossed over the other, raven-black hair cut bluntly to her chin, lipstick on.

Joni threw down her pack.

'Joni!' Maggie shrieked, launching to her feet, chair tipping over. She flung her arms around Joni.

'You are kidding!' Helena laughed, joining the hug.

They pulled Liz into the crush too, and the four of them were hugging and squeezing and bouncing on the spot. Joni breathed in the herbal scent of Maggie's shampoo, the expensive moisturiser Helena had worn for years, the clean laundry scent of Liz, and felt tears well in her eyes. This was home!

Maggie pulled back, breathless. 'We didn't think you were coming! What about the tour? Did Liz know?'

'I wanted to surprise you all!' Joni grinned. She reached out and touched Maggie's cheek. 'God, I've missed this face. You look so beautiful, you mama! How's Phoebe?'

Maggie's eyes sparkled. 'She's glorious!'

Joni turned to Helena. 'And you! I love the fringe!'

Helena's dark bob had barely been touched for years and now a blunt fringe ran squarely across her forehead.

'Hides the frown lines,' Helena said.

Joni reached for Liz's hand. 'You organised this. Norway! Like our geography project! D'you remember? We're here, just like we said.' She felt an explosion of happiness in her chest. It was so delicious, so golden and rare, that the precise beauty of it almost winded her.

Her gaze fell on the map on the table. 'Is this us? Which mountain are we climbing?'

Helena and Maggie looked at one another. Said nothing.

'What? That's what we're doing, right?'

Maggie kept her gaze lowered.

Joni said, 'I just bought up an entire outdoors store. Please tell me we're climbing a fucking mountain?'

Helena, eyes on Maggie, asked, 'Mags?'

Slowly, Maggie lifted her head. Then her face split into a grin. 'Okay, we're climbing a big fucking mountain!'

Liz laughed with something that sounded like relief. Then she began explaining the route they were taking, pointing to places they might camp. They talked over one another in a rush of enthusiasm.

Joni found her attention being pulled towards the bar, where bottles of spirits glistened on a rack. 'First up, I'm getting a round in!' She slipped away from the others.

'What can I get you?' the barmaid asked.

'A bottle of champagne, please. And a double shot of vodka.'

'Champagne?' the barmaid said with a raised brow. 'We don't get asked for that every day.'

'Anything with a cork will do! Whatever you've got.'

The vodka arrived first. Joni tipped it back with a grimace, wiping her mouth on her hand.

The barmaid produced a bottle of dusty champagne. As she placed it in an ice bucket, she glanced at Joni from the corners of her eyes. 'I know you. You are in that band, yes? My son listens. Horse Fly.'

49

Joni wanted to say, *You don't know me. You don't know that when I sing, those lyrics are empty. Or that the only things I ask for in my rider are vodka and crisps. Or that when a kid says to me, 'I want to be like you!' I want to grip them by the shoulders and say, 'No. You don't!'*

'That's me!' Joni answered, giving a dazzling smile. Then she hooked an arm around the ice bucket, slotted her fingers through the stems of the champagne flutes, black nail varnish flashing, and returned to the table.

The others were still grinning, laughing, pulling over a fourth chair.

'Champagne!' Maggie exclaimed, clapping her hands together.

She caught the roll of Helena's eyes. Flashy? Was that what she thought?

Joni popped the cork and filled their glasses, champagne frothing over the rims, dripping onto the map, a patch of the trail distorting beneath the fizz of bubbles.

She raised her glass high into the air. 'Here's to being together – and losing ourselves in the wilderness!'

12

MAGGIE

The lodge bar was packed. A crowd of people were dancing in front of a stage, where a guy was strumming a guitar and howling into the mic. A group of men suddenly cheered and hooted, thrusting their beers to the ceiling.

Maggie was feeling pleasingly light-headed from the champagne. She didn't drink much at home – it never felt quite right opening a bottle of wine for one while Phoebe was sleeping. That's where the biscuits came in.

The man from the reception desk, Leif, was threading his way through the room, T-shirt flattened to the muscles of his chest, a beer bottle in his grasp. As he neared their table, he looked up, smiling. 'Having a good night?' he asked.

'Absolutely,' Liz said, grinning, her features softened by the wine. She signalled to an empty chair. 'Join us?'

The spindles strained beneath his frame as he lowered himself down, folding his legs beneath his seat. He sat forward, a thick forearm resting on the table. Maggie couldn't stop looking at the ridges of muscles in Leif's arms, the prominent veins, the neatly cut nails, and strong fingers. A climber's arms. Alcohol wasn't the only thing she was missing in the evenings.

'This is Joni,' Liz said. 'And this is Leif.'

Joni smiled, lips parting over straight white teeth. 'Good to meet you.'

A sunburst of lines appeared around his eyes as he smiled. 'You're the singer in Horse Fly!' He uncurled his fingers from his beer, wiped them against his T-shirt, then reached across to shake her hand.

She shook it, smiling easily.

'Joni surprised us!' Maggie beamed. 'The four of us holiday together every year – but we didn't think Joni would make this one.'

'Every year?' Leif asked.

'Since we were eighteen,' Joni said proudly.

'Although the trips usually involve a pool and cocktails,' Helena added.

'How long have you known each other?' Leif asked.

Maggie leaned across the table to refill their glasses. 'Forever,' she said, catching the edge of a slur in her voice. 'These are my best people.'

'We met at secondary school,' Helena said. 'Maggie and I used to bus in from the wrong end of town.'

Their school covered a large catchment area, from the council-owned houses where she and Helena lived, to the leafy village where Joni and Liz grew up in detached houses with pretty gardens.

'Wrong or right end, it didn't matter,' Liz said, who was leaning back in her chair. 'We were all in the same tutor group. Four to a bench. It was love at first sight.'

Leif smiled. 'You've stayed close all this time.'

'We're family,' Joni said, putting her arms around Liz and Maggie, who were sitting on either side of her.

Liz said, 'Remember that school residential trip when they put us in separate rooms? We snuck out with our sleeping bags and slept in the boat shed so we could be together!'

'Which would've been fine,' Helena said, 'except Joni decided to take out a rowing boat so we could stargaze – and one of the security guards spotted us.'

'Always leading us astray,' Liz said, grinning at Joni. 'Remember when you dared us to nick a top-shelf DVD from Blockbuster, and that kid on the counter chased us down the street?'

'Or the time you organised a rave in the quarry,' Maggie said, 'and it got shut down and we were delivered home by the police!' It had been worth the month-long grounding just to dance in that echoing quarry, music thumping through her whole body.

There was something about Joni that always made Maggie feel excited by life. When she and Aidan married, Joni had given them a wedding gift for their home, but she'd also bought something separate, *Just for you*, she'd whispered, pressing it into Maggie's hands. Maggie had opened the beautifully wrapped package alone and discovered a set of stunning paintbrushes and acrylics, with a note reading, *Stay you. Always create*. A flush of shame travelled through her insides as she pictured the paints, still unused, tucked at the back of her wardrobe ready for the right time. She pushed the thought aside. Tonight wasn't about regrets.

'You have a lot of history,' Leif said, smiling.

Maggie liked seeing their friendship, through Leif's eyes, as something golden and easy. The four of them had travelled through career highs and lows, failed romances, the arrival of children, the loss of parents – and been there for each other throughout it all.

Their annual holiday was more than just a quick blast of sunshine or fresh air. It meant everything to Maggie. When the four of them were together, she was reminded that her younger self was still there, glimmering beneath the responsibilities of adulthood, polished fresh by her friends' company.

'Have you been to Norway before?' Leif asked.

They shook their heads.

'You'll love the mountains. They change you. You can't go into the wilderness without uncovering your wild self.'

Helena asked, 'Have you always lived here?'

'Yes. My grandfather built the original lodge. Then my parents took over and ran it for twenty-five years. We lost my father three years ago and it's been too much for my mother to manage alone – she isn't in good health – so now I look after it. We renovated last year for the first time since the Seventies.'

'You've done an incredible job,' Helena said. 'I love how the lodge has a traditional feel, yet the open glass sides feel so fresh and expansive.'

'Thank you,' Leif said, his face flushing with pride.

'When a place is passed down through the generations, does it become a pressure?' Maggie asked, interested. 'Do you feel like you *have* to stay here?'

Leif shook his head. 'It's everything, this place. We have the mountains. The coast. The lake. Hot sun in summer. Snow in winter. There's nowhere I'd rather be.'

Maggie smiled to hear him talk so passionately about his home. Raising her glass, she said, 'To you and your lodge.'

Leif lifted his beer and clinked it against her glass.

Ahead of them, the dining-hall door swung open, and a rangy guy who looked to be in his late twenties exploded into the room. A faded rucksack hung off one shoulder, and an orange beanie was pulled low over the back of his head, a wash of dark hair falling across his forehead. He was unshaven, a black tattoo stamped on the near side of his neck.

The barmaid stopped mid-step, eyes stretching wide in surprise.

A group of young women paused from drinking, a whisper passing between them.

Leif was completely still – eyes pinned to the incomer.

The man crossed the space, his gait loose, arms swinging. His gaze searched the crowd, jaw jutting forward, as if silently demanding, *What are you looking at?*

'Who is that?' Maggie whispered, feeling the atmosphere in the room tighten.

Without taking his eyes off him, Leif answered: 'My brother.'

The table jarred as Leif got to his feet, sending their drinks sloshing.

The brother's gaze landed on Leif – and he halted.

Leif and his brother faced each other.

Every person in the lodge seemed to be holding their breath. The singer had paused between tracks. Leif's brother said something in Norwegian, his face serious.

Leif returned his stare.

Then Leif's brother opened his hands expansively, his face cracking into a smile. He stepped forward.

There was just a beat of hesitation before Leif did the same, embracing him as he said, 'Erik!'

As they clapped each other on the back, Maggie caught Leif's sidelong glance. His gaze searched out Bjørn and Brit, who were sitting at a corner table.

Brit's eyes had widened and the drink she held had begun to tremble. Bjørn sat rigid, hands gripping the sides of his chair, knuckles white. Both of them were staring at Erik as if they'd watched the devil walk in.

13

HELENA

The atmosphere in the lodge was briefly stalled by Erik's arrival. Helena noticed the low voices, strange sidelong glances, and groups of drinkers talking with their heads bent together. But soon enough the music restarted, the guitarist turned up the amp, and the party buzz returned.

Maggie got to her feet and Helena watched her weave through the room towards the stage, hair swaying at her back.

Helena loved drunk Maggie. Her body became completely boneless, as if she were dissolving beneath the love she felt for everyone around her.

'What's she doing?' Liz asked.

Maggie, standing on tiptoes, whispered something into the singer's ear. Then she turned, looking back towards their table, pointing, beaming.

Helena nudged Joni. 'Think your night off is over.'

Joni looked up.

Across the room, Maggie was grinning, beckoning Joni.

'Oh God . . .' Joni groaned, shaking her head at Maggie, mouthing, *Don't!*

But the singer was already leaning into the mic, announcing

in lilting English, 'I am told we have one special guest in the room tonight.'

Several pairs of eyes swung immediately to their table.

Liz, cigarette tucked behind an ear, placed her forearms on the table. She leaned forward until she was nose to nose with Joni. She slapped one palm against the table, then the other. She eyeballed Joni, a steady drumbeat beginning to build, as her face split into a wide smile. 'Joni-Gold! Joni-Gold!' she chanted.

Helena picked up the rhythm, her rings clinking against the table edge, champagne glasses trembling.

At the bar, another group joined the chant. 'Joni-Gold! Joni-Gold! Joni-Gold!'

The voices grew louder, everyone looking in their direction. Liz stood, reached out her hand, and pulled Joni to her feet.

Joni grabbed her champagne, tossed it back, then let herself be led across the room as the crowd cheered. At the front, Maggie was clapping delightedly as Joni squeezed past the amp. The musician said something in Joni's ear, then unhooked the guitar from his neck, and Joni put the strap around hers.

Helena picked her way to the front, standing with Maggie and Liz.

'I can't believe she's going to do this!' Liz said, beaming wildly, as Joni checked the tuning of the guitar.

'I can,' Helena said. Applause was Joni's sustenance. She'd never been the girl calling, *Hey, look at me over here!* She waited until she was wanted. Until her name was chanted. Until the tables were pounded and everyone in the room was swept up in the excitement and was hoping, hoping that she'd perform. Then – and only then – would she step forward.

Helena studied Joni. She wore an old T-shirt with a pair of ripped shorts, her slim legs stuffed into heavy boots. A sleeve of leather bracelets flocked up her right arm, and her septum was pierced with a silver bar. She wore just a flick of kohl around her eyes, her prominent cheekbones and sharp green irises doing the rest of the work.

Everyone was watching. The stage was hers.

Joni closed her eyes, her body began to rock, the rhythm already playing in her head. Instinctively, she angled her face towards the microphone. With her mouth almost touching it, her lips parted, her eyes opened. 'Hey.' One word, smoky, low, deep.

The room fell silent.

And into that silence she began to sing.

Oh, Jesus! That voice.

Dusky, deep. The resonance ripping through the lodge, sending shivers down Helena's neck.

She was a rock star.

Every pair of eyes was trained on Joni. As she strummed the guitar, the music drew the crowd forward, heads nodding, hips swaying, feet moving. No one could take their eyes off her. That was the thing about Joni: her talent was shocking. You could feel it, raw and beautiful and throbbing. You wanted to reach out, touch it, because you understood that what you were witnessing was something special.

Helena's skin buzzed with the electricity in the room. Watching Joni perform was mesmeric. Her voice was textured – gravelly and deep one moment, then soft and haunting in a single note change. It was like she was singing not just with sound, but from a place deep inside her. The guitar became part of her, her long fingers dancing instinctively across the fret board, strumming chords, picking notes. You could see the song moving through her body, the flex of her spine, the arc of her neck, the mellow close of her eyelids. She became fluid, transformed.

Joni didn't play music. She *was* the music.

The room swelled with energy. Helena let the music flood her body, her spine softening. She took out her phone and hit the *Video* button.

Liz tugged free her hairband, shaking loose her ponytail. Maggie swirled, expression ecstatic, dress lifting around her knees. Behind them, a girl whistled, fingers thrust hard between her lips. A man with a shirt unbuttoned to his navel threw his hands in the air.

Maggie's arms circled Helena and Liz, the three of them leaning in together. Helena turned the phone briefly on them as they grinned, and then at Joni, who looked up from the mic, straight at them, and beamed. They could have been twelve, or eighteen, or twenty-five. That was the magic of old friends: the years were stripped away. Joni was theirs and they were hers. All the hurt and anger and resentment disappeared because Joni shone so bright that her light banished the darker memories, left Helena so dizzy and struck that she forgot to be mad.

At the song's end, the crowd burst into applause. Joni smiled, eyes shining, revealing perfect white teeth, with the tiniest gap between the front two. Her first manager had asked for her teeth to be corrected and Joni had said, 'Sure. Right after you have your personality corrected.' That was the thing about Joni, she didn't take shit. She did what the hell she wanted – and it was intoxicating.

It was meant to be one song. That's what Joni had said. *Just one.* But Helena felt the heat of this crowd. There was no way they were letting her go. As Joni removed the guitar strap from her neck, the previous singer stepped forward to the crowd, asking, 'Who wants another?'

The room erupted.

'Me!' Liz yelled, jumping up and down on the spot. 'Play "Black Shell"!'

Liz's shining pride in her best friend was loveable. She was never jealous of Joni's beauty or success or fame. She accepted her long absences with grace, not complaint. Liz seemed flattered that, despite the glamour of Joni's world, she'd still get on a plane for her.

'This one is for my girlfriends,' Joni said huskily into the mic. Then she strummed the first chord of 'Black Shell' and the crowd surged.

Helena loved this song, too. She remembered being sent the track when it was fresh from the recording studio. 'Listen to this,' she'd told her mother, playing it for her. Tears had filled her mother's eyes, her hands pressing to her heart as she'd listened. 'Tell Joni I'm so proud of her. She must visit when she's home next.'

In their teenage years, Joni had come over to Helena's after school most weeks. Helena's mother had taught her how to play the keyboard, how to read music, how to use the incredible range in her voice. For Joni's seventeenth birthday, her mother had spent her wages on a Moleskine notebook, pressing it into her hands, saying, 'For writing your own songs.'

When Helena's mother died, she'd left Joni her old keyboard and an antique wooden box containing the sheet music that they used to practise together. Helena had planned to give it to Joni when she returned for the funeral – only Joni had never shown up.

The crowd writhed, but Helena remained still. If her mother were alive, she'd have been cheering Joni's name. She would have waved away her hurt that Joni hadn't called or visited when she was sick – because her mother had always seen her talent, her beauty, her vulnerability, her fragile confidence, and she'd wanted to protect her. Her mother would have forgiven her. Like everyone did.

But Helena couldn't.

Near the exit, someone was leaning back against the wall, not dancing. She turned her head more fully.

It was the man from the bar, Austin. His ice-blue eyes weren't on Joni Gold.

He was watching her.

Helena met his gaze. Could sense the desire in his expression. His gaze slid to her mouth. She felt the drum of anticipation begin to beat in her chest.

The crowd surged again; drinks spilled; arms were raised to the ceiling. When the crowd poured back, Austin moved away from the wall towards the door. He held it open, eyes on her. An invitation.

Helena glanced briefly towards her friends, who were lost to Joni's spell, and then she was slipping through the crowd, other bodies closing the space where she had been.

14

JONI

Joni leaned close to the mic, voice husky. 'This is the last one.'

The crowd whistled and roared.

At the side of the makeshift stage, a man with thick, wavy hair handed her a shot. She threw it back, wiped a hand across her mouth, then tossed the empty towards him.

Joni looked down at the guitar in her arms and hesitated, as if she couldn't quite recall how it got there, or where she was. The room fell quiet. She swayed lightly. Her head felt blank, suspended.

She lifted her gaze to the sea of faces. She could see Liz at the front of the room. Her brow furrowed as she grew alert, stepping forward, ready.

Liz was always there, ready to catch her when she fell.

Joni didn't deserve her. When she disappeared for months at a time, Liz would try calling, or emailing, or sending packages of vitamins and supplements to her record label, hoping they'd get passed on.

In breaks between tours, occasionally Joni would stay with Liz and Patrick, rolling in exhausted, her skin wan. Liz would make up the spare bed, pick flowers from the garden and arrange them in a jug on the windowsill, and – on that first day – Joni would sleep and sleep. Then she'd emerge quieter, a little softer, drawing Liz's children into her arms. Evie would perform dance routines, eager for praise, while Daniel would shyly lay out his latest karate belt, hoping to be asked for a demonstration, tiny legs and fists flying at the sofa cushions. In the evenings, Patrick would make nourishing meals from root vegetables he'd grown through the winter, and the adults would stay up late, Joni and Patrick listening to old, obscure albums and crushing on riffs and chord progressions, Liz warmly teasing them, hiding her yawns behind her hands.

Liz kept encouraging her to buy a house in the village as a base to return to between tours. Her childhood home had been sold a decade ago, after her grandmother died. She knew Liz wanted her to have roots – and bed them in the earth near her.

But Joni couldn't come back.

Now Liz took a step towards the stage. 'Joni?' she called, concerned.

Joni blinked. She gave the lightest of nods, silently communicating that she was okay. Then her fingers began to move, picking at the strings. Three notes. A curling pause. Then her voice kicked in.

She felt the riptide of energy and endorphins and alcohol carrying her away, until she was soaring with the sound-waves.

She watched Liz smiling, relieved.

On stage, Joni moved to the music, hairline beaded with sweat, the inside of her thighs damp. Her hips sank lower. Her hair swung loose against her neck.

I'm flying so high/Touching the clouds, she sang, throat open, diaphragm pushing up, fingers plucking the strings.

The small crowd moved to the words, arms thrown in the air, faces flushed, T-shirts clinging to hot, sweating bodies.

Her mouth lowered to the mic as she sang, *But they don't see/I'm not flying.*

A single, final strum of the guitar. Then a last breath, drawn deep in her body. Her head rising, lips brushing the mic. *I'm falling . . .*

She held the last note, feeling the sound deepen and hollow as it left her body, chest tightening, abdomen firing. Then she dropped her head, emptied of sound, dark hair curtaining her face.

The lodge erupted with cheers.

She kept her eyes lowered, applause washing over her. For a few moments, she felt bathed in it, connected through her music with these strangers. They were her words. Her emotions. Poured out. And when they hit another person, just right, it was like a spark in the darkness. She'd forgotten the feeling of a small audience an arm's length away. No dazzling stage lights or costumes or big screens. Just a girl with a guitar and something to say.

Slowly, she raised her head, a grin splitting her face, golden warmth spreading through her as she took in the room. Two younger guys jumped on the spot, arms around one another's shoulders. Maggie and Liz were clapping madly, calling her name.

Joni dipped her face to the mic. 'Thank you for having me,' she said in a low voice. Then she was unhooking the guitar strap, handing it back to the musician who was grinning, and then Maggie and Liz were stepping forward.

'That was incredible!' Liz cried, hugging her.

'You were phenomenal!' Maggie said, joining the hug.

Joni concentrated on the feel of her friends' arms tight around her, the buzz of the music still deep in her chest, the energy humming in the room. It was so close to being just right. Almost perfect.

She looked up, scanning the faces. Her brow dipped. 'Where's Helena?'

15

HELENA

Helena walked slowly towards Austin, each step purposeful, her gaze held by his. She felt sexy and wanted and in control. There were no words. There'd be no conversation.

She came right to him, stopping inches away. Their bodies faced one another's.

He had a pleasant face. Clean hands. Good trainers.

It was enough.

She pursed her lips. Made a small movement of her head. A suggestion.

He nodded.

She knew this dance. Maybe she'd known it was happening when she accepted the bottle of wine. It was a routine she'd moved to many times before.

Austin ran a hand through his white-blond hair. There was an energy – a brittle, fizzing confidence about him – and she wondered if he was high.

He grabbed her hand. His was warm, slightly clammy. He pulled her lightly after him. A room. A cubicle. A store cupboard. An empty corridor. It didn't matter.

He shouldered open a door to a disabled toilet.

Helena shut it behind them. Locked it. The light was garish

and harsh, illuminating a greasy shine across the bridge of Austin's nose. His pores were large and open and there was a faint spray of acne scars pitted at the edge of his hairline.

He looked at her hungrily and with a touch of self-congratulation – like he couldn't quite believe his luck. This wasn't a city club. This was a lodge in the foothills of mountains. She hooked her finger into his waistband. Pulled him close. Kissed him.

Cider and meat. Something sour. She pressed herself to him, felt the hardness of his cock through his jeans. She didn't even want this. It was how some people felt when faced with the last strip of chocolate. They didn't want to eat it, but knew they would, so needed it over with. Done.

She needed this done.

She shimmied her black trousers and knickers to her knees, and he lifted her onto the edge of the wet sink. Then he was inside her. Too fast.

She tried to rock herself into a rhythm she'd enjoy. A balled-up tissue on the toilet floor fell in her eye line. She looked away. Caught sight of herself in a mirror nailed to the back of the door. She didn't look like a woman in control. Her lipstick had rubbed off and she looked sad and empty and hard-faced and lonely.

She screwed her eyes shut.

Austin grabbed her breasts, squeezed. She tried not to yelp. They were tender. They shouldn't be tender. She pushed herself into him more firmly, rocking fast, speeding this up.

He came with a shudder.

Then she slipped down from the sink, pulling up her knickers, buttoning her trousers.

He looked at her wide eyed. 'Wow. That was . . .'

His cock was still out and the sight of it embarrassed her.

She moved to the door.

'Wait! You are leaving? Already?' Austin looked suddenly boyish, vulnerable.

'Yes.'

'Can I . . . see you again?'

'I'm off hiking in the morning,' she said, hand on the door.

'When you are back at the lodge?' he called.

She stepped through the doorway into the low-lit atrium. 'Sure,' she tossed, needing to get away.

'See you again!' he called, and she felt guilty for the catch of happiness in his voice.

As her boots clipped along the wooden floor, she was startled to pass Vilhelm and his dog, who'd returned to their silent watch on the bench. His cap was drawn low, and she couldn't see his eyes, yet felt them following her as she passed, her skin prickling with shame.

16

LIZ

The lodge bar had emptied, the crowd pulling on coats and moving outside to continue the party lakeside.

'You coming?' Liz asked Maggie.

'My bed is calling, and I must go,' she said, swaying lightly on her feet, hands in the pockets of her yellow dress.

Liz smiled. 'Okay, g'night. Love you.' She planted a kiss on Maggie's warm cheek, the earlier irritation between them already forgotten.

Liz followed a group of women speaking in quick-fire German as they exited the lodge. The night was cool, sharp mountain air pinching her face. She paused, stepping out of the throng of people, and letting her eyes adjust to the darkness.

A crescent moon hung above the lake. A fire was roaring in a large oil drum, a crowd of people huddling close, music playing. A string of fairy lights hung between the trees. Some people danced, while others lounged back on wooden benches. Laughter and voices drifted across the water.

She searched for Joni, guessing she'd been swept up by a group of fans. It'd been incredible to see her perform tonight. The last time she'd seen her play had been four months earlier at a venue in Dublin. Joni had phoned to say – 'Can you get over here? I've put you on the guest list.' Patrick booked the flights. The kids had an impromptu sleepover with Liz's brother and sister-in-law. Liz packed a small bag, and they left. It had felt impossibly exciting – like bunking off from life.

Joni had arrived on stage wearing a mermaid-esque sequin cape, dark hair flowing, silver gems in the corners of her eyes. She looked like some beautiful, glittering ocean creature. When her face was illuminated on the big screen, the crowd screamed and writhed.

'She is the most beautiful woman in the world,' Liz had marvelled, her head resting on Patrick's shoulder.

'But she looks sad,' Patrick responded.

Liz had stared at her best friend, her face pixelated onto a fifty-foot screen, and thought: *He's right. She does.*

After the gig, Liz had wanted to spend proper time with Joni, but a migraine had swooped in and cut the night short. She didn't hear from Joni again for weeks because, when things were hard, that's what Joni did: shut down, closed herself off.

But now she was in Norway! They'd have the next four days to walk and talk.

She spotted Joni – not with a crowd, but sitting alone. She was perched on the backrest of a bench facing the lake, boots on the seat, phone pressed to her ear. Her leather jacket was hunched around her ears, long bare legs tucked beneath her. She was listening closely, nodding, eyes lowered.

As Liz walked through the dew-studded grass, she caught Joni's voice. It was low, worried. 'I don't know what to say . . .' She wrapped a hand around the back of her neck, a chunky silver ring catching in the moonlight, black nail varnish glossy.

There was something about Joni's posture and the tone of her voice that caused Liz to hesitate.

Joni continued to talk, lips close to the phone, voice thick with emotion. 'Course not!'

Liz waited in the dark, arms hugged to her middle.

Joni shifted. Then, as if suddenly becoming aware of Liz, she swung around, eyes widening, face washed pale in the moonlight. Into the phone, she said, 'I need to go.'

She ended the call and slipped the phone into the pocket of her leather jacket.

Liz climbed onto the bench beside her. 'Who was that?'

'Kai.'

'Being a dick?'

She nodded.

Liz bumped her arm against Joni's. 'You okay?'

There was a beat of silence. The lake was still, not a breath of wind stirred. Behind them, the bass of music pumped. 'I'm in Norway. With you. Course I'm okay!'

Liz smiled. There was so much she wanted to ask Joni – about why she'd left the tour, whether it was over with Kai, what came next – but it could wait. They had four days of walking for that.

Joni plucked the cigarette from behind Liz's ear, slipped it into Liz's lips, and took a lighter from her pocket.

The flame illuminated Joni's dark irises, and Liz saw her own image reflected in them. She took a shallow drag of the cigarette, hot smoke pushing into her lungs. She didn't want the cigarette. She removed it from her lips and handed it to Joni.

Joni took a deep draw, then pushed to her feet. 'Come on, let's go to the fire! I want to dance!' She grabbed Liz's hand and led her towards the crowd. A man threw on another log, sparks dancing high into the night. Music blared from a speaker propped on a hay bale. A group of men called something to Joni as they passed; she threw them a smile but didn't stop.

Joni staggered closer to the fire pit. A girl in a dark hoodie scooped two beers from a cooler and handed them to Joni and Liz.

Liz thanked her but held the chilled can in her grip without opening it. Wood-smoke stung her eyes. 'We should probably get some sleep. We've got an early start.'

Joni laughed and squeezed Liz's arm as if she'd said something amusing. She snapped the ring pull back and took a thirsty drink, then danced towards the fire, her body mirroring the mesmeric pattern of the smoke, fluid and curving.

Across the other side of the flames, she noticed Erik, Leif's brother, standing alone in the shadows. He was holding a bottle of something at his side, orange beanie pulled low to the base of his head, a spill of dark hair curling towards his jaw. He moved distractedly from foot to foot, his gaze on the glow of the fire, shadows carved into his face.

Nearby, Leif was standing at the centre of a group of men who were talking and laughing. Although Leif's posture was relaxed and easy, his eyes kept sliding towards his brother.

Liz returned her unopened beer to the cooler and wiped her wet hands on her thighs. Ahead, Joni staggered slightly, reaching out towards the flaming oil drum. 'Steady,' Liz said, stepping forward and catching her free hand, moments before Joni placed it on the scalding metal.

Joni wrapped an arm around Liz's waist, smiling distantly.

The music suddenly cut, a string of lights going out. A cheer went up as they were plunged into music-less dark. A guy wearing a backward trucker cap lurched towards a generator and held up a cable, laughing. His friends jostled him as he tried to plug it back in.

A sharp voice cut through the night. '*Du!*'

Liz turned. Bjørn and Brit – the older couple from the lodge – were passing the party. The husband lifted his hand, pointing straight at Erik's face.

Erik stared back. He took a slug of beer, eyes not leaving Bjørn's.

71

Bjørn unhooked his arm from his wife's and stepped forward, chin lifted. '*Du er modig som viser deg her!*' he spat.

Erik stared at him for a long moment, then shrugged.

Bjørn's features tightened. He took another step forward until he was positioned only inches from Erik. A ball of tension worked at the side of his mouth, fury causing the muscles in his arms to twitch, fingers clenching at his sides. '*Jaevel!*' he yelled.

'What's he saying?' Liz whispered to the girl in the hoodie beside her.

Before she could answer, Bjørn turned to the onlooking crowd, shouting, '*Han drepte Karin!*' He banged his fist to his chest. '*Det vet jeg!*'

The girl in the hoodie rubbed her collarbone uneasily. 'He's saying . . . he's saying that Erik killed his daughter.'

Liz and Joni glanced at one another. *What had they walked into?*

Erik was still glaring at Bjørn, chin jutting, shoulders back, bottle hanging from his fingertips. Tension spilled from him. He looked ready to launch.

Then Bjørn's wife hurried forward, grabbing Bjørn by the arm. He tried to brush her off, but she linked her arm firmly through his, speaking in a quiet, quick voice close to his ear.

Bjørn spat on the earth at Erik's feet. Then he turned and allowed himself to be drawn away. Liz watched Bjørn lean into his wife, the two of them creating a terrible picture of defeat as they dragged themselves towards the car park.

Around the fire, the crowd's collective gaze moved to Erik. He stood before them, face blanched, glowering. '*Hva?*'

The crowd was silent.

With a wild growl, Erik launched his foot, kicking over the fire drum.

Liz and Joni jumped back as burning wood and embers spilled across the ground. Sparks filled the night sky.

'*Hei!*' a guy with short dreadlocks yelled, stepping forward as if to confront him, but Leif was suddenly there, holding up his palms, pacifying. He said something in a low voice, then put an arm around Erik's shoulder, attempting to steer him away.

Erik shrugged him off, his expression ravaged. He lurched towards the lake, stopping only at the edge to kick off his boots. Then he waded right in, fully clothed, the water rippling around him as he struck out.

Liz and Joni watched as he swam on and on, following the silver channel of the moon, Leif's protests echoing through the night.

17

HELENA

Helena returned to her room, brow tight, tears hot in her eyes. She could taste alcohol on her breath, feel a soreness between her legs.

She pulled her backpack onto the narrow bed and yanked at the zipped side pocket. She began pulling out items: a head torch, a small wash bag, spare socks.

Outside in the corridor, she could hear footsteps, then the fumble of the lock.

She tried a second pocket, stuffing a hand deep into the tightly packed contents. After rummaging for a moment, she pulled out what she was looking for.

Maggie opened the door, hair loose, her smile making her eyes glitter. 'There you are!' Then Maggie's brow crumpled with concern as she took in Helena's expression. 'What is it? What's happened?' Her gaze lowered towards the item Helena was gripping in her hand. She stepped closer. 'Is that . . . a pregnancy test?'

'Yes.'

Maggie blinked. 'For you?'

'I need to do this right now. I need you to be there. And I don't want to talk about it.'

'Okay . . .' Maggie said slowly, carefully.

Helena's hands were shaking so hard that she fumbled with the box, dropping it. 'Damn!'

'Here,' Maggie said, coming forward and gently taking it from her.

She looked so lovely in her lemon-yellow dress, eyes bright, hair loose. Next to her, Helena felt soiled, the smell of Austin still on her skin.

Maggie carefully removed the test from the box, then flattened out the instructions on the bed. She read for a moment, then removed the cap from the pregnancy test and said, 'Wee on this part.'

Helena took the stick, heart thundering, and walked into the en suite like a condemned woman. She peed with the door ajar, feeling a hot stream of urine splashing over her fingers. When she was finished, she placed the test on the cistern, and washed and dried her hands.

'I'm timing three minutes,' Maggie said, setting the timer on her phone.

Helena could feel the pulse of blood in her ears. Three minutes. She rubbed her collarbone. Water. She needed a glass of water.

No bloody glass in this toilet. She went to her backpack and rooted around for her water bottle, hands shaking. She took a long gulp, liquid dribbling over her chin.

Maggie watched her. 'I've got questions.'

'Too bad.' Helena began to pace. Their room was small, furnished simply with two single beds and a wooden desk.

Looking at her watch, Maggie said, 'We have two minutes and thirty-four seconds to fill. I get to ask any questions I want until the time is up.'

Helena eyed her suspiciously. 'And then we never talk about this again?'

'If that's what you want.'

'That's what I want.'

'Okay then,' Maggie said. 'First question: How late are you?'

Helena began pacing again. 'Eight days.'

'Eight?' Maggie repeated loudly.

Helena's cycles were like clockwork. Twenty-nine days. Ovulate on day fifteen. Irritated as hell on days twenty-seven to twenty-nine. Then bleed. She was never late.

Helena paced from the window to the door. Six steps. Turn. Repeat.

'Why do you think you could be pregnant? Was there a problem with the contraception?'

'Yes, there was a problem.' She looked at Maggie, chin lifted. 'I stopped using it.'

Maggie's jaw dropped. An actual, physical dropping, like it fell off its hinge. 'But you . . . you always use contraception.'

'Contraception queen. Yes, yes, I know.' Helena had been on the pill since she was sixteen – *and* she used condoms. She'd never wanted children, so why be slapdash when it came to contraception?

Maggie was still staring at her, large hazel eyes shining in confusion. 'Why have you stopped using it?'

That was the question, wasn't it? The one that Helena had been avoiding thinking about. 'Time?' she barked.

Maggie checked her phone. 'One minute forty to go.'

She stopped pacing and slumped on the end of the bed, the contents of her backpack bouncing beneath her weight. 'I . . . I don't know . . .' She couldn't put it into words. Or at least none that made sense to her. 'Something's changed, Mags, and I don't know how to explain it – to you, to me, to anyone.'

'Is this about Robert?'

Oh, Robert. Her Robert. Her handsome, funny, kind ex-

76

boyfriend. Robert Louth. Helena had spent most of her twenties single – and happy about it. Until Robert. He shook up her world in all the right ways because suddenly here was a man she was completely mad about – and who felt the same about her. Neither of them wanted children and she'd allowed herself to believe she would spend her life with him. That's why, two years ago, when they'd been sitting in bed on a Sunday morning, drinking coffee, surrounded by the papers and buttery flakes of croissants, Robert had set down his mug and said, 'There's something I need to say,' and Helena had put down her coffee and thought: *This is it. He's going to propose.*

'I've changed my mind,' Robert had told her. 'I do want a family.'

If he'd told her he'd cheated on her, it would've been less of a blow. That was something they could work through. Get over. But having children – well that was a do or don't.

And she was definitely *Don't*.

The break-up was excruciating. They were still in love and wanted each other. They just no longer wanted the same future. Helena had thrown herself into work, into socialising, and into the beds of other men.

Then, a year ago, she had answered the call she'd been dreading. Robert had met someone. They were engaged. His fiancée was pregnant. 'I wanted to be the one to tell you. I'm sorry, I know this is hard.'

Maggie lowered herself onto the bed beside Helena and took her hand.

Helena said, 'I saw a photo of Robert with his daughter. She was so perfect. She has his nose. His colouring. That funny little widow's peak. And God, it was like glimpsing what *our* child could have looked like.'

Maggie squeezed her fingers hard.

'I always knew he'd be an incredible father – and I've no

doubt he is – just not to our child.' She removed her hand from Maggie's and moved to the window. She pulled the curtains open onto the black of night. In the reflection, she could see Maggie's concerned expression. She opened the window, letting in a cool blast of mountain air.

'The timing with Robert's baby . . .' Maggie began. 'It was all so close to losing your mum . . .'

Helena nodded. Her mother had died ten months ago and the loss had almost destroyed her. You don't know how much you love someone until you realise you're never going to see them again. That you must live in a world where they no longer are. The finality of it, the utter endlessness of grief – it was overwhelming. She couldn't fix it. Or change it. Or bargain with it. Or control it. It just happened and she was powerless. Grief was so brutal that she didn't know if she'd survive. Some days she'd find herself walking the streets of Bristol looking around, thinking: *How many of you have lost someone you've loved? How are you still standing?*

She said to Maggie, 'When Mum died, all I could do was hold her hand. That's what life gets reduced to in those final moments – the person you choose to hold hands with. I couldn't do anything to keep Mum alive. I couldn't take away her pain. But I could hold her hand. I could do that. I'm her daughter, Maggie, and I was with her, holding her hand as she left.' She sucked in a breath. 'When I die, I want someone to hold my hand.'

In the reflection, she saw Maggie was biting down on her lip. If she cried, it was game over. Helena would crack right open and God knows what would spill out. 'Time?' she barked, pushing to her feet, hands on her hips.

Maggie jumped. Looked at her phone. 'Fifty-eight seconds.'

Her stomach lurched. She glanced towards the open bathroom. Her future was written on a stick. She was sweating.

Damp patches had formed under her arms. She crossed the room, resuming her pacing.

'Maybe this isn't anything to do with Robert or losing Mum,' Helena said. 'Maybe my biological clock struck midnight and sent some ridiculous hormone message to my brain that said, *Go forth and procreate!*'

She pushed her hands into the roots of her hair. 'What a mess. I'm a mess. This –' she said, pointing into the bathroom – 'this is a mess!'

'Forty-five seconds,' Maggie offered.

Her stomach churned. She wiped her palms down her thighs.

Maggie asked: 'Who did you sleep with?'

'Who didn't I sleep with? I've been steadily working my way through the suited half of Bristol.' She'd been accepting booty calls from guys on dating apps and sleeping with people she met in bars. Every week there was someone. She'd been through promiscuous patches in the past and had sat in the therapist's chair enough times to know it was wrapped around self-worth issues and needing to be wanted, loved. God, it was all so pathetic and predictable. 'I just shagged that guy, Austin, in the lodge toilets as it gave me thirty seconds of respite from my own thoughts. Healthy pattern, right?'

'Oh, darl—'

'Time?'

Maggie glanced at her watch. 'Twenty seconds.'

A hot wave of fear tore through her. 'I can't look at it. You tell me.'

'Okay.'

As Maggie walked into the bathroom, she hesitated, turning back to Helena. 'What do you want the test to show? That you're pregnant – or not pregnant?'

'I . . . I . . .' She stopped pacing.

She thought about her mother's hand, cool and still in her

own as the breath left her body for a final time. She thought about Robert, with a baby strapped to his chest, his eyes bright with joy and pride. She thought about her sparkling flat, the walls kept bare except for expensive light fittings and art, while her friends' homes were covered with photos and crumpled paintings by their children. Did she want that?

But she barely liked children. Except for Phoebe. Helena couldn't have a baby. She was too selfish. She was too busy at work. She'd resent taking a step back in her job. She didn't even have a partner, for god's sake! Her apartment was completely impractical for raising a child. And wine – she loved wine! She'd be no good at motherhood. She had never wanted children. She'd always been clear about that. Everyone knew. It was part of who she was. How she saw herself.

Maggie's gaze lowered to the pregnancy test.

Helena's insides bunched tight. Her skin felt painfully hot. Her future hinged on this moment. She swallowed. 'Tell me.'

DAY 1

18

MAGGIE

Morning sunlight beamed through the lodge window. Maggie and Helena stood shoulder to shoulder, staring at Maggie's backpack, which lay prone on her single bed. It was enormous. Bloated. Bone-compressingly heavy.

Hands on hips, Helena said, 'You can barely lift it. How are you planning on hiking with it?' Helena was dressed in black, slim-fit hiking trousers, red merino wool socks that matched her lipstick, and a moisture-wicking long-sleeved top. Somehow she'd managed to make hiking gear look fashionable.

'I've read *Wild*. I was thinking there'd be blisters and sweat, but ultimately I'd triumph over adversity.'

'Cheryl Strayed walked solo for two months through desert and mountain snow. We're going for four days. You need to ditch five kilos before we leave this room.'

Helena was right. She was right about most things. Even though she had never climbed a mountain, or slept in a tent, she researched, she asked intelligent questions, spoke to the right people, bought the right gear. She got shit done.

Maggie began pulling items out of the backpack. 'You gave me half of this stuff.' Parcels had kept arriving at her address, Helena telling her she'd ordered two of something by mistake.

Two down sleeping bags? Really? They both knew that Helena had sent her these things because Maggie didn't have the spare money to kit herself out for this trip.

'Yes, the useful half,' Helena said, picking up a pair of pink binoculars. 'Taking up bird-watching?'

'What if we need to see something in the distance?'

'Like what?'

'I don't know. A path? The best route?'

'We're following a trail. We have a map. Liz has a compass.' She lifted the binoculars to her face, squinted. 'Are these Phoebe's?'

'Maybe . . .' Maggie admitted. She was a terrible packer. Belongings made her feel secure. She was one of those people who always carried a huge handbag without ever quite knowing what was in it. She didn't trust people who strode about with small, practical handbags. Too much efficiency. Too much disciplined decision-making. She liked it when someone asked, 'Do you have any hand cream?' and she'd dig around for a few moments, finally emerging with a tube of something she'd not seen in twelve months. 'Yes, I do!'

Focus.

Did she just think that instruction, or had Helena said it? Maggie so often channelled Helena's voice that it was hard to tell. Faced with a difficult decision, she'd ask herself, *What would Helena do?* – but now that she was standing next to Helena, it was hard to remember if it were the real or imagined Helena who'd just spoken.

'Maybe these could go?' Maggie said, lifting a tin of Peppa Pig plasters.

Helena eyed them with disdain. 'Correct.' Then she plucked a sewing kit from the bed. 'What are you planning on doing with this?'

Maggie lifted her shoulders. 'Repair something?'

Helena tossed the sewing kit aside. 'Next. Do you need a book?'

'I like to read before bed.'

'So do I, but *Shantaram* is 930 pages, and it looks like you've only got fifty left. Anyway, Lin resumes his heroin habit and ends up in an underworld opium den. The end.'

Maggie clutched her chest. 'Where was the spoiler alert?'

Together they slimmed and cropped, snapping off the end of a bamboo toothbrush, removing the packaging from her stove, setting aside Wet Wipes and spare T-shirts. She was allowed two pairs of socks. No pyjamas. Three pairs of knickers. A spare base layer. It was brutal but Helena was focused and busy – and busy for Helena was happy.

Last night, when Maggie had attempted to talk about the pregnancy test result, Helena had cut her down. 'No more questions. No meaningful looks. I'm not open for talking. You've had your three minutes of questions.'

'But Helena—' she'd tried.

'No buts. We're done. We have a mountain range to cross. That's what I'm focusing on.'

The conversation had ended.

Now Maggie kept glancing sideways at Helena, wondering how she was feeling; wondering why she'd stopped using contraception; wondering—

'Here,' Helena said, interrupting her thoughts as she handed Maggie her backpack. 'Try now.'

Maggie heaved the bag onto her shoulders. It was heavy and cumbersome and still compacted her spine, but she smiled cheerfully as she said, 'Can barely tell I'm wearing it.'

They trudged through the entrance of the lodge.

'There you are,' Liz said, smiling briefly. A map in a clear wallet hung from a cord around her neck. Her hair was pulled back into a neat ponytail and her hiking laces were double-knotted.

'I'm signing the logbook for us,' she said, drawing a pencil across the ledger, noting each of their names.

Liz Wallace
Joni Gold
Helena Hall
Maggie Padden

Under the 'expected return date' column, Liz hesitated, the pencil hovering for a moment. She checked the date on her watch, then scribbled down four days from now.

'Did you check the weather?' Helena asked.

'Looks mixed. We'll probably get a bit of everything. But it's gorgeous this morning,' Liz said, glancing towards the open doorway.

'Do you think we'll get rain?' Maggie asked. Hiking in the rain would be miserable.

'Four seasons in a day. That's what they say,' Liz said cheerfully.

Outside, the sky was pure blue. The mountains rose sharply, their peaks kissed with morning sun. A light breeze lifted from the land, carrying the scent of grass and something faintly earthy.

Joni was sitting on her pack in the shade, shoulders rounded, sunglasses on. Her dark hair was piled on top of her head, a honey-coloured bandana keeping loose strands from her face. She was wearing shorts and the same cut-off T-shirt she'd worn last night. From the pallor of her skin and slump of her shoulders, Maggie wondered if she'd even made it to bed.

'How are you feeling?' Maggie asked, sliding her pack from her shoulders.

'Like I've been dug up.'

Helena was eyeing Joni's backpack. 'Looks light. Got everything you need?'

'I stopped at a hiking store en route. Asked the kid behind

the desk to pack everything I'd need to survive for four days. Guess we'll see how he did.'

'I'm going to try Aidan,' Maggie said, slipping her phone from her pocket and stepping apart from the others. She walked a little way towards the lake until a bar of reception showed, then dialled. She held the phone to her ear, pacing, as she waited for him to pick up. She was desperate to hear Phoebe's voice, to tell her she loved her, to know if she'd slept through the night, to check she didn't need to come home.

She watched the tread of her boots back and forth, listening to it ring. She waited a full minute. Then another.

Her stomach plunged with disappointment as Aidan failed to pick up. Tears pricked at her lower lids as she thumbed out a text message for him to show Phoebe, filling the screen with heart emojis. MISS YOU! I'LL BE HOME SOON!

'Couldn't get through?' Joni asked, as Maggie trudged back towards her.

She shook her head. 'What if Phoebe thinks I've forgotten her?'

'She's the most loved child on earth. And think how proud she'll be when you get back and tell her that you've climbed a mountain.'

Maggie pressed her lips together, nodding. Joni was right. Climb the bloody mountain. That's all there was to it. Once they were out the other side, she'd be on her way back home, back to Phoebe.

'We need a group photo before we set off,' Liz announced as she exited the lodge. 'Let's stand by the trail head.'

The others obliged, settling their packs on their shoulders and crossing to the edge of the lake, where the beginning of the trail was marked by a wooden post reading, *Svelle Trail*.

They crowded close. Maggie tried to reach her arm around Helena's waist, but the packs were too large, so all four of them gripped hands.

As Liz was angling the phone, jostling everyone closer into position, Maggie became aware of someone watching them.

Erik was standing further along the path, his face drawn, eyes dark. A tired backpack sagged against his shoulders. He was staring at her, a heaviness in his features. There was something unnervingly distant about his gaze. A hollow feeling spread across her insides.

'Mags! Smile!' Liz instructed.

She pulled her gaze back to the screen to see it filled with Helena's red lips, Liz's bright smile, Joni's eyes hidden behind dark sunglasses.

The shutter was pressed. The picture of the four of them froze for a beat, Maggie's expression hesitant, uncertain.

As her friends released her, she turned. She saw the back of Erik's pack, the lope of his tanned legs stuffed into worn boots. She watched, uneasy, as he disappeared onto the trail they were about to begin.

THE SEARCH

Leif leans in the open doorway. It's been four days since the end-of-season party and the lodge guests have thinned to a trickle. The serious climbers will be flocking to warmer places to see out the winter in Greece or Spain, while the skiers won't arrive until the first heavy snows. Leif finds the lodge strange in the shoulder season; he misses the buzz and influx of new-comers.

The blue skies of a few days ago are gone. Now the wind is blowing hard, raking the lake into ridges. The mountains have been swallowed by billowing dark clouds. There will be poor visibility up on Blafjell today.

Autumn arrives early in the mountains, he thinks, noticing the leaves are already starting to fall. As kids, at this time of year he and Erik would mess around in the long, browning grasses before school, the sweet smell of turning leaves filling the air. Their mother would send them out to pick the final wild blueberries, ready to make jams to see them through the long winter. They'd return, fingers stained purple, boots muddy, a bag of fruit swinging between them.

He can remember the sweet, honeyed smell of the jam bubbling on the stove in the lodge kitchen, the thick embroidered material of his mother's skirt, his father coming in with the smell of the outdoors on his skin. Those days feel like a lifetime ago – before their father died; before their mother's MS had really taken hold; before Erik walked out.

He runs a hand down the door jamb, reminding himself: *We still have the lodge.*

Lots of people his age move away. Go to Oslo or Bergen. Winter somewhere warmer. He tells anyone who asks that he loves this place – it's home – and that's the truth. But more recently he's found himself fantasising about leaving – that incomparable freedom of starting over somewhere new.

With Erik on his mind, he pushes away from the door and returns to the reception desk. Sliding the logbook towards him, his gaze travels down the short list of hikers out on the Svelle trail.

There. Erik's name written in his loose, scrawling hand. He's surprised he even signed himself out. Leif wishes he hadn't gone – but what could he do? Chase after him? Say, *Don't go?*

He lifts his gaze, looking through the open doorway, studying the green flanks of the nearest mountain. The Svelle route leads through valleys and woodland to reach a remote section of coastline, before ascending steeply over a mountain ridge onto Blafjell – and then returning to the lodge. The route takes most hikers four days.

Typically, they liked to make an early start on the final morning, so they would be back at the lodge in time for lunch. He checks his watch. Midday.

All morning he's had a strange plunging, lurching sensation in his gut – like he's at the top of a rollercoaster and is tensing, ready for the drop.

His knuckles move back and forth beneath his chin. Leif knows these mountains better than most. Knows the switch of the weather. Knows how fog can roll in and swallow everything that's familiar. Knows how the changing shadows of the mountains can challenge even the best navigators. Knows how panic can be fatal.

His gaze runs across the low foothills. For any hiker who has taken the Svelle trail and climbed Blafjell, this is the only route back to the lodge.

He keeps on looking, feeling the rising beat of his heart.

The path is completely empty.

19

LIZ

Liz strode across the valley, sun on her face, long grass brushing her lower legs. The air smelt of ozone and pine.

She smiled: they were out here, the four of them, hiking beneath a wide, blue Norwegian sky, tents on their backs! She felt strong and fit, her hiking boots sturdy on the even, giving ground.

Patrick always joked that Liz was really a six-foot person trapped in a five-foot body. The twins complained that she walked too fast – but she loved striding out, feeling her heart rate climb.

They'd already passed the lake and ascended a hillside, where they'd stopped for lunch, leaning against their packs while eating sandwiches prepared for them in the lodge kitchen. Now they were enjoying the last of the flat terrain as they crossed the valley bottom. Layers of undulating green stretched as far as the eye could see, meadow rolling into tree-lined hillside, climbing into mountain. The breeze was gentle, the sun full and bright.

She paused, glancing back. The others were a distance behind her, the drift of their voices mingling with the far-off tinkle of sheep bells. Maggie was at the rear, spine curved under the weight of her pack. Liz had recently read an article about the demotivating effects of being at the rear of a group – and made a mental note to make sure Maggie took a turn leading.

Up ahead, a fallen log lay at the side of the path. She paused there to give the others the chance to catch up. She shrugged her pack from her shoulders and took out her water bottle, absorbing the view.

The path through the valley intersected farmland. In the distance, there was a traditional red clapboard barn. A tractor was parked in front of it, huge cylinder bales of hay shrink-wrapped in plastic sheeting. Beside the barn was a small house, chimney smoking. She wondered what it must be like to live somewhere so remote. It looked beautiful on a sunny day like this, but what about in winter when the fields were covered in snow and the track leading in and out wouldn't be ploughed?

Liz felt a prickling sensation at the back of her neck and had the feeling she was being watched.

She turned.

A thickset woman in dark trousers was standing at the edge of the field, leaning her forearms on a fence post. She looked a decade older than Liz, her skin tanned and weathered.

'*God morgen!*' Liz called.

'Hiking the Svelle trail?' she asked in perfect English, eyes warm.

'Yes, that's right.'

She pushed her lips together, then turned and looked west in the direction of the coast. 'Have you checked the weather?'

'Yes.' She'd checked three weather apps this morning, until she found one that gave her a forecast she liked. The first two had shown lightning and thunderstorms tomorrow evening. The third hadn't.

'A low pressure is coming. It will bring a storm tomorrow.'

The Hike

Liz glanced up at the clear, bright blue sky. 'We've got water-proofs.'

The woman smiled lightly, but her voice was firm as she said, 'Better to wait until it passes, *ja?*'

They couldn't wait. This was their window. It was either set out today, or not do it at all. She wasn't disregarding the woman's advice – this was her territory, not Liz's – but they couldn't derail the entire trip based on one person's opinion. If there was a storm, they'd take shelter. They would handle it. She glanced over her shoulder and, spotting Joni, felt a guilty flush in her neck.

'Tell your friends to turn back,' the woman said quietly, seriously. Then she pushed away from the fence-line and crossed the field.

Turning around just wasn't an option. Liz needed this. She pictured returning home to the uncertainty of everything that awaited her and having failed at this one thing. No. She wouldn't let that happen.

Liz glanced at her friends. Joni was singing, fingertips dusting the long grass. Maggie's cheeks were flushed with the sun. Helena was walking straight-backed, no phone pressed to her ear. They all needed this just as much as Liz did. She wouldn't make a choice based on fear.

When they reached her, Joni asked, 'What did the lady say?'

Liz hesitated only for a moment. 'That it's a beautiful day for hiking.'

20

HELENA

Helena was aware of the hot, uncomfortable rub of her heels within her boots. She didn't even want to think the word, yet there it was popping right into her head, shiny and bloated: *blisters.*

Oh God, she was going to be *that* hiker. The one who complains all trip. How much sympathy can reasonably be mustered for someone else's blisters?

She'd bought her hiking boots over a month ago and had very much planned to break them in. The problem was, where? She could hardly strap them on and yomp to her Bristol office in her blazer and hiking boots. The only time she'd put them on was in the evenings in her apartment, effectively meaning she'd broken them in by walking to her fridge to fetch wine.

She was desperate to kick them off, peel away her sweaty socks and wiggle her toes. She pictured herself lounging back in a comfy chair, feet freed from their chambers. But, of course, there would be no comfy chair. They were wild camping, that's what Liz kept calling it. It had sounded faintly romantic when talking about it over dinner in a restaurant that served polenta chips and rosemary-infused seabass. She'd never understood the appeal of campsites – paying money to sleep in a tent beside families with whingeing kids who wake at dawn. At least *wild* camping held a sense of adventure and glamour, pitching up somewhere picturesque and empty. That's what she'd thought. But now that they were in the middle of nowhere, she was thinking a campsite with a picnic bench, flushable toilet and coin shower could be adjusted to.

She kept on walking because that was the deal. Put one foot in front of the other and walk.

It was that easy.

It was that hard.

If she could concentrate on the rhythm of her footsteps, then it would be easier to ignore the rub of her boots and the tension in her shoulders. Harder to ignore her thoughts, though. They kept circling back to the pink cross on the pregnancy test. She recalled the slow, single blink of Maggie's eyes before she'd turned the test towards Helena, saying, 'You are pregnant.'

It felt unreal. A ludicrous fact.

Helena Hall is pregnant.

The statement belonged to a different person's life. Not hers. Her life was made up of other statements:

Helena Hall likes cocktails.

Helena Hall enjoys city breaks.

Helena Hall dislikes other people's children.

And yet here she was. Pregnant. In Norway. In hiking boots.

Helena Hall has a baby in her belly.

Helena Hall has never changed a nappy.

Helena Hall has no mother to ask: What do I do?

Helena Hall has stopped walking.

Helena Hall finds tears leaking from her eyes.

There was a warm hand on her forearm. Maggie was beside her, face creased with concern. 'What is it?'

'I'm just having a small, quiet breakdown. Feel free to walk around me.'

'Right. Get this off you,' Maggie said, unbuckling the chest strap of Helena's pack, and helping her out.

'You know I'll never get it back on.'

Maggie took off her own pack, and then she stepped forward and hugged Helena, putting her lovely soft body, which smelled of the outdoors and a hint of apricot moisturiser, against Helena's.

She buried her face in the thick auburn waves of Maggie's hair. Ever since her mother had died, she'd had to get used to crying and accepting hugs. She was coming to like them. It was as if they hit a release valve, allowing her own tears to flow.

'It will be okay. It will all be okay,' Maggie said soothingly.

When Helena was finished with the releasing, she wiped her face, then reached into her pack for a gold tube of lipstick. Reverently, she removed the lid and breathed in: rose mixed with a hint of vanilla.

Helena and her mother had always worn lipstick. It was armour. *Here I am, world. Do your worst!* Even in the last weeks of her mother's life, when her muscles wasted and her breathing became laboured, she still applied lipstick. And when she was too ill to do it herself, Helena had done it for her. Lipstick fixed nothing, but it was a way of holding onto a piece of identity when illness stripped away the rest.

Now Helena traced the colour over the full curves of her lips.

'She's back.' Maggie grinned.

'Do you ever look at your life and think: *This isn't the one I'm supposed to be leading?*'

Maggie eyed her. 'I'm a divorced, single mother, in rented accommodation, receiving benefits. I thought I'd be an artist, with a horde of children, living in a rambling country house, with a husband who adored me, and an art studio in the garden.'

Helena laughed. 'But I love your life! You are acing your life!'

Maggie shook her head, although she was smiling.

'You know why I came on this trip?' Helena asked.

'Because you're scared of saying no to Liz?'

'I came for Mum.'

Maggie's head tilted to one side.

'Right at the end, you know what she told me? That she regretted not seeing more of the world. She worked so damn hard, Mags. Two jobs. Never wanting me to go without. Bringing up a kid on her own – you know how tough that is – and Mum did it with grace.' Her mother had been a teaching assistant by day and worked a nightshift on the weekend at a care home to bring in extra money.

'Just when she was planning her retirement, she goes and gets cancer. Life's a piss-take, isn't it? Do you know, I was going to take her to Barcelona? We'd been looking at travel brochures, planning a city break. I was just waiting for a window with work . . .' Tears pricked her eyes. 'Never wait, Mags.' She lowered her head, a well of grief waiting for her to drown in.

Maggie didn't rush to fill the silence.

Helena pressed her lips together. Tasted the sheen of her lipstick. Dragged her gaze up. And there was the view: a carpet of green, stretching into a startling vista of mountains, reminding her that life was also beautiful.

She drew in a breath, turning to face Maggie. 'Mum asked me if I'd scatter her ashes "far and wide".'

Maggie's eyes crinkled with warmth. 'You've brought her ashes?'

She eyed her pack. 'Some of them. They weigh four kilos and I had to decide between those and rehydrated meals. I went with a bonus mushroom risotto.'

Maggie laughed.

'I'm going to do it when we reach the coast.'

'That is the loveliest,' Maggie said, eyes glistening. She went

Lucy Clarke

to say something further – and Helena sensed she was going to use the intimacy of the moment to bring up the pregnancy test result – but Liz had started signalling that they should catch up.

Helena saluted. 'Can't keep Brown Owl waiting,' she said to Maggie, then heaved on her pack.

Side by side, they continued to walk.

21

JONI

Joni took a deep breath, filling her lungs with fresh, pine-scented air. Her ears buzzed with silence. Tall grasses bent and shivered with the afternoon breeze. In the distance, the lower, green slopes of mountainsides were bathed in golden sunlight. She didn't care about the weight of her pack, or the thunder of her hangover. All she could think, was: *Look where I am!*

Where she *should* have been was at a sound-check in a huge arena in Germany. She would have been breathing in tour-bus-engine fumes, or the stale sweat of the roadies, or the blunt fug of the dry-ice machine. There would have been people clamouring for her attention, speakers and guitars and drum kits being tested, radio microphones clipped to costumes, the press of warm battery packs at her waist, layers of make-up to paste on, eyelashes to glue.

She'd never pulled out of a gig before. Not once. Not even when she broke her ankle five hours before going on and was so dosed on painkillers and coke that the roadies carried an armchair onto stage and she sang from the crushed velvet, her broken ankle raised on a footstool, silver nail polish glittering in the spotlights.

The show always went on.

Until now.

She'd stepped out. Walked away.

Kept walking.

And look where she was!

She gazed around, drinking in the lush valley, the dense thatch of forest ahead, the mountain peaks rising jagged into a blue sky. It was dizzying, impossible to gauge distances with so much space and horizon and sky.

She reached Liz's side, who was waiting with her hands hooked around the chest straps of her pack. Her head was tipped to the mountains. 'The scale is something else, isn't it?'

'The space – I can barely grasp it,' Joni marvelled. It was an age-old landscape and her body responded to it with ancient instincts, as if waking her from a deep, dreamless sleep. She felt alert, aware, as if the rest of her life had been sleep-walked through.

'We didn't get to talk properly last night,' Liz said as they fell into step together, the sun on their faces. 'How are you feeling?'

Joni concentrated on the hard press of the earth beneath her boots. She wanted to be honest with Liz, but how did she even begin to explain? Liz's life made sense. She had a husband, two children, a job. She had ticks in all the right boxes. Fame was the opposite of sense. It was confusion. It was the white noise of drugs and alcohol. It was the haze of tour buses and hotels and jetlag. It was the tabloid hall of mirrors, being celebrated on a Tuesday and shamed on a Wednesday. It was the claustrophobia of strangers shouting your name. It was the relentless hounding of the press. It was having no way out.

Seeing Liz and Patrick in the audience at her Dublin gig had exposed every story she'd told herself about her life. Joni believed – or wanted to believe – that she was wild and free and happy. But there, in the crowd, arms around one another, were Liz and Patrick, whooping and hollering her name, their faces bright, their children tucked up in the care of family, a home to return to.

What if *that* was the story Joni wanted?

Liz glanced sideways, waiting for a response. There was so much she couldn't tell her. 'I'm burned out,' she settled on.

Liz nodded gently. 'In Dublin, you needed me, didn't you? I'm sorry – I feel like we came to the gig, enjoyed the free tickets, then disappeared.'

'Don't do that. You had a migraine. Don't apologise for things that aren't your fault.' She looked at Liz in her neat hiking trousers, her hair brushed into a ponytail, her honest, open heart. Joni stopped walking. 'You have always been there for me.' She thought of the time Liz had driven across the country when she'd broken up with a guy she was seeing in Manchester and had no money to get home. Or how Liz had come over in the middle of the night when her grandmother died and didn't leave for a fortnight. 'You're my good thing. I hope you know that. You always have been.'

In the middle of the valley, they hugged. Liz's cheek was warm and smooth against her own. She could feel a surge of emotion pushing upwards, feelings she didn't want to examine.

Joni's phone vibrated in her pocket.

'You've got reception out here?' Liz asked.

Joni slid it from her pocket, glancing at the screen. 'One bar.' There was a message from Kai. As she read it, the blood drained from her face.

'What is it?' Liz asked.

Joni pushed her sunglasses onto the top of her head and stared at the screen. Then she turned the phone towards Liz.

The message read: *You're going to need a lawyer.*

Beneath, there was a video. She clicked *Play*.

Liz stood at her shoulder as the video buffered. Then suddenly

103

Joni saw herself in shot, singing on a makeshift stage, a borrowed guitar in her arms, a small crowd bobbing up and down.

'Oh no . . . no . . .' she said, head shaking.

Maggie and Helena had caught up. 'What are we looking at?' Helena said, lurching her pack from her shoulders, breathing heavily as she peered at the screen.

Joni said, 'A video of me playing at the lodge.'

They all looked to the screen, but the clip had frozen.

'It puts me in breach of my contract! I'm supposed to be signed off! Your doctor's note,' she said to Liz, 'which exempts me. Means I'm insured. All the ticket holders get a refund. The band still gets paid. But not if I'm gigging on the same night someplace else!'

The video began to play again. Whoever was recording it had been dancing too, pointing the screen at the stage. Joni watched herself, mouth lowered to the mic, fingertips strumming the guitar, eyes closing as she hit a high note. Then the camera panned to the crowd, travelling over a sea of heads, hands thrown in the air. It paused on Maggie and Liz, who had their arms wrapped around one another and were swaying, beaming directly at the camera as they sang along with the lyrics. Then the image jolted as the camera was turned around, an arm briefly in the frame, before it refocused on Helena. She pouted, thrusting her index and pinky fingers into a *Rock on!* sign.

The video ended.

There was silence.

'It's *your* video?' Joni said, turning to face Helena, her voice cut with disbelief.

'I wasn't thinking. Sorry! It was just on my Instagram. I've got about ten followers.'

Joni's chest tightened. 'Those followers shared it with their followers, and now it's *everywhere!* There are 300,000 views already! The tabloids will crucify me!'

'Sorry, okay? I didn't know the gig was secret.'

'It wasn't a gig!' Joni shot. 'Maggie dragged me on stage!'

Maggie recoiled. 'Oh. God. I didn't mean to . . .'

'You've got nothing to be sorry about,' Helena said, back stiffening. Joni recognised Helena's tone – the switch to something sharper, defensive. 'Joni was hardly *dragged.*'

'What does that mean?' Joni demanded.

Tension pulsed in Helena's neck. 'You could have said no.'

'You expected me to get on the mic and explain I wouldn't be singing because of legalities and insurance provisions?'

'I expected you to get on stage because you love it. A roomful of people chanting your name? Begging you to perform? It's an ego trip.'

Joni felt winded. The weight of her pack was cutting into her shoulders. She snapped off the buckles, let her backpack crash to the earth. She turned away from Helena, hands lifting to her hairline.

Panic rose hot and spiked in her body. 'I'm screwed! They'll sue me for this. They'll figure out that the doctor who signed me off was my mate. Liz is in the video!'

Liz blanched. 'Oh, God. Am I going to get in trouble? What if the surgery finds out? You didn't even have a consultation. I shouldn't have written a doctor's note while on annual leave!' she said, wringing her hands. 'They could revoke my licence for this!'

Helena shook her head. 'That won't happen. Your doctor's note said Joni is suffering from exhaustion and stress, right?'

Liz nodded.

'Then it will be fine. You wrote the note – but it's not up to you to decide what Joni does with the advice.'

Joni felt scalded by Helena's tone – as if she were a schoolgirl who had caused trouble. It was just like when they were teenagers – the others turning together, protecting each other

105

whenever Joni went too far. Liz's solid career couldn't be threatened; Maggie wasn't to be blamed for dragging her on stage;
Helena couldn't get in trouble for simply posting a video. It
was Joni – she was the flawed one. The bad girl.

She looked at each of them in turn. 'You've screwed me.'

Helena gaped. 'You're blaming *us*?'

'I came out here to be with you all. To have some space from
the crazy mess of my life. Not to be hauled on stage . . . and
then splashed across social media just to get a few likes from
people you barely know!'

There was silence.

Maggie shifted.

Liz's gaze was on her boots.

'That is your take on our friendship?' Helena said, voice
deathly quiet. 'We've heard nothing from you on the group
WhatsApp for weeks. Then you swan in, all smiles and champagne. You put on the *Joni Gold Show*. Sprinkle us with your
own brand of glitter. What comes next? Hike with us for a few
days and then disappear for another two years?' She shook her
head sharply. 'Don't expect a round of applause from me for
your part-time friendship.'

Joni felt like she'd been gut-slammed. She looked at each of
her friends. Their gazes were averted.

'And by the way,' Helena said, hauling on her pack. 'I didn't
post the video to get a handful of likes from people I "barely
know". I did it because I was proud of you. I was happy that
you showed up for us. That's why I shared it.'

22

LIZ

Liz watched Helena striding off across the valley floor, pack riding high on her shoulders.

Maggie turned and looked helplessly at Liz, lifting her palms. Then she heaved on her backpack, grimacing as she fought to push her arms back through the straps, and went after Helena.

Joni had snapped her sunglasses back on and turned in the opposite direction, walking some distance and then flinging herself down in the long grass, a starfish of limbs, as she glared at the sky.

Liz was too hot beneath her fleece – confrontation always made her sweat – and she yanked at the zip and then tossed the fleece on top of her pack.

Helena and Joni had clashed often in their teens. They could both be strident and opinionated, quick to rile and slow to back down. Liz and Maggie had become mediators, trying to smooth out the knots in the fabric of their friendship.

Somehow, Liz and Joni never fought. Perhaps it was because they didn't set themselves against one another. They'd always been so different – Liz with her studies and focused, determined attitude, and Joni with her music and chase for wild freedom. Like magnets, they were drawn together by their opposing forces.

She waded through the tall grass, the sun hot on her shoulders. She found Joni still lying down, fingers pushed into the roots of her hair.

Liz reached out a hand to her.

'Not ready.'

With a sigh, Liz sank down beside her, flattening a little space in the long grass. She didn't say anything for a while, giving Joni the space to breathe. From her experience with patients, she'd learned that often it was the pause that was the key.

She examined the grass for ticks, wondering whether Norwegian ticks carried Lyme disease. She'd have to look it up when they had a signal. Then she glanced up, watching a bird of prey circling above the treeline, its wingspan dark against the flare of sun.

Eventually Joni said, 'Helena's always looking for an excuse to bring me down. She thinks I've got my head up my arse. Did you see the look she gave me when I bought the champagne last night? She's always had a chip on her shoulder about money.'

'She's had to work hard for everything she's got.'

'And I haven't?' Joni said, sitting up. 'Sure, my grandmother owned her house, but we were hardly rolling in it.'

Liz knew that. She and Joni had lived on the same street – detached houses on a tree-lined road, with room in the driveway for two cars. It wasn't riches, but it was enough.

'I'd have given away the house in a flash to have what she had. What you all had.'

Family.

Joni's mother – a Chilean model who was to thank for Joni's wide, dark eyes and striking bone structure – had died a week after giving birth, from an infection caused by a part of the placenta not being expelled. Joni's father, a British photographer, had dumped Joni in her grandmother's care when she was seven.

Now he only got in touch if he needed VIP passes to whatever festival she was headlining.

Joni took off her sunglasses and squeezed the bridge of her nose. Her skin looked pale and there were mauve shadows beneath her eyes. Then she looked up at Liz, face filled with concern. 'I hope I haven't gotten you in trouble over the doctor's note. I wasn't using you.'

'I know that,' Liz said, and she did. Joni could be impetuous and a little self-centred at times, but she was never manipulative. 'It'll be fine. The surgery will have my back.'

'I shouldn't have put you in that position. And I shouldn't have bailed on the tour, on my bandmates, on Kai . . .'

'Do you think really think legal action will be taken?'

She shrugged. 'I'm in breach of my contract.'

'What did Kai say when you spoke to him last night?'

Joni looked blank.

'Down by the lake. You were on the phone to him?'

'Oh. Yes.' Joni glanced away. 'He was trying to get me to finish the tour.'

Liz nodded. 'When he calms down, maybe it'll all settle. You said it was over with him?'

She nodded. 'We're bad for each other. We've been doing too much coke. Too much of everything. I can't see him letting this go. He's got a mean streak.'

Joni's romantic life had always been tumultuous. She pinwheeled from one relationship to the next. There was a dancer from Spain she was briefly engaged to. A club owner in Ibiza she lived with for two years. An Australian surf instructor who wanted to take her back to Bondi. And then Kai.

Liz said, 'It was brave of you to get out.'

'But the way I did it . . . I've messed everything up, coming out here, getting you into trouble. I've made so many mistakes,

Liz. Hurt so many people. If you knew . . .' She broke off, shaking her head. 'I should never have come.'

'Don't say that! You've made this trip for me! Helena and Maggie were thinking of pulling out. If it wasn't for you, I'd be spending four days in the lodge taking gentle strolls around the lake. I need you!'

'You need me?' Joni managed a laugh. 'Liz, you're the strongest, most capable person I've ever met. You don't need anyone!' A shadow passed over her eyes. 'Especially not me.'

23

HELENA

Tight balls of tension worked at Helena's clenched jaw. Her blistered heels burned with every stride, pack bouncing on her shoulders.

Liz and Maggie never stood up to Joni. It was as if she were too special, too golden, to handle the truth.

Then she remembered the way Joni's face had fallen as she'd said that stuff about her part-time friendship. Beneath the burn of anger, she felt the smallest niggle of guilt.

She paced on. The valley led into woodland, where thin silver birches clustered close, a light breeze stirring their branches. The forest floor was dusted with the first fallen leaves of the season.

'Wait up!'

Helena turned and saw Maggie attempting to jog beneath the bounce of her pack.

She eventually caught up, face flushed, hairline damp. 'You've got a stride on you!' she said, breathless.

'Walking off the rage.'

'How's that going?' Maggie asked, wiping her brow.

'Ask me on the peak of Blafjell. Might be out of my system by then.' She glanced back to where Joni and Liz were finally rejoining the trail. 'What's the bet Liz will defend Joni?'

111

Maggie didn't comment.

'Doesn't it frustrate you that Joni turns up – unannounced – when we've not seen her in eighteen months? She doesn't call. Doesn't check in. The rest of us have been preparing for this trip for weeks, buying the right gear, getting fit—'

Maggie looked a little sheepish.

'Okay, fit-ish. But you did your best, right? Joni, though – she decides on a coin toss! Then she just orders some poor star-struck teenager in an outdoors shop to sort her gear, and just like that, she's here – singing in the lodge, partying through the night. Then she's up and out on the trail this morning, running her fingers through the meadow grass like she's found her bliss. If I drank my bodyweight in booze, partied until dawn, and slept in my make-up, the next morning you could wear me as a Halloween mask. Yet Joni wakes up in smudged kohl liner, piles her hair on top of her head, ties a bandana, and looks like a bloody rock star.'

'She is a rock—'

'Fine! The point is,' she said, not entirely sure what her point was going to be, 'the point is . . . Joni bought her hiking boots yesterday and hasn't worn them in, but is she going to be the one with blisters? Of course, she's not!'

At her side, Maggie was trying not to smile.

'Why are you making that face?'

Maggie's smile widened. 'The things that frustrate you about Joni – her impulsiveness, how she doesn't give a shit about plans, that she'll throw herself into any situation – those are also the reasons why you love her.'

Helena paused on that comment for a moment. She was saved from having to concede that Maggie was, in fact, completely right, because the trail had delivered them through a narrow band of trees and onto a riverbank.

'Oh,' Maggie said, as the trees parted, revealing a glacial blue river rushing between two deep grassy banks. Water-smoothed boulders studded its surface.

'This must be where we need to cross,' Helena said, noting the two red T-markers painted on opposite sides of the river.

Three flat boulders looked like possible stepping stones, but they'd need another dozen if they were to make it across with dry feet.

'It looks too deep,' Maggie said.

But Helena was already thinking about the relief of peeling off her sweat-soaked socks and lowering her feet into the cool water.

When Liz reached the riverbank, she planted her hands on her hips and said, 'We can't cross here.' She consulted the map she wore around her neck. 'I think we should keep on walking – see if there's a narrower section up there.'

Helena could feel the pulsating heat of her blisters. Liz wasn't even sweating. She looked hydrated, energised. Like Joni, her heels were no doubt blister-free. 'I'm crossing here,' she snapped, unlacing her boots.

Joni was standing several feet away, sunglasses on, arms folded across her chest.

'It's too dangerous,' Liz warned. 'Anyway, you're meant to keep your boots on for grip during a river crossing.'

Helena tossed her head. 'And what, walk in soaking wet boots for the next four days? My heels are already pulp. I don't think damp pulp is going to help.' She was being short-tempered with Liz but couldn't seem to rein it in. She peeled off her blood-stained socks, grimacing as they snagged against the damaged skin.

'Your feet!' Maggie cried, wincing.

'They're fine,' Helena said, choosing not to look. She removed her trousers, stuffing them in her pack, then secured her boots to her backpack by their laces. She lugged the pack onto her shoulders and made for the riverbank.

'Helena, don't,' Liz said.

Helena moved carefully between the first three stepping stones, and then lowered her feet into the icy water. The cold rush made her gasp with pleasure and pain.

Beneath her soles, the riverbed was lined with large, round stones coated in algae. She took a moment to find her balance, bare toes clinging to the curves of stone. The weight of her backpack forced her to tilt slightly forward as she made one tentative step and then another.

The water was soon above her knees, the tow of the current surprisingly fierce. She was aware that everyone was watching her. She kept going, gradually reaching the middle of the river. Liz was right; she'd underestimated the depth and tow.

'It's too deep!' Liz called.

It was the clipped bossiness of Liz's tone that propelled her on. She took another step and, as she did, she felt the sole of her left foot slide over the algae-slick surface of a stone. She tried to grip with her toes, but there was no purchase. She was thrown off balance, her body lurching forward, the weight of her pack toppling her further. She reached out – but there was nothing to grab.

She felt the icy slap of the river smack her face. In an instant, she was under. The freezing water sealed above her head, the fizzing rush of it filled her ears and nose. She could taste its earthy, mineral bite as it gushed into her mouth.

Her backpack was strapped fast, forcing her down. Her knees met the riverbed, rolled over loose stones. She tried to push back to the surface – but the weight of her pack, which had filled with water, kept her pinned under. She heard the distorted screams from the others on the riverbank.

Her fingers grappled with the chest strap, fumbling, panicked.

She managed to wrench the clip open and tried to pull it from her shoulders, but it was still attached at her waist with a second buckle.

Her lungs were burning, eyes wide to the blurry sting of the river. With blundering fingers, she scrabbled underwater to release it. Her wet hair fanned in front of her face.

The urge to breathe was becoming desperate. She clawed at the buckle.

Fire burned in her chest.

This is how I'm going to die, she thought.

Suddenly there was a strong yank above her, and she felt the pack being raised out of the water, Helena drawn with it.

She burst to the surface, gasping, sucking air into her lungs.

Joni, soaked, was in the river. She unclipped the buckle of Helena's pack, releasing her from its weight.

'You're okay,' Joni said, calmly. Her sunglasses were studded with water. 'You're safe.'

Adrenalin spiked in Helena's veins as she dragged in another breath, hair pasted to her face.

'Let's wade to the other bank, okay?'

Helena nodded, a hand gripping Joni's arm as they moved across the riverbed together, Joni holding the pack high above her head, muscles taut.

Reaching the opposite bank, Helena crawled out on her knees, chest heaving. Shock ricocheted through her body. She flopped down on the grassy bank, wiping snot from her face.

Joni clambered out beside her, clothes sodden, boots wet, and hauled the backpack away from the edge. She crouched in front of Helena, water dripping from her clothes. 'Are you hurt?'

'I could've drowned,' Helena said, her voice small. 'I was in waist-high water, but I couldn't stand. I shouldn't have crossed . . . I'm sorry,' she said, humiliated. She'd started to shake with the cold or shock.

'Here, take off your wet things.'

Helena nodded, peeling off her soaked top.

Joni searched through Helena's pack for the spare clothes that were thankfully stored in dry bags, and handed her a warm fleece.

Helena felt a deep rush of gratitude – and shame. Joni was the one who'd launched straight into the river. Never hesitating. Never considering the consequences.

Helena looked at her. That was Joni, wasn't it? Impulsive, brave, unthinking. It was her curse – and her gift. Just like Maggie said. You start choosing the parts of someone that you'd change or alter, and you realise those very parts are what also makes you love them.

Helena pushed her wet hair back from her face. 'I'm sorry about earlier. For all of it. For posting the video. For what I said.'

Joni shrugged. 'I'm sorry for blaming you. It's my mess. My responsibility to clean it up.'

From the opposite bank, Liz and Maggie were calling to them both, asking if they were okay.

Joni and Helena held each other's gaze for a long moment.

'We're okay,' Helena said eventually, something like a truce settling between them.

THE SEARCH

Leif grips the metal nail between his lips, while he lifts the door back into position, aligning the hinges. Using his full strength, he holds it in place with a single arm, while pinching the nail from his lips and slotting it into the hinge. He twists the screw-driver, securing the first hinge, then repeats it with the second.

He tries the door, moving it back and forth, hearing the satisfying click as it closes smoothly. Done.

He returns the tools to the locker at the side of the lodge. While he's there, he clocks Vilhelm's old blue truck parked on the gravel. He knew it was there – he'd seen it earlier – but its presence draws a shadow over his mood.

Last week, Vilhelm had delivered his mother a freshly caught river fish – and she had invited him to join her when she cooked it. Leif had walked into the lodge kitchen and seen Vilhelm, feet under the table, where his father used to sit. He'd looked up as Leif entered and smiled easily.

Now Leif pauses by Vilhelm's truck. He glances about, then opens the driver's door – no one keeps their vehicles locked in the mountains. He's not looking for anything in particular, rather just wants to get the measure of him. It's strange how you can live in the same village as someone for years without

117

ever really knowing them. Inside there is a dog blanket neatly folded on the passenger seat. A roll of fishing line and a pair of binoculars stowed in the glove compartment. There's nothing beneath the seats except for the original vehicle manual, its pages browning and water stained.

He takes out the binoculars and balances them against the bridge of his nose, adjusting the magnification so they focus on the distance. A gust catches the strap and it flutters around his neck.

A flash of movement fills his vision.

He blinks, startled. He adjusts the focus so he can see the foreground.

Emerging from the treeline only a hundred metres away is a woman. Her dark hair is loose, shielding part of her face. Instinctively, he knows something is wrong. It's the way she's moving: fast, a half-run, half-stagger.

Her head jerks around as she looks over her shoulder.

Behind her, Leif sees a second woman. He tracks her with the binoculars. The pack on her shoulders seems to weigh her down, her mouth hangs open as she pants.

Leif drops the binoculars and begins to run.

24

MAGGIE

They'd agreed to camp by the river for the night, too exhausted to walk any further. A large clearing was bathed in lowering sun, and Liz toed the ground, looking for a dry, flat area to lay their tents.

Maggie rolled back her shoulders, feeling a spasm of muscles shooting down the left side of her spine. She stretched one way and then the other, lips pulled into a grimace. She couldn't remember feeling so exhausted.

Looking towards the woodland they'd be hiking through tomorrow, she was struck by the sheer density of the trees. The landscape seemed to press up against them, a thick buttress of green. She reached into her pack to check her phone for signal.

The screen eyed her blankly. Not a single bar. She felt the hot, panicky sensation of being too far from Phoebe. Too far from everything.

Behind her, Helena, heels blistered, hair still wet from the plunge into the river, was laying their tent across the grass, looking defeated.

All Maggie wanted to do was sit. Not move. She wished that were the full scale of her requirements – but she knew she had to help.

119

She dug into her pack for the bag of pegs and poles, having split the weight of the tent between them. She emptied them into two piles beside the groundsheet.

Helena's face was set, eyes dull.

'You okay?' Maggie asked.

'Fine.' Helena didn't look at her.

'The instructions are sewn into the tent bag, remember? The poles are colour-coded. That's sexy, isn't it?' Good organisation always improved Helena's mood.

'Very.'

Maggie began snapping poles into long lines, then she threaded them through the fabric hooks of the tent. She and Helena had had a practice run in her garden a few weekends ago, Helena bringing wine and olives for the performance. They had recorded it on time-lapse and laughed till their ribs ached, watching themselves back as they'd scratched their heads, laid and relaid it, Phoebe tunnelling beneath the groundsheet.

This time around, there was no wine to motivate them, or Phoebe to make them laugh. In a few minutes they'd arched the poles together, pegged in the groundsheet, and were looking at their home for the night.

Helena disappeared inside, laying out her roll mat and sleeping bag and organising her belongings in the tent pockets.

Maggie padded barefoot across the spongy grass towards the riverbank. Sunlight dappled its surface with gold flecks, colourful rocks wavering in and out of view through the clear water.

She stepped out of her trousers, trying not to look at her pink, dimpled thighs. She peeled her sweat-damp top over her head. The icy cool was glorious as she took a tentative step into the river. She'd not forgotten Helena's earlier ordeal and decided she'd anchor herself to the riverbank.

She sluiced water beneath her underarms and across the back of her neck, washing away the day's exertion.

Her skin was studded with goosebumps as she climbed back onto the riverbank. She didn't have a towel, so she sat facing the sun, letting the last of its warmth dry her skin. She closed her eyes, listening to the soothing rush of the stream flowing over rocks, the low hum of Liz and Joni's chatter as they set up their tent, the high cheep of a bird in the tree canopy.

She heard the lightest sound on the water. Like a whip of wind, followed by a light plink. She opened her eyes and looked at the stream, searching for a bird, or one of her friends throwing in a pebble, but Helena hadn't left their tent, and Joni and Liz were still wrestling with theirs.

A whirring noise was coming from the far riverbank. Perplexed, she glanced about, then noticed a tiny current running across the surface of the river. She angled her head, peering at it, confused. It ran in the opposite direction to the flow of the river.

Then she caught the line shimmering in and out of view, only noticeable because of the water dripping from its thin stretch. A fishing line.

She blinked, following the line, which travelled to the opposite riverbank, where, obscured by a cluster of bushes, she made out the figure of a man.

Maggie startled. She grabbed for her top, pulling it to her chest.

He was wearing dark green trousers, a plaid shirt and a peaked cap. She recognised him immediately: Vilhelm from the lodge.

His eyes were lowered to the river – but he must have seen her. Seen all of them. The noise and the chatter as they put up tents, the pops of colour in amongst all this green space. Had he been here when they arrived, silently watching?

She shivered. His hook had landed only a few feet away. What if it had snagged her? She thought of a metal hook at the back of her neck, the tug and tear of skin.

'Hey!' she called out in a loud voice, wanting him to know, *I'm here. I see you!*

Slowly, Vilhelm raised his head. His dog lay at his feet, muzzle on its paws.

'It's Vilhelm!' Liz whispered, coming to her side with Joni.

'He almost hooked me when I was washing. It's creepy, him all this way out here.'

'He did say he'd be fishing on the trail,' Liz said.

Maggie wrapped her arms around herself, their little slice of tranquillity feeling suddenly threatened.

'He's packing up,' Joni whispered, as he reeled in his line, then put the rod into a sagging bag.

Without looking at them, he lifted the pack onto his shoulders, turned and walked east into the forest, his dog trotting behind him.

It was an eerie, lonely image in the ebbing light.

'Where's he going?' Joni asked.

'There's no path that way,' Liz said, voice low.

They watched, silent, as he was swallowed by the forest.

25

LIZ

Night gathered close, a hush settling over the landscape. The river ran blindly beyond their camp, polished stones turning in the dark. The breeze had quietened, lulled by the late hour.

The four of them circled close to a small fire that smouldered rather than burned. The wood they'd collected earlier from the forest floor was too green to flame.

Liz scraped her fork against the side of the pan, scooping up the last of the noodles. 'I could eat that all over again.'

She pushed to her feet, backside numbed from the hard log where she'd been perched. She flicked on her head torch and carried the pan to the river edge.

She cast the beam to the opposite riverbank, thinking of Vilhelm's strange presence there earlier. A cluster of tiny winged insects darted in and out of the light, but the bank appeared empty.

Kneeling on the damp grass, she plunged the pan into the icy flow. She scooped up water and used her fingers to flush out the noodles that had burned at the edge of the pan.

Away from the glow of the fire and her friends, a strange, unnerving sensation tickled the edges of her senses. Her back felt exposed, the curve of her spine vulnerable as if, behind her, lurked some unnamed threat.

Vilhelm's warning about the landscape drifted into her mind, dark and unsettling.

She shook her head briskly to dislodge the thought, annoyed for allowing her imagination to spin so wildly. She rinsed the pan clean, then hurried back to the fire, grateful for its faint glow and the presence of her friends.

Maggie was handing around a bar of chocolate. 'You sure?' Liz asked. Supplies were precious when you had to carry everything you planned to eat for the next four days.

'Course.'

Liz gratefully snapped off a small square, bringing it reverently towards her face, breathing in its sweet, milky scent. She dropped it into her mouth, chocolate melting against her tongue.

'We've survived day one,' Helena said, stretching her bare feet towards the modest warmth of the fire. She and Joni had propped their wet hiking boots beside it to dry. 'We hiked, crossed a river, put up tents, cooked on a camp stove – and now we have fire. Well, smoke.'

'Wish Aidan could see us!' Maggie said triumphantly.

'How is your delightful ex-husband?' Joni asked.

'Still bitter that you didn't sing at our wedding.'

Joni laughed for the first time in hours.

'God, what did I see in him?' Maggie asked.

'Don't ask me.' Helena shrugged.

'I think I was so swept up by how romantic he was – surprising me with weekends in Amsterdam and Paris, sending flowers all the time, making me feel adored – that I didn't see—'

'What a self-absorbed, jumped-up, narcissistic arsehole he was?' Helena suggested helpfully.

'Don't hold back,' Maggie said wryly. 'I knew things weren't right, but then I fell pregnant, and the wedding was already booked, and I felt obliged to go ahead. Isn't that insane? I married him because I was too embarrassed to say I'd changed my mind. God, I'm weak.' Her expression looked doleful in the firelight.

'You're not weak,' Joni said, elbows on her knees. 'I think you were hopeful. You were pregnant with his baby. You wanted it to be right. You wanted him to be a wonderful father. You wanted the marriage to work. So you hoped and hoped. That's what happened.'

Behind them, in the dark line of trees, Liz thought she caught a movement. She froze, staring. She blinked into the darkness, but the shadow dissolved into the woodland.

'How do you and Patrick manage it?' Maggie asked Liz.

She blinked. 'Us?'

'You've been together for years. You've always been so solid, so strong. So in love. I remember Patrick recording you mix tapes – all the track titles handwritten.'

Liz smiled. She still had those tapes, filled with songs by the Red Hot Chili Peppers, Lenny Kravitz, Beastie Boys. She used to play them over and over as she tried on outfits for their dates to the cinema, or to get fish and chips in town. She hadn't owned a tape deck in two decades, but she had kept every single one.

Maggie continued, 'You survived university in different cities. You got through your medical placements. You managed to keep it together with kids. What's the secret?'

Liz still hadn't said a word. She kept her eyes on the fire. She attempted to smile, but her mouth seemed to wobble.

'What is it?' Maggie asked, head tilted to one side.

Liz could feel the others looking at her across the fire. She wanted to reassure them that everything was fine. That yes, she and Patrick were still wildly in love. But she couldn't seem to make her mouth work. Tears began pricking at her eyelids. Heat rushed to her cheeks.

'Oh, Liz,' Maggie said, scooting close, placing a warm hand on her back.

Her breath snagged. 'Patrick and I . . . we're on a trial separation.' She wanted to say, *But it's fine. It's a good thing. It's not even a real separation – it's a trial.* She wanted to emphasise that word *trial*. That was the important part – that they were just trying it out to remind themselves how much they loved each other – but she couldn't say any of this because, alarmingly, she'd started to cry. 'Sorry,' she said, wiping her face.

'Don't apologise for having emotions,' Maggie said, producing a pack of tissues from a pocket.

'I wasn't planning on saying anything. I didn't want to be a downer.'

'We are your oldest friends!' Maggie cried. 'We do the good and the bad. The whole messy journey, okay?'

Joni nodded emphatically.

'I know.' Maybe she hadn't talked about it because then it would be real, or perhaps it was that she liked people thinking of her as strong and capable. She was the one who other people came to for advice. Those were the foundations of her identity. Without those things, then who was Liz Wallace?

'Why are you separating?' Helena asked.

Wood-smoke drifted towards her, thick in her throat. 'Things have been . . . hard . . . for a while. I can't even explain what's gone wrong.' She shook her head. Could feel the others watching her, waiting. 'We've just . . . lost something,' she tried. 'We haven't laughed together in ages. We used to talk about things, you know? Bands. Adventures. Books. Dreams. Everything. Now all we have time to talk about is who's ordered the school dinners, or what after-school clubs have been cancelled. We're living out the *before* kids and *after* kids cliché.' She'd seen the same thing happen to her parents' marriage: kisses moving from mouths to cheeks; a double bed traded for separate rooms; irritation in place of laughter. *Not us*, she'd thought.

126

But it was them. Liz kept her gaze on the fire as she admitted, 'We've stopped having sex.' It wasn't that one of them was pulling back. It was that they both weren't bothered. It was as subtle and devastating as that. Desire lay in the space of anticipation and mystery. In the beginning, she'd had no idea what Patrick would do in bed – so everything felt surprising and exciting. But in a relationship, she realised that you become so intoxicated by those spaces that you want to know more, you want to be pulled so incredibly tight together – and you inadvertently close them. And then you look up and there are no spaces or mysteries left.

'Do you still love him?' Maggie asked quietly.

'Whose idea was the separation?' Joni asked.

'Mine.'

'But, why?' Helena asked.

'I wanted to hear Patrick tell me it was a crazy idea.' She sniffed. 'Only he didn't. He said *it sounds like a good idea.*'

'Oh, Liz!' Maggie cried.

'It's all been so polite. So civil. We agreed to it. Made a plan. Diarised it. We're taking it in turns to be at home for a week at a time. The kids don't know what's happening yet. This is my week to be away.'

'Maybe this will be a good thing,' Maggie said. 'Like pressing a reset button.'

She nodded, desperate for Maggie to be right.

She wiped her face, looked down at her hiking boots. That was why she needed this trip. Needed to walk with these women. She felt so lost – in her marriage, in herself – that the only thing that made sense right now was to follow a trail from one point to another, step by step.

127

26

HELENA

Helena lay in her narrow sleeping bag, hands at her sides as she had nowhere else to put them. Did people *enjoy* sleeping in tents? Every time she moved, her inflatable roll mat crackled, and her sleeping bag crinkled violently. It was like going to bed in a crisp packet.

She pressed her bladder, testing whether she needed to pee. The thought of rustling out of her sleeping bag, unzipping the tent, pushing her blistered heels into her boots, and then stumbling in the dark to squat with her trousers around her ankles made her want to cry. She was homesick for her en suite.

She became aware of her hands, which had shifted and were now resting over her womb. She could feel the warmth of her body beneath her palms. Somewhere in there was a . . . foetus. Yes. *Foetus.* That was the word. *Baby* was far too emotive. Babies were real, with feelings and needs. A foetus was . . . scientific. Abstract.

Her palms moved in small, slow circles. It felt nice, so she didn't stop. Her plan was to not think about the pregnancy, or talk about it, but the problem was, her body seemed very busy steaming right ahead – pumping out hormones that made her exhausted, her body tender, her appetite fierce. Or was that just how everyone felt after a day of hiking with a hulking great backpack?

She should sleep. She slid a hand free from the sleeping bag, reaching for the small torch Maggie had left glowing, and switched it off. She lay still, waiting for her eyes to adjust to the darkness. She lifted a hand in front of her face. Couldn't see it. Waited.

'It's so dark I can't breathe,' Maggie whispered.

'Thought you were asleep.'

'Too scared.'

Helena heard Maggie rolling onto her side. 'You all right, after the Joni argument?'

'I'm surprised Joni bothered pulling me out of the river.'

'You know Joni loves you, don't you? Her not showing up, it's never about us. It's about her.'

'I know,' she said quietly. Then she bunched onto her side, too – God, everything ached – and lowered her voice further. 'It was a shock about Liz and Patrick separating.'

She could feel Maggie's breath against her face as she asked, 'How did Patrick seem when you met recently?'

'Happy to be let off the leash.'

'Helena!'

'What? You know he likes a few drinks when Liz isn't around.' She paused. 'Don't you feel a bit duped? Liz planned this trip to fit in with her separation schedule.'

Maggie didn't say anything. She could be counted on for many things, but bitching wasn't one.

Her silence only encouraged Helena. 'Why does her life have to be this neat, perfect thing?'

'Shush,' Maggie said.

'It's true! It's all smiles and plans and maps and checklists, but why couldn't she have just picked up the phone and said, *You know what? Patrick and I are having a rough time. I could do with getting away. Will you come?* And we'd have said, *Yes!*'

'I was saying shush because I can hear something!'

'Oh.' Helena stopped talking and listened. Beyond the tent she could hear a light wind moving through the branches of the trees. Was it pine needles whispering together?

Maggie's voice was hesitant as she asked, 'Vilhelm . . . where do you think he went?'

'Home to his bed if he has any sense.'

'He had a camping pack.'

That was true. He'd looked just the sort to be able to survive out in the wilderness for weeks, probably setting traps for rabbits or living off fish he'd caught.

Maggie's voice lowered further. 'He knows we're camping out here, alone. All that stuff he was saying about thin places . . . it's spooked me.' Maggie reached through the darkness for Helena's arm.

'That's my boob.'

'Oh.'

Beyond the tent, Helena heard movement.

Maggie went still.

There it was again. Footsteps? Then the crack of a branch underfoot.

'Someone's out there!' Maggie whispered.

Helena held her breath, listening to the distinct sound of footsteps approaching. Her muscles contracted. There was a sudden rush of motion and Helena cried out as she took a blow against her shoulder.

Maggie screamed in the dark.

Disorientated, Helena punched back at the tent. Her knuckles met the solid mass of something human on the other side.

A scream!

Helena lashed out again in the darkness.

'Ow!'

Then Maggie was pinning her by the arms. 'Stop!' Maggie shouted.

Beyond the tent, she heard Liz's voice. 'It's me! Are you trying to kill me?'

Helena wriggled from her sleeping bag, unzipped the tent, and pushed her head out. In the moonlight, she could see the outline of Liz staggering to her feet.

'What the hell?' Joni said, emerging from her tent and flicking on a torch.

Liz held a hand in front of her face. 'I went for a wee and tripped over their guy rope!'

'You landed on me!' Helena said, who was still catching her breath, heart drilling. 'We thought we were about to be murdered in our beds!'

Joni laughed, the sound breaking the tension, the torch beam shaking.

'Sorry!' Liz said.

Joni was still laughing. Maggie, too.

Helena supposed it *was* funny.

As she was up, she might as well go for that wee now. She couldn't face pushing her blistered heels into her hiking boots, so she padded barefoot across the damp grass. She squatted a little distance from the tents, hearing the hot stream of her piss hit the earth.

She wondered why Liz had been close enough to their tent to trip over the guy rope – and whether she'd heard them talking.

Still. Helena hadn't said anything she hadn't meant.

She finished her wee and resettled her trousers. When she looked up, she heard a movement beyond the dying flames of the fire. She fumbled with her torch, shining it in the direction of the sound – but there was nothing.

She directed the beam across the grassy area, circling slowly, eyes squinting to focus. Trees loomed tall, black shadows huddled between them. She felt watched, although she couldn't remember being further from civilisation.

Oddly, an image drifted into her thoughts of the man she'd shagged at the lodge. Austin. She recalled the taste of cider and meat on his breath. The cold blue eyes. The way he'd called out to her, *See you again!*

Helena took a final look around, then crawled back into the tent, pulling the zip behind her.

THE SEARCH

Leif runs hard, boots slamming into the earth, binoculars gripped in his fist. His gaze is pinned to the two women lurching towards the lodge.

Out front, the younger woman runs with her coat knotted at her waist, hair flying around her. Sweat patches darken her top. When she spots Leif, the rhythm of her run crumbles, relief slackening her muscles.

Leif recognises her. A young German woman. Eighteen perhaps. The woman behind is her mother. The two of them set out yesterday. They were doing an overnight hike, he seemed to recall. They'd had dinner at the lodge the night before they left, their expressions serious as they studied their map.

'What's happened?' he shouts, closing the gap between them.

The young woman stalls to a halt, breathing hard. She bends forward, hands on her knees, chest heaving. Her forehead glistens with sweat.

Her mother staggers to her side, cheeks deep red.

Both mother and daughter turn, raising their hands towards Blafjell.

His gaze lifts, squinting into the hazy light. He's not sure what he's expecting to see. Other people? Smoke trailing from its crown? But from here, the mountain rises tall and square and desolate.

The daughter speaks first. 'A woman—' she says, breaking off.

Her mother drags in a breath. 'Fallen.'

Leif feels his pulse in his throat.

'We shouted! But too far!' the mother says. 'We were on the lower path! Long distance from her.'

'We could not climb that section of the mountain—'

'We tried to call mountain rescue—'

'—but no signal,' the daughter finishes.

'We run here to get help.'

Leif's chest squeezes tight. 'Is the woman . . . alive?'

Mother and daughter look at one another.

Cold fear slices across his body.

Perhaps the mother imagines her daughter's fate playing out on that mountain top, as her eyes film instantly with tears. Then she turns to Leif. Her voice is quieter now, the panic fading as something darker settles. 'We do not know. She was not moving.'

DAY 2

27

LIZ

A rush of cold air met Liz's skin as she unzipped her sleeping bag and crawled out.

Beside her, Joni slept with an arm flung behind her head, a flock of tattooed starlings migrating from elbow to wrist. Her breathing was light, lips parted, eyelids flickering beneath a dream.

Liz clambered from the tent, disturbing a shiver of water droplets that had gathered on the fabric. A blue sky hung above them, but the clearing where they had camped remained in shade, the sun yet to crest the tallest peaks.

Coffee. That's what she needed. She set up the stove on the dew-studded grass, then carried the pan to the river.

She knelt on the bank, dew soaking into her trousers as she scooped up a pan of water. The river was running slowly, tiny midges circling above it like dust motes. A small fish darted out of a patch of weed, disappearing just as quickly. She had the urge to call, *Fish!* like she would have done when the twins were younger.

She had loved the point-and-name stage – *Look! Digger! Fire engine! Bird!* – and the instant giddy joy it delivered. Already the phase was ending, folded quietly beneath the next layer of childhood.

A low feeling of gloom settled over her – the sensation of so much being behind her. Had she given too much of herself to the surgery and her patients, rather than her family? A memory landed: returning late from work to find Patrick lumbering across their lawn, the kids hanging from each arm. The children were already in their pyjamas as he called to her: 'Found a couple of ferrets. What do you want me to do with them?'

Liz was standing in her work shoes on their shaded deck. 'Much meat on them?'

'I'll check,' he said, tossing them onto the grass, and sizing up their limbs through squeals of delight.

She should have joined them, played and tumbled on the lawn, nibbled their bath-fresh skin, but something had been nagging her about a patient she'd seen earlier, so instead, she'd returned inside to write a note on her phone. By the time she'd finished, the children were in bed and she'd missed their night-time kisses.

Memories like that left her bruised. But she couldn't cut corners as a doctor. Liz didn't get to have an off-day or not show up – the stakes were too high. She knew that.

She shook her head, trying to dislodge her introspective mood. She carried the pan to their camp area and lit the stove, a blue flame hissing to life.

From the tents, sleepy voices began yawning awake.

'Coffee's on!' she called, ready for company.

There were murmurs of enthusiasm and she set about locating everyone's camping mugs, enamel clinking as she gathered them, dusting dirt from their bases. As she turned, something caught her eye.

She jerked back.

A large brown fish, the length of her forearm, had been laid over a rock by the burned-out fire. It had river-green spots across its body, glistening and slimy. It was dead – freshly so –

138

its black bulbous eyes bright. There was a thin line of red at its belly. Leaning closer, she could see the clean slice across its underside, the guts already removed, a blood-red space left behind.

Hairs lifted on the back of her neck. She looked up. The clearing was empty save for their tents, but the treeline beyond was shrouded in darkness.

She jumped – but it was only the sound of a tent unzipping. Joni emerged, bleary-eyed, pulling on a jumper, a glimpse of toned stomach revealed.

From the adjacent tent, Maggie exited yawning, waves of auburn hair loose around her shoulders.

'Feel like I slept in a tomb,' Helena said behind her, kinked fringe stuck to one side of her forehead.

Maggie stopped when she noticed Liz's expression. 'What is it?'

Liz pointed at the fish.

Joni, rubbing her forehead, came closer to examine it.

'Vilhelm left it!' Helena declared.

'Keep your voice down,' Liz whispered.

Maggie hugged her arms around herself, glancing around the clearing. 'You think he's . . . listening?'

Liz's gaze searched the treeline.

Helena whispered, 'Why would he leave a fish here?'

'Maybe he caught more than he needed,' Liz suggested, reasonably.

Helena looked unconvinced. 'Why not give it to us, then? Why sneak around in the dark and leave a dead fish in our camp? I knew I'd seen someone last night!'

'What?' Maggie said.

'When I was peeing, I heard a rustling. Must have been Vilhelm.' She shuddered theatrically.

'What are we going to do with it?' Maggie asked.

139

The four of them stared at the fish.

Helena said, 'There's no way I'm eating that thing!'

'We might be grateful for it after four nights of noodles,' Liz said.

'You want to put it in *your* backpack?' Helena said.

'Chuck it in the river,' Joni suggested.

Helena folded her arms. 'I'm not touching it.'

With a sigh, Liz stepped forward and picked up the fish by its spiny, wet tail. Arm outstretched from her body, she carried it to the river's edge and tossed it in with a splash.

The fish floated on its side, belly gaping open, a swirl of blood dispersing into the river.

28

MAGGIE

Maggie was at the rear of the group. Again. She was coated in sweat and breathing hard. She hooked her thumbs beneath the straps of her backpack but the knot of muscles between her shoulder blades continued to spasm.

With every step the forest seemed to deepen, the blue sky long swallowed by a green ceiling. The air felt heavy with the damp, earthy smell of moss, fern spores, and the sweet rot of turning foliage.

They'd walked through the morning, stopping only for a short, unsatisfying lunch of crispbreads, nuts, and cheese, before continuing. She had no idea how far they had to go until they reached the coast.

The trail ascended gradually, the incline barely visible, but she could feel it in her calves and the forgotten muscles in her backside.

Head down, she slogged on. She watched the rise and fall of her thick thighs in purple leggings. She wished she were fitter. She'd never fully succeeded in shifting the baby weight after having Phoebe. She didn't know how Liz had managed it, with twins and a career to juggle. But then Liz was one of those disciplined people who would never raid a biscuit drawer.

She lugged herself onward, her breathing coming in uneven draws. The earthy ground was rooted and dark. Rocks coated with acid-yellow lichen studded the forest floor. Moss clung to the trunks of thin saplings, so that everywhere was licked green.

Up ahead, the others had stopped. Their packs were off, water bottles raised to mouths, heads tipped back. A shaft of sunlight had found its way through the thick canopy of trees, and it struck them beautifully, lighting the planes of Helena's face. How was she managing this, pregnant, her heels pocked with blisters? Maggie felt ashamed to be the one at the back, complaining, slowing them all down.

By the time she reached the others, they were already twisting lids back onto their bottles, heaving packs over shoulders.

Liz was studying the map hanging at her neck. 'Only another couple of kilometres until we're out of the woods and on the mountainside. From there, we should be able to see the coast.'

It wasn't far. Maggie could do it. She *had* to do it.

Already the others were returning to the track, pointing at the next red T-marker ahead.

'Just having a wee,' Maggie called, frustrated that she hadn't had a chance to rest.

She ducked off the path, boots pressing into the soft bed of moss that was kissed emerald-gold by patches of sun. Struggling to undo the waistband of her shorts, she had to shoulder off her backpack.

She squatted beside a tree, listening to the quiet of the forest, the whir of insects, the gentle dance of the breeze through the leaves. When she was finished, she dug a hole in the earth with the toe of her boot, then buried the tissue paper there. She was meant to carry the paper out – she knew that – but then she'd have to dig around in her pack for the Ziploc bag she'd brought and, honestly, she just didn't have the energy.

She grimaced at the pain as she pulled on her pack, re-fastening the buckles across her chest and waist.

She stepped forward, then faltered. Which direction was the path? The mossy, root-veined ground all looked the same. Had she overshot the trail – or was she on it? She felt weirdly disorientated – like when you step out of a shop in an overly bright retail park and find your orientation scrambled.

She turned on the spot, searching for the path they'd been following. It was right here, surely? She peered through thick-trunked trees trying to catch a glimpse of the others, but they'd been swallowed by dense forest.

The first prickling of panic inched across her scalp. 'Helena?' she called.

No answer.

'Joni? Liz?'

She waited.

The faint rush of water sounded from a distance.

'Where are you?' she shouted, louder this time, urgent.

But there was no response.

They'd walked on.

Maybe they hadn't heard her saying she was stopping for a wee. She could only have been a few minutes at most. One of them would look around soon and notice she was missing.

A tightness spread across her chest, breath shallowing as she felt the forest pressing close. The scale and size felt ominous, looming. Her gaze skittered anxiously.

Above her there was an explosion of movement in the canopy. Maggie reared away, arms drawn defensively towards her face – but it was only a bird taking flight.

The beat of panic picked up its pace, her heartbeat thundering.

She couldn't stop her thoughts racing ahead: what if she didn't find the others? She pictured the map of the area – the huge expanse of wilderness. If she'd lost her friends in minutes, how would anyone find her?

She scrabbled in the side pocket of her pack, pulling out her phone. She held it in front of her face, willing the screen to reveal a magical bar of reception.

No signal.

She wiped her mouth.

She thumbed to the map on her phone, squinting. Before leaving the lodge, she'd photographed the trail map. The light quality must have been poor as when she zoomed in, the map pixelated to a blur.

Shit!

She shoved the phone away and glanced about.

In her panic she'd been turning on the spot and had now lost all sense of direction. The forest had become a wall of green, the sunlight swallowed by the dense canopy.

Maggie was lost.

THE SEARCH

Leif makes the call to Mountain Rescue. He presses the phone to his ear, sharing the few details he has with Knut, who mans the desk at the rescue base.

Over the years, Leif has met most of the team of volunteers. His father used to be one of them. They're a solid, experienced team of climbers, mountaineers and retired medical staff. If a rescue operation is needed, there is no crew he'd rather call upon.

He tells Knut, 'The woman was sighted near the eastern ridge of Blafjell mountain. There's no GPS location, but the hikers who saw her think she's about twenty metres down.'

Knut doesn't comment on the information, but Leif knows what he'll be thinking: the odds on surviving a twenty-metre fall onto rock aren't good. 'Any sign that the woman was still alive?'

'The hikers called to her, but there was no response.'

'Weather conditions on Blafjell?'

Leif glances through the open doorway. The peaks of the mountain are still shrouded in cloud. 'Visibility looks poor. The wind is up. Can't rule out rain incoming.'

Knut's voice is calm and authoritative as he delivers the bad news: 'The rescue helicopter is already out. There's another incident over at Hyvik.'

'The rock?'

'Yes.'

Hyvik rock is a tourist hot spot and there has been a chain of accidents this summer – mostly tourists standing too close to the edge with their selfie sticks. There is talk of putting in a safety barrier.

'The helicopter's only just been sent out. Could be a few hours. Then we'll need to refuel. You can have the second truck and team. First is already en route to Hyvik.'

Leif understands. 'I'll go on foot. Get a head start. See what the situation is.'

'Good man,' Knut says. 'Keep your radio on.'

Leif's done his basic rescue training and first aid. Most of the good local climbers have. If you spend a lot of time in the mountains, you need to be prepared.

Just before Knut hangs up, he asks a final question. 'Do we know who this woman is?'

Leif slides the logbook towards him. He opens it, scanning the list of names, a heaviness settling in his chest. 'No. Not yet.'

29

HELENA

The trail twisted through the dank forest. Helena missed the open, expansive landscape of the valley, and the muscular movement of the river. The woodland felt claustrophobic, trees swallowing the view and light.

She was trying to ignore the pain in her heels, which was difficult when she could feel the damp leak of her blisters against her socks.

Everything was irritating her, like the bob of Liz's ponytail as she walked – it looked so damn perky, keeping pace with her busy strides. Or Joni's light humming as she sang to herself, lost in her own lyrical thoughts.

Helena's thoughts were tightly knotted around the pregnancy. She wondered if it was crazy of her to have gone ahead with the hike. Exhaustion was real. She wasn't sure how much longer she could walk for – and the hardest days on the trail were still to come.

The sight of Maggie struggling would cheer her, she decided, turning. That was exactly the sort of sick friend she was: she liked her misery to be kept company.

She turned, scanned the landscape.

The track behind Helena was empty.

She waited a moment, peering harder through the cluster of trees.

No Maggie.

She put her hands on her hips. 'Mags?'

When there was no response, she called to the others. 'Hey, wait! Where's Maggie?'

Joni stopped singing and turned. Liz, too. They both eyed the empty track. She watched their faces, expecting someone to say, *She overtook us – she's just up there.*

'We'll be walking until dark at this pace,' Liz said, swatting at a mosquito.

They waited for a minute.

Then another.

Joni let her pack slump to the ground.

Liz checked her watch.

Helena eyed the empty path, a beat of unease stirring.

Three minutes, then four.

'Maggie?' she called.

No answer.

A small frown line had appeared between Liz's brows. 'When was the last time anyone saw her?'

Joni stared into the woods. 'Not since we stopped for water.'

'Same,' Helena admitted. She'd been so preoccupied with her own problems that she hadn't glanced back to check.

Liz's forehead creased. 'But that was ages ago. Forty minutes. Maybe more. Why didn't you check?'

The admonishment made her bite. 'If you hadn't been striding ahead, Maggie would have had a chance to catch up!'

'So it's my fault?' Liz snapped.

'It's no one's fault,' Joni said. 'She's probably just around the corner.'

'I'm going to look for her,' Helena said, pushing past them both.

Liz called after her. 'We should all stick together.'

'So come!'

'Let's just think about this for a moment,' Liz said, catching up with Helena. 'What would you do if you'd come off the path?'

'Stay where I was,' Helena said instinctively. 'Wait for someone to come.'

'I wouldn't,' Joni said. 'No way would I stay put in a creepy wood all on my own. I'd try and find a way out.'

Liz asked, 'But what would Maggie do?'

Helena thought for a moment. 'She'd shout for us.'

30

MAGGIE

'Helena! Liz! Joni!' she cried.

She lurched on, panting, with no idea if she was moving towards the others or sinking deeper into the wilderness. Every direction looked the same. Trees crowded close, blocking out the light. The air was weighted, hard to breathe.

'Helena!' she called again.

The forest answered with its murmur of creaks and whispers.

Fear swam hot and spiked through her body. She made herself keep moving. She was coated in sweat, breathing unevenly.

Thick, gnarled roots reached from the dark earth. A bird screeched urgently. Her foot snagged against a root and suddenly she was shot forward, the weight of her pack propelling her. She felt a jolt of pain in her spine as she twisted, landing hard on her front, cheek slammed into the dirt.

She lay still, the taste of soil in her mouth, tears hot in her eyes. She whimpered, pinned beneath the weight of her pack.

There was no one to hear her. No one to help.

She lay in the dirt, scared, alone.

If Phoebe fell, Maggie would come to her side, tell her, 'Up you get! That's it. Dust yourself off, you brave girl.' The image of her daughter gave her a shot of strength.

Wincing at the pain in her back, she pushed herself onto her hands and knees, then staggered to her feet. Her vision swam. She took a breath, slowed her exhale.

Took another.

Think.

She stood still for a moment, listening. Just trees. Forest. Nature. She heard the rush of the river.

Then she remembered something: all rivers ran downhill. The Svelle trail led them up a mountainside, so Maggie needed to follow the river uphill, which would lead her up and out of the woods.

She pushed on, tears drying on her cheeks. A new pain had emerged in her back, a hot twist of it around her lower spine, but somehow it was better than the fear, so she leant into it.

She kept close to the river whenever she could, calling intermittently for her friends. The river weaved and curved in places, drawing her in strange patterns. She began doubting herself: did rivers *always* flow downhill, or were there exceptions? What if it didn't bring her out of the treeline, but led her deeper into the wilderness?

She had to concentrate on where she placed her feet – it would be so easy to turn an ankle in high, stiff boots. Her muscles burned as she lugged herself onward. Further and further through the forest, eyes wide in her search for a cairn or flash of red paint to mark the trail.

Time passed. The earth softened beneath her boots, a cushiony spring to it, layers of decaying plants making for rich soil. Orange and grey mushrooms sprang from the dank ground. Had she been here before?

Maggie could feel herself growing weary. She stopped to drink water, emptying her bottle. The light felt like it was at a different angle than earlier. She'd lost sense of how long she'd been separated from the others. Was dusk coming? Her heart rate spiked at the thought of darkness encroaching.

She couldn't spend the night alone in these woods.

She turned slowly on the spot, desperate to see a path. As she did so, the hairs began to prickle across the back of her neck. She had the unnerving sensation that the forest was watching her.

Goosebumps spread down the backs of her arms.

There was the slightest shift in the air.

Vilhelm's warning crept up, dark and insidious. *That feeling of unease, of not being alone, that isn't immediately explicable.*

Something moved between two trees.

She froze, her mouth dry.

Every fibre of her being tensed. She narrowed her vision, searching.

There, beside a gnarled tree trunk, a man was standing alone, watching her.

31

LIZ

Liz was peering into the depths of the forest. 'Maggie! Maggie!'

For the first hour they'd retraced their footsteps along the trail. They'd since turned around and cut through the woods in case Maggie had overshot the path and come out further up. But there was still no sign of her – and Liz was aware the sun was beginning to lower.

Liz lifted the map around her neck. Her brow wrinkled as she studied the deep spread of green on either side of their trail, which stretched for tens of kilometres in all directions. If Maggie had strayed from the path, she could be anywhere.

'Check your phones,' she instructed, taking out her own. She eyed the empty space where the bars of reception should have been.

'Still nothing,' Helena said.

'Me neither.' Joni rubbed the side of her face. 'What do we do?'

'Go back to the lodge, raise the alarm?' Liz suggested.

'It's a day and a half's walk. Maggie can't spend the night out here – she hasn't even got a tent,' Helena said.

Liz baulked. 'What?'

'We split it. Maggie took the pegs and poles. I've got the material.'

Liz knew exposure was the biggest killer among lost hikers. It got cold overnight out here. Last night the temperature must have fallen as low as five or six degrees.

'We'll find her,' Liz said, but the promise sounded flat, even to her ears.

Without communicating it, they all picked up their pace, gazes swinging to the spaces between the trees.

Suddenly, Liz froze, holding out a hand to signal for the others to stop.

She could hear her pulse in her ears as she waited, alert.

The forest hummed with the stirring of leaves and unseen insects.

She could pick it up more clearly now – the low sound of movement, the hurried pad of feet against earth.

No one spoke, waiting.

Ahead, the bushes parted, a dark shape travelling towards them, fast. The shape, the speed, sent a spike of dread through her middle.

Behind her, Joni gasped.

A dark, wire-haired dog, ears flattened to its head, came galloping from the forest. Its mouth hung open, tongue lolling. A frill of blood dripped from the long hairs of its muzzle as it came at them.

The dog bolted past on the narrow trail. Liz felt the brush of its fur against her legs, its warm, animal smell, muddied with the scent of blood.

'Is that Vilhelm's—' Helena began to ask.

From deep in the woods, they heard a scream.

32

MAGGIE

A man was standing half hidden behind a tree, watching her. His hands were gripped to the straps of a sagging, worn pack. There was no smile. No hello. She took in the dark stubble, the narrow jaw, the orange beanie pushed back on his head.

Erik.

She remembered the way he'd walked through the lodge bar, a strange hush falling over the room.

She remembered the way Bjørn and Brit had both glared, watching Erik, as if the devil had walked in.

She remembered the way he'd set out on the Svelle trail yesterday, turning and looking back over his shoulder – at her.

And now he was here.

He stared, eyes as dark as the woods. 'Karin . . .' he said quietly, his voice barely audible.

Her skin turned to ice.

She forced herself to shake her head. Say, 'I'm Maggie.'

Erik blinked slowly. Ran a hand over his face.

The trees crowded close. She was aware of the silence that had gathered around them. He was staring at her with unnerving intensity.

Her heart kicked hard against the cage of her ribs.

155

He glanced left, then right. 'Are you lost?' he asked in English, his voice thick, as if he hadn't used it all day.

As a woman, she'd been taught to walk with confidence, to look like she knew where she was going. To not show weakness, because a predator senses it. How do you do that in the middle of the Norwegian wilderness with no clue where you are?

No phone signal.

No help.

No one to hear her scream.

She took a breath, then forced her voice to come out confidently. 'I'm with my friends.'

He looked around him.

'We got separated.' Her breathing was speeding up. 'They'll be looking for me.'

'Where are you going?'

'The coast.'

'You know the direction?' he said, his Norwegian accent strong.

She hesitated.

He was looking right at her.

She could tell him, yes, she knew. But then he'd watch as she set off and would know she was lying.

'I've lost my bearings,' she said.

His expression was unreadable. 'I will take you.'

He could lead her anywhere. It could be a trap and she'd have no idea. He could've been tracking them all day, waiting for one of their group to separate. But if she said, *No*, stayed here, what then? Night would close in and she'd be out here alone. She had no tent. The temperature would drop. How long would she last?

Erik turned and began to walk, moving through the trees, ducking to miss a low hanging branch, pushing aside a sweep of ferns.

Maggie felt certain he was leading her in the wrong direction. Was he taking her deeper into the woods?

'I . . . I thought the trail was that way,' she said, pointing east.

He shook his head. Walked on.

Maggie, heart skittering, followed.

She kept a few paces behind, trying to get the measure of him. His pack was sun-bleached and half-empty, worn hooked over one shoulder. He had on tatty cargo shorts and his legs were tanned and lean, rangy muscles in his calves and thighs.

Maggie had read that if you were feeling threatened by someone, you were meant to keep them talking, humanise them and yourself. Build up a conversation. 'You're Leif's brother, aren't you?'

'Yes,' he answered.

'He said your family own the lodge? It's a beautiful place to grow up. I'm from a village in the south of England. I thought it was rural until I came here.'

Silence.

'I have a daughter. Phoebe. She's three. I miss her. She's staying with my ex-husband for the week. He's not had her before . . .' Her throat tightened and she trailed off. She shook her head, tears pricking the corners of her eyes. *Don't you dare cry!*

She was cloaked in sweat, her breath laboured. She didn't want to go any further. It felt like the woodland was growing denser. The ground was descending – when she was meant to be rising. He was taking her further from the path, she was sure.

Quietly, she unclipped the buckles of her pack in case she needed to turn, run. The pack slackened, putting more weight into her shoulders. She could hear her own breath, feel the panic building.

Her gaze flitted nervously through the darkened forest. In

the mossy grass, she spotted a fist-sized rock. She took a couple of steps towards it and quickly snatched it up. She straightened, fingers closing around the cool, solid rock.

When she looked up, Erik had stopped. He was standing very still, arms loose at his sides, watching her. Their eyes met.

The forest fell quiet, the world shut out.

Erik asked, 'Why do you pick that up?'

Her face flamed. 'I . . . I just . . . I thought it was pretty.'

They both looked at the rock in her hand. It was a plain grey rock as big as her fist, its edges jagged.

He returned his gaze to her face, staring right at her. 'Liar.'

THE SEARCH

Leif stuffs his pack with provisions – climbing gear, a radio, a first-aid kit, two water bottles and a couple of energy bars – then swings it onto his shoulders, barely noticing the weight.

Adrenalin pumps hard through his body. He knows the rescue team won't make it into the mountain for hours. It's up to him.

The two German women who reported the sighting are standing by the noticeboard examining the trail map. The mother taps the area where she believes the woman lies. 'Here.'

Leif peers at it.

He knows that it took these women five hours to return to the lodge from that area of the mountains. But he is fit, fresh. If the weather conditions aren't too treacherous up there, he estimates that he can get there in half that time.

He thanks them and turns to leave.

He's almost at the door when he thinks of something. It's been nagging at him that these German hikers have only mentioned one woman. No one else has called it in or reported a companion missing. He's checked the logbook – there are no single hikers out on the trail – at least none who have signed in.

'Are you sure the woman was alone?'

'Yes,' the mother answers.

Then the daughter straightens. 'We did see someone earlier, though.'

'That's right,' her mother says. 'It was strange, yes?'

The daughter explains, 'Before . . . A younger man. He was alone. Head in his hands.'

Leif feels his pulse spike. 'What did he look like?'

The daughter thinks. 'Mid-twenties, maybe. He was slim. Dark hair shaved close. He had a tattoo on his neck.'

He swallows. 'Of what?'

The girl pauses. Looks to the window as if suddenly understanding something: 'The mountain.'

Leif remembers Erik having it done. They'd lost their father two years earlier – a rescue mission in the mountains that went wrong. His father and Knut had been sent out to find two inexperienced hikers who were a day late returning from a trail. Unknown to Leif or Knut, they'd canned their hike early, forgetting to sign out of the logbook or tell anyone about their movements. Out on the mountains, bad weather rolled in, and their father fell, slipping in the scree, sliding down the mountain face, faster and faster. His body was recovered with thirty-six broken bones.

Erik struggled with his loss. He disappeared for long stretches of time, full of anger and loathing. He hated the mountains. Hated tourist hikers. Hated the whole damn world. He disappeared to Bergen, returning several months later, thin and hollow eyed, a black tattoo on his neck.

Leif was his big brother: it was his job to look after him, to make things better. But Leif didn't know how. Instead, he threw himself into running the lodge, believing it was the life raft that could stop his family from sinking.

He knows Erik is out there on the Svelle trail – and has a

bad feeling about it. He replays the hiker's description of Erik, alone, *head in his hands.*

As he looks towards the mountains, Leif thinks: *Erik, what have you done?*

33

JONI

The scream cut through the woods, high-pitched and urgent, causing the hairs on the back of Joni's arms to stand on end.

Helena began to run. 'Maggie!'

Joni followed. Trees rushed by. Undergrowth clawed at her bare legs. The thrust of her pack slammed up and down on her back. Liz raced at her side, arms pumping.

The scream grew louder, inhuman in its shrill desperation.

The three of them skidded to a stop, breathing hard.

A figure was crouched low; something lay prone on the ground in front of them.

Another high-pitched cry tore through the forest.

Joni realised the figure was Vilhelm. He had one knee in the dirt, his right arm raised, a rock in his fist. He brought the rock crashing down, even as Joni was moving forward, yelling, 'No!'

There was a dull thud of rock against flesh.

The screaming was silenced.

The forest fell quiet.

Vilhelm dropped the rock, then pushed to his feet. Joni could smell the warm ooze of blood.

Now that he'd moved, she could see the limp body of a hare at his feet, its skull crushed from the blow.

163

Vilhelm wiped his hands on his dark trousers. He shook his head sadly. 'Runa caught him. Never kills them outright. Gets the scent of blood and bolts for the next meal.'

Joni stared at the dead hare. Its fur was wet from the dog's mouth, puncture wounds marking its breathless belly.

'Something else will get a meal out of it, I hope.' He pulled on his pack, his rangy frame handling the weight with ease.

'The scream . . .' Joni said.

'Terrible noise, isn't it? Wrong to let it suffer.'

Vilhelm whistled loudly for Runa. A few moments later, the dog came bounding towards him, tongue lolling. 'You don't know any better, do you?' he said, stroking its head.

Joni felt her heart rate slowing.

Vilhelm asked, 'You enjoyed the fish I left? It was a good one. Too big to feed just me.'

They glanced at one another.

'Yes. Thank you,' Liz said, cautiously, still trying to get the measure of him.

Vilhelm looked between them. 'You are one down.'

'Yes, Maggie. She got separated,' Joni told him. 'We were walking in the woods . . . thought she was behind us.'

Vilhelm looked concerned. 'How long has she been missing?'

Missing. The word felt unnervingly serious. *A missing person.* That implied police. A search . . .

Liz looked at her watch. 'For two hours. Do you have a radio? Our phones don't have signal. We need to call for help . . .'

'No radio,' Vilhelm said. 'But I will help you find her.'

34

MAGGIE

Maggie faced Erik, the rock still gripped in her hand.

Her pack was unbuckled – she could slip it off, run – but Erik looked faster, fitter. He would catch her. And anyway, where would she run?

'You don't trust me,' Erik said, face pinched, jaw tight.

Blood bloomed to the surface of her skin, hot enough to make her body pulse with it.

'What have they told you?'

She kept her mouth shut.

He looked agitated as he waited for her answer, thumb scratching at his chin. Suddenly, Erik glanced over his shoulder.

Maggie tensed, alert.

The sound of movement echoed from behind Erik. She held her breath, listening.

There it was again, the tread of boots over earth. Then she thought she heard a female voice.

Maggie began to shout. 'Helena! Liz! Joni!'

Erik's eyes widened.

Blood throbbed in her ears as she waited. Then, from the silence, her own name reverberated off the dense trees. '*Maggie? Maggie?*'

'I'm here!' Maggie cried, stumbling towards the familiar voices.

Relief coursed through her as she saw Helena emerge, running towards her, yelling her name.

Liz and Joni were only paces behind, packs bouncing on their shoulders, faces flushed. She spotted a fourth person – Vilhelm? – before she was swallowed by her friends' embraces.

She held on tight in a clash of packs, arms, elbows. A rush of pure, warm relief flooded through her body, almost buckling her knees.

'We lost you! My God, are you okay?' Helena said, holding her tight.

'I'm so sorry!' Liz kept saying, the four of them still in a clumsy knot of limbs. 'You weren't behind us! We didn't realise! I'm sorry!'

When they pulled apart – Maggie wiping tears from her face – she saw Vilhelm standing with his dog at his heel.

'Vilhelm's been helping us search,' Joni explained.

Maggie swallowed. 'Oh. Thank you.' Then she turned, scanning the silver trunks of the birches, her gaze moving over logs and dense bushes. But the treeline was empty, Erik gone, melted back into the forest as if she'd imagined him.

'What is it?' Helena asked, noticing her expression.

'Erik . . . Did you see him?'

Her friends looked at one another, shook their heads.

'He was right here.'

They turned, as did Vilhelm, peering deep into the forest.

'When I was lost, he was in the woods, just standing there . . .' she lowered her voice, '. . . watching me.'

'What the hell?' Helena hissed. 'Did he try anything? Are you okay, Mags?'

Maggie looked down, noticing the rock still gripped in her fist. She opened her fingers and let it slip to the forest floor. 'I'm fine . . . but it was just . . . odd . . . the way he looked at me. He called me Karin.'

Vilhelm was staring at her.

'Erik said he was leading me towards the coast – but this feels like the wrong direction.' She turned to Vilhelm. 'Is it?'

Slowly, Vilhelm turned and pointed in the opposite direction. 'The coast is that way.'

Something cold moved through her stomach. 'Where was Erik taking me?'

Her friends looked at one another.

'A shortcut, perhaps?' Vilhelm posed, although his voice lacked conviction.

Maggie glanced about, as if she expected him to be half hidden amongst the trees. She lowered her voice as she addressed Vilhelm, 'At the lodge, it seemed like the locals are wary of Erik. Why?'

Vilhelm adjusted the peak of his cap minutely before responding. His voice was low, quiet. 'Erik was hiking the Svelle trail with Karin when she disappeared. He was the last person to see her alive.'

Maggie blinked, taking in the information. 'What happened?'

Vilhelm shook his head slowly, as if to suggest he was at a loss. 'There was an argument, I understand. Erik says he walked off. Left Karin.'

'Do you think he hurt her?' Maggie asked.

'No one knows for sure,' Vilhelm said. 'There are no witnesses in the wilderness.'

'Let's get out of these woods,' Joni decreed.

Maggie nodded. She needed to see sky, breathe in fresh air.

'How far is it to the sea?' Liz asked Vilhelm.

'The forest thins in another kilometre, and the coast is only over that next ridge,' he answered. 'But there's bad weather coming in soon. You'll be exposed on the coast.'

The sea – that's what Maggie craved. Wide open space,

somewhere to wash herself clean. The light was lowering and she didn't want to camp in the woods overnight. 'I want to keep going,' Maggie said decisively. 'I need to get out of these woods.'

The others nodded their agreement.

'In the morning, maybe then we think about turning back?' Maggie suggested.

'Reaching the beach – that's enough for me,' Helena said. 'I'm crippled by these blisters.'

Joni said, 'I don't think I've the energy to make it up Blafjell.'

'It was a pipe dream,' Liz admitted. 'I shouldn't have pushed us so hard. We don't need to climb a mountain. I just wanted us to be together. I'm sorry. We walk to the beach. Camp there. Then turn back in the morning and head for the lodge.'

Maggie's shoulders softened with relief.

'Are you sure?' Vilhelm said. 'I'm returning to the river now. I could show you the way back?'

'We're fine,' Liz said. 'But thank you for all your help.'

He looked uncertain about letting them hike on, but their minds were made up. Vilhelm dug around in his pack and pulled out a small bar of chocolate, still wrapped, and handed it to Maggie. 'To keep up your strength,' he said.

'Thank you,' she said, surprised by the warmth of the gesture.

Vilhelm called Runa to heel, and man and dog departed, disappearing into the gloom of the forest.

The four of them walked on, Maggie snapping the chocolate bar into quarters and sharing it out. 'Mmm, this tastes incredible,' she said, letting the chocolate melt on her tongue.

'A definite upgrade from a gutted fish,' Helena added.

Maggie's heartrate had begun to settle now that the trees had thinned. Early evening light filtered through the sparse branches. A deep weariness spread through her limbs and, although she was exhausted, she was thankful that she was here, safe, with her friends.

Eventually the earthy trail turned drier, rock replacing roots.

As they walked, Liz came to her side and quietly slipped her arm through Maggie's. 'I'm sorry we let you down in the woods. That *I* let you down.'

'You didn't. I'm not your responsibility.' She'd allowed the others to carry her along on this trip, Helena paying for her flight, sending her the right gear, reorganising her backpack; and the same with Liz, who'd planned the route, checked the weather, sent her the list of things to bring. But Maggie was the one who had to walk across this wilderness and out the other side. No one could do that for her.

She looked up at the blushing evening light, the tips of mountains visible in the distance. It was wildly beautiful, but she'd also seen how dangerous it could be. She needed to start taking responsibility. Taking it seriously.

They all did.

'We look out for one another from now on,' Maggie said.

Liz held her gaze. Nodded.

Joni, who'd struck out ahead, suddenly stopped. She turned, shouting, 'Guys! Quick! You've got to see this!'

35

JONI

The four of them stood shoulder to shoulder on the crest of the ridge.

The ocean.

There it was – breath-catching in its wide, shimmering blue.

Sheltered by sheer-sided mountains was a sugar-white beach. It stretched into a crystal-clear bay, the water an otherworldly arctic blue. It was like no place she'd ever seen.

Joni stood rooted to the spot, heart lifting. 'My God!' Her blood fizzed with a pure energy. A fresh breeze, kissed with salt, brushed her neck like a lover.

Beside her, Liz shaded the lowering sun from her eyes, head shaking slowly. On her other side, Helena tipped back her head and laughed.

At the far end of the wide beach, Blafjell mountain rose high and vast in stoic shades of grey, guarding its jewel-blue secret. A lone red fishing boat was leaving the bay, a white wake all that was left as it disappeared in the lee of the mountain.

The trail down to the beach descended through a series of switchbacks, zigzagging steeply. Joni let the natural angle of the path tip her forward, propelling her into a run. She forgot about her aching muscles and the weight of her pack, leaning into the delicious momentum.

She heard the others follow, whooping and hooting as they bounded towards the waiting sea.

The hard-packed earth gave way to wind-sculpted sand.

'Not a footprint!' one of them marvelled.

Wordlessly, packs were dumped, boots were unlaced, damp socks were removed.

Joni shimmied out of shorts, a vest, underwear. Her skin was hot, cloaked in sweat. She tugged free the bandana knotted at her head, and ran naked towards the glittering blue, called by water, salt, wind.

She felt the smack of water against her legs. It was startlingly cold. She ducked under, the sea sealing above her briefly before she surfaced with a whoop of delight. The sea felt like an ice-cold drink quenching a deep thirst.

She shook the water from her hair like a dog. She turned to see Helena, running into the shallows, arms clamped to her full white breasts. Then Liz followed, rushing into the water, naked and lean, strap marks from her pack leaving red indents on her shoulders.

Maggie hesitated on the shoreline, only her boots and socks removed.

'Come on!' Joni called.

Helena yelled, 'We need you, Mags!'

She froze for a moment, uncertain. Then, with a shrug, she peeled off her remaining clothes and tiptoed, squealing, into the icy water, her gorgeously curvy body jiggling, auburn hair trailing behind her.

Here they all were with their beautiful, real bodies, in the middle of nowhere! Blistered heels. Blood-stained knees. Dirt-encrusted nails. All of it!

Joni dived, sweat and dirt sluicing from her skin. She flipped onto her back, breasts to the sky, staring at the cloudless blue.

She filled her lungs, tasting the salted clarity of the ocean, tinged with forest and the thin bite of mountain air. Each breath felt purifying.

Liz swam over, grinning, her face washed clean, eyes glittering. The relief of being weightless and present and together was almost overwhelming. They trod water, looking out over the empty horizon. Nothing between them and Greenland.

The evening light softened the lines of Liz's brow, her expression open and clear. Joni suddenly understood why Liz had brought them out here. If there had been a road to this beach, if they'd stepped out of a car, their pleasure at reaching this place would have been diminished. Joy was the reward that followed a struggle.

Joni felt the thought broaden, clear something in her mind. Wasn't it that joy and struggle were so deeply emmeshed that you couldn't experience one without the other? She'd been taking short cuts. Blocking the harder feelings with drugs and drink and the clamour of other people.

She reached for Liz's hand, lacing their wet fingers together. Her black nail polish had chipped, the bolt of lightning fading to a golden crack. 'Thank you,' she whispered.

Liz looked at her, head tipped to one side, wet hair pasted to her head.

Liz had always been her person – there throughout Joni's wild highs and her crashing lows. She understood Joni's need to disappear, to go into herself, and then emerge when she was ready. She championed Joni's songwriting, not her fame, and carried her during the dark months after she lost her grandmother. And here she was now, leading this trip, fulfilling a promise they'd made to each other about one day coming to Norway.

172

'Thank you for bringing us all here. It doesn't matter that we won't climb Blafjell. We came for this.'

Liz's eyes sparkled as she nodded, water beaded on her eyelashes.

The tour she'd left behind, the threat of legal action, her mistakes . . . it all felt so much further away. Maybe she could let it go. All of it. For a beat, she felt hopeful. Lighter. She let herself picture a simple cabin, a guitar, a notebook gradually thickening with lyrics.

Joni dived, kicking towards the sea bed, until the undulating contours of sand grazed her naked belly, and she hung there, suspended, weightless.

When she broke through the surface, the first cloud had appeared in the wide sky, casting a long shadow over the beach.

36

HELENA

Helena floated on her back, the water cradling her head. The cold felt deliciously anaesthetising.

She let the fizz and clicks of the ocean fill her ears. Her breasts felt swollen and tender, and it was bliss to float there, naked. She tried to picture herself pregnant – well, she was pregnant, but to picture herself *really* pregnant. Swollen belly straining at her top; tits so huge that they needed a whole new set of underwear. She didn't know how it made her feel.

Hell, she was too knackered to know how anything was meant to feel.

As she floated, her thoughts drifted to her mother. Grief was like that – pockets of memory bubbling to the surface unbidden. Her mother had always loved to swim and, throughout the summers of her childhood, they'd holidayed in north Devon, renting a seaside flat for a week, her mother swimming each morning in all weathers. She'd float on her back, lipstick on, body surrendered – and Helena used to love seeing her that way: relaxed, still, held by the sea.

This is where I will sprinkle your ashes, Helena found herself promising. At dawn. Her mother's favourite time of day. Pleased with the decision, she rolled onto her front and swam to shore.

Her skin was puckered with goosebumps as she waded out, nipples like bullets. The sun had been swallowed by cloud now and she shivered. She had no towel, so she used the back of her fleece to dry herself, then pulled on her only fresh top.

Liz and Maggie were already dressed, arms hugged to their bodies, stamping their feet to stay warm.

Joni was the last one out, her expression beatific as she walked up the beach. She lifted her hands, squeezing the water from her dark rope of hair. A tattoo of tiny birds inked the inner skin of her wrist. A new tattoo Helena had never seen stretched from hip to pubic bone. There had been a time when she knew each of Joni's tattoos and what they meant – but that closeness had evaporated. Joni always had the power to lift and drop you like a wave.

'Look,' Maggie said, turning and pointing out to sea, brows pulled together.

Everyone followed her gaze. A brooding army of rain clouds was marching in from the horizon.

'We should set up camp,' Liz said.

The last of the sunlight had been swallowed and now darkness was pulling close, and with it, a rising wind. Helena's gaze skirted away to the sea, the tips of waves beginning to whiten and crest. The air held an earthy sweetness of approaching rain.

Helena used the heel of her hiking boot to stamp the final peg into the ground. Then she stepped back, assessing the tent, a knot of worry squirming in her stomach.

'Are you sure this is a good spot?' she said to the group. 'Aren't we too close to the mountain?'

They had set up camp at the bottom of the trail, where the mountain met the beach. Maggie hadn't wanted to walk a step further than necessary, campaigning that they'd be in the right place to hike out in the morning.

Helena peered up at the steep, earthy slope.

'There's nothing overhanging us,' Joni said with a shrug.

'We can't pitch the tents on the sand,' Liz said. 'The pegs wouldn't hold.'

Helena felt the first drop of rain fall from the sky, plump and heavy. One landed on the back of her hand, another on her cheekbone.

'Time to get inside,' Liz said, disappearing into her tent with Joni.

Maggie dusted the sand from her pack, then heaved it into the tent. She grimaced as she crawled in after it.

'Y'okay?' Helena asked, as she zipped shut their tent.

'Just my back,' Maggie said.

A gust of wind shouldered the tent, blowing the fabric against them.

They both did their best to make the tent cosy, inflating their mats, unrolling sleeping bags, making pillows of their coats. There would be no camp-stove dinner tonight, so they took out a breakfast bar each, knowing that would have to suffice. Helena shuffled into her sleeping bag and nibbled at the dry, honeyed oats, while listening to the rain, which had begun to pour in earnest.

The light had leached from outside. She felt the low flutter of anxiety she always experienced as day became swallowed by night. Helena flicked on her torch. She pulled her phone from her pack, checking it reflexively for messages – but of course there was still no signal.

'Nothing?' Maggie asked, who was raising and lowering her shoulders to release the tension in her back.

Helena shook her head, pushing the phone back in her bag.

They were both quiet for a time, listening to the strengthening wind.

'Earlier, in the woods,' Helena said, voice raised above the elements, 'what did you make of Erik being out there?'

'I don't know . . . It was like, like he knew where I'd be.'

'You think he was following us?'

'No. I don't know. Maybe.' Maggie looked down at her lap. 'It was just the way he was suddenly there, staring at me. The way he called me Karin. And then . . . he disappeared when you all turned up.'

Helena watched her closely.

Maggie looked towards the tent door. 'Do you think he's still out there?'

'We're safe,' Helena said, reaching for Maggie's hand and squeezing, just as another gust of wind hurled itself against their tent.

THE SEARCH

Leif runs along the trail into a cold headwind.

He moves with speed and agility. His thoughts are fixed on only where he's putting his feet. The terrain has changed from spongy grass to a rocky trail, stones flying out beneath his heels.

Lactic acid builds, a burning sensation that tightens his calves. He keeps his breathing steady, in and out through his nose.

He can feel a thirst building in his throat but tells himself he won't stop until the next peak.

He is aware he may be running towards a body – yet if there's the smallest chance that the woman has somehow survived, then every second counts. He's known a climber who fell fifty metres, landed on a bed of pine needles, and only broke an ankle. He's known a man who fell from a three-rung step-ladder and snapped his spinal cord.

He raises his gaze to Blafjell. Finds himself thinking of his father's bravery in these mountains, the chances he took, the people he saved, the people he lost. Leif wonders what his own scorecard will look like by the end of the day.

He pushes forward, breath high in his chest. He glances at

his watch. If he keeps his heart rate at 150 bpm, he can run on and on.

He's always stayed fit. Hard not to with this on your doorstep. He remembers exploring out here when he was a kid with Erik, Austin, Karin, and a couple of the other local kids. They made up a game called Search, where one of them would close their eyes and, with a random stab on a trail map, they'd pick a point to race to.

It wasn't only speed that counted, but how well you could read the mountains and weather, how well you knew the terrain and your own capabilities. Leif may have been the fittest, but Erik had an edge, taking risks, jumping between ledges, not pausing to think about a precarious landing or unstable ground. Austin rarely arrived first – he lacked stamina – but he was happy enough to have a reason to be out of the house all day. He often turned up with a black eye or split lip, and the others knew better than to ask. Karin was the one Leif liked competing against because she was fast, tough, but most of all she had endurance. That's what won out on the mountain. Your ability to overcome.

Now, as Leif runs, he tries telling himself this is just another game of Search. Racing towards a random end point on a map. He doesn't want to believe that he could be running towards a body. Doesn't want to believe the description of Erik on the trail, *head in his hands*.

And yet he can't shake the fear.

He springs over a boulder in his path, his pack feeling light, his body able and strong. He's grateful for it, knowing life is full of cruelty. Out here a woman was able-bodied hours ago – and now she lies twenty metres down.

The mountains are brutal. Impervious. They don't care who

is left broken and bloodied. They don't care for weeping or joy.

It is why people lose themselves out here. There's no judgement. You can be anyone in the wilderness.

37

LIZ

Liz woke to the howl of wind. Something cold and damp was pressing against her cheek. Thick with sleep, she reached out, palms meeting a tomb of wet fabric above her. The tent was buckling!

She fumbled in the blackness for her torch, while outside the wind shrieked and waves hurled themselves to shore.

Finding her torch, she filled the tent with light. She saw Joni sitting with her knees bunched to her chest, eyes squeezed shut, rocking.

'Oh! Joni! Are you okay? The weather will pass—'

Even as she said it, another rush of wind battered the tent, flattening it against them. Liz opened her arms above her head to keep the fabric from their faces. Then a shock of lightning filled the sky, illuminating the tent.

Joni shrank further into herself, head buried against her knees.

Liz silently counted the seconds that followed the lightning. A boom of thunder reverberated around the basin of mountains. She estimated that the storm was still a few kilometres away.

Suddenly the tent door was unzipped, fabric sent flapping by

183

the wind. Liz raised a hand in front of her eyes as a torch beamed into the tent.

Rain drilled down on Maggie and Helena, who were huddled in the entrance.

'Our tent isn't holding!' Maggie cried.

'It's leaking, too! Everything is soaked,' Helena said.

'Get inside!' Liz said, shuffling over as rain sheeted in behind them.

They crawled into the cramped space and zipped the tent tight. There was barely space to move – the domed roof pressed to the crowns of their heads. The air filled with the wet-dog stench of damp woollen socks and unwashed bodies. Everywhere was gritted with sand.

Lightning tore from the sky, illuminating the tent.

Liz began to count. After eight seconds an almighty crack of thunder struck the mountains, the amplified sound feeling physical in its strength.

Joni shrieked.

'Where has this storm come from?' Helena shouted. 'Was it forecast?'

Liz's skin prickled as she thought of the weather apps she'd checked, most of them showing the lightning icon. The forecast had felt so unthreatening on screen, just a tiny zigzag of yellow. With a guilty swallow, she recalled the farmer's warning. *A low pressure is coming. It will bring a storm tomorrow*, she'd said. *Tell your friends to turn back.*

Only she hadn't. She'd told them nothing.

Her cheeks flushed as she said, 'Vilhelm told us all the weather was turning, didn't he? I checked the forecast and it looked mixed – I told you that. I'd no idea it would be this bad. I thought the storm might not arrive—'

'Storm?' Helena said. 'You knew there would be a storm?'

'We'd already set off and—'

'Wait, what do you mean we'd already set off?'

The sting of guilt seemed to drive the truth from her mouth. 'The woman I saw in the field on that first morning – she mentioned that the weather might turn.'

In the torchlight, Maggie's face stretched in surprise. 'You didn't tell us.'

'I didn't want to spook anyone. We were committed—'

'What did she say?' Helena demanded.

Liz flinched. '*Tell your friends to turn back*. But when she said it, the sky was clear. It looked perfect for walking . . . I—'

'Jesus, Liz!' Helena shot. 'It wasn't your call to make! It was for all of us to decide – as a group.'

'Then why didn't anyone else check the forecast? I can't be responsible for everything!'

The others blinked, as if surprised by her tone.

She shouldn't have snapped, but sometimes Liz tired of being expected to take care of everything. 'Look. I'm sorry. I really am. If I'd known it would be like this, I'd have turned back—'

A gust whipped down from the mountain, shouldering against them.

Liz knew she'd messed up, but right now they needed to deal with what was here. 'It's not safe to stay in the tents.'

'You want us to go out in that?' Maggie gawped.

'The tents have metal in the poles. They'll conduct electricity.' She'd treated a victim of a ground strike during her first medical placement. It was horrific. The current had been so strong it had blown off their shoes, burning the soles of their feet, and causing vicious thermal burns and lacerations across their body. 'We need to put on waterproofs and hiking boots – they've got rubber soles.'

Everyone's gazes lifted as lightning broke somewhere beyond them, illuminating the tent. Thunder followed only a moment later. The storm was close.

185

'Now!' Liz yelled.

Maggie and Helena scrambled from the tent, but Joni remained hunched in the corner. She was shaking. Liz placed her hand on her arm. 'We need to go.'

Joni didn't move.

'I'll keep you safe, I promise,' Liz said, pulling Joni to her feet.

Outside, rain lashed at them as they pulled on waterproofs, tightened hoods, shoved feet into boots in a blur of weather and torchlight.

Liz was helping Joni into her wet weather gear when Helena yelled, 'The guy ropes aren't holding!'

Running her torch over the bowing sides of the other tent, Liz saw the ropes hadn't been pegged far enough from the tent. She grabbed the nearest one and knelt on the damp ground, squinting against the driving rain, pulling the peg from the earth. As she did, the wind billowed beneath the fabric of the tent, snatching the rope from her grip. It flew madly through the air.

'Look out!' she cried, as the rope lashed back down, whipping the wet earth inches from Helena.

Helena lunged for the rope, and Liz held down the side of the tent, while fixing the metal peg back in place. The ground was already sodden from the heavy rainfall, the pegs loosening in the earth. She'd no idea if either of their tents would stand up to the strong winds.

Once she was done, she turned on the spot, trying to think. She knew they needed to get away from the mountains – electrical charges sought out the tallest thing – but they also sought out open space. Most people weren't hit by an actual bolt, but by a ground strike, where the energy is discharged through the earth and transferred to whatever – or whoever – is nearby.

She turned and turned, her head torch scanning the landscape. 'I think there may be a cave at the far end of the bay, by Blafjell.'

She'd seen a dark hollow earlier when she'd been swimming. 'We can shelter there.'

She led them across the dunes. The rain was driving at them sideways, sheets of white illuminated in her head torch. It was creating water run-off from the mountains, narrow streams threading down the rockface.

Wet sand sucked at her boots, her waterproofs flattened to her body by the wind.

A crack of lightning burst from the sky almost directly above them, followed by an almighty clap of thunder. For a startling moment it was like daylight. She saw Maggie's eyes turn skyward. Helena was rooted to the spot, blinking rapidly. Joni screamed and dropped to her knees, arms clasped to her head as if she'd been shot.

'It's okay!' Liz shouted above the rain, gripping Joni's shoulders. Guilt burned in her gut. 'This way!' she called, pulling Joni to her feet and leading them to the far end of the beach, torchlight scanning the foot of the mountain, looking for the cave entrance.

Wind whipped the ocean into dark waves, flinging foam high into the night. Gusts tore through the dune grass, howling and wheeling against the mountain face.

'There!' she said eventually, shining the torch into a gap in the dark rock. 'We'll be safe inside!'

38

MAGGIE

The wind snatched back Maggie's hood. Squinting against the sheeting rain, she stared at the cave. Its black, glistening entrance was arched like a church door.

'We need to get inside!' Liz yelled, beckoning for them to follow.

Maggie had left her torch in the tent. She wanted that bright golden beam in her hands – something to light up her way, steady her thundering heart rate.

Liz went first, guiding Joni behind her.

Maggie stuck close to Helena as they picked their way into the cave, the sand running silver with water.

There was a different quality to the darkness inside, almost suffocating in its thickness. The air smelt stale and dank, tinged by the faint scent of ammonia. Water trickled through cracks in the rock, everywhere gleaming and damp.

She paused, glancing back towards the entrance, watching the curtain of rain.

'Maggie!' Helena called, the beam of her head torch swinging to her. 'You need to come deeper!'

She stayed rooted where she was.

Helena came back for her. 'You've got to get out of the

entrance! Lightning travels down vertical surfaces to reach the ground. It's not safe.'

Maggie felt the reluctance deep in her body – something primal and instinctive warning her not to move deeper into the darkness.

'Here, wear my head torch!' Helena pulled it off and handed it to her.

Suddenly, there was a deep rumbling far beyond the cave. The earth began to tremble beneath her feet. She waited for the flash of lightning – but it didn't come.

'Did you feel that?' Maggie whispered, breath shallow.

Helena, eyes wide, peered towards the beach. 'Yes.'

'What was that?'

Helena shook her head. 'Maybe lightning struck something?'

'There was no flash.'

They were both silent for a few moments. 'Let's keep going,' Helena said eventually.

They followed Liz and Joni deeper into the cave. Maggie walked with her arms stretched out, feeling for obstacles in the darkness, the rock rough like pumice beneath her fingertips. Eventually the narrow cave opened out into a wider space, the size of a modest room.

'Look! Lobster pots!' Liz called from up ahead, casting her torchlight over a dozen or more pots stacked in the corner of the cave.

The sight of them – something human and man-made – was faintly comforting. She could smell their briny scent, salted and strong.

'Let's wait it out here,' Liz said, guiding Joni towards the pots.

Joni sat on one, spine rounded, knees hugged to her chest.

Maggie, too unsettled to sit, paced back and forth, shining the torch into the dark, cavernous cracks. She pointed the beam upwards, wondering whether there were bats roosting above. The image of sticky wings beating against her hair made her pull her hood tighter around her face.

Several minutes passed, the storm outside echoing into their hollow shelter. Maggie kept moving, examining the inside of the cave, noticing that some of the rock seemed to glitter in her torch beam. As she was running her fingers over the nooks and ledges, her eye was caught by something delicate and silver. She angled the beam of her head torch, illuminating a small natural hook on which something slender was snagged.

She tilted her head, looking more closely.

'What is it?' Helena called.

'I've found something,' she said, running her fingers over the nook and slipping free a silver chain.

As she freed it from the rock, it glittered beneath the torch-light, a cobweb entangled around the clasp.

She could see it more clearly now. 'A bracelet.'

The torchlight glinted across it and she saw that, threaded into the silver links, were several letters. 'There's a name on it.'

She narrowed her gaze, turning it through her fingers. Her skin grew cool as she read the five letters.

'*K-A-R-I-N.*'

'It's hers . . .' she whispered. 'Karin – the girl who disappeared.'

'We don't know it's the same Karin,' Helena pointed out.

'Vilhelm said that she was out here – on the Svelle trail – when she disappeared,' Maggie said. 'And look, the bracelet is covered in cobwebs – so it must have been here for some time.'

She passed it to Liz, who examined it, turning it methodically through the beam of her torch.

'What do you think?' Maggie asked.

'It seems likely,' Liz said. 'The bracelet is made for an adult wrist. It's her name.'

Maggie asked, 'But what's it doing in the cave?'

'Maybe she was sheltering in here, like us?' Helena suggested.

She lifted her head torch, raising it to the domed roof of the cave, looking into the cold hollows, wondering whether Karin had once been sitting in this very spot, just as she was.

39

JONI

Joni pressed her nails into the flesh of her bare calves, braced ready for the next flash of lightning.

The others were passing the bracelet between them, discussing Karin. Joni couldn't hold onto the conversation, her thoughts skittering with fear.

She glanced back over her shoulder, saw the narrow gap of the cave entrance. A streak of lightning bolted outside in a brilliant series of flashes. Her heart flared in her chest; the roar of blood filled her ears.

Beside her, Liz asked, 'You okay?'

She tried to make a noise, reassure Liz that she was fine, but no sound emerged.

Just beyond the cave, a second burst of lightning cracked the night open. Then a bellowing roar of thunder raged from the sky.

Joni gasped.

Liz was turning, talking, promising the storm would be over soon, but her voice sounded distant, as if Joni were at the far end of a tunnel.

Panic rose in her throat as she felt herself slipping away from the others, being swallowed by a memory of that first storm.

She had been six years old. She'd joined her father on a

photoshoot. The house they'd rented had been noisy with models, stylists, make-up artists, and her father's voice, booming above them all. She'd kept out of the way, like she'd been told to. One of the assistants brought pizza up to her room and, despite the voices and the music, at some point she'd fallen asleep.

She woke hours later to a growling rumble outside. Beneath her covers she froze, terrified. She'd fumbled for the lamp, but the power was out, and there was only more darkness. At her window, the forest lit up in a flash, eerie and wild. She screamed, stumbling onto the pitch-black landing, calling her father's name.

But he wasn't there.

No one was there.

She was a child. She didn't understand that there'd been a power cut. That her father and his friends were drinking in the pub next door, a generator keeping the lights on. She didn't know that she hadn't been abandoned.

Hours later, when her father had returned with the others, he'd found her asleep on the doormat, her pyjamas soaked with urine. Someone had put her back in bed – him? An assistant? – without changing her.

In the morning her father was hungover, grouchy, preoccupied with the shoot. He didn't ask if she was okay. Didn't apologise for leaving her. She knew her fear, her emotions, her presence, were an inconvenience to him. She shrank inward, trying to make herself invisible.

A few weeks later, her father had a shoot in France, and he left her at her grandmother's house in Oakscombe, like he had done before. Only this time, he didn't return.

She really was invisible.

The next flash of lightning struck, and she felt the terror rise up, tightening at her throat. She screwed her eyes shut, dug her fingertips into her skin, clamped down her teeth. Her breathing was ragged, high and shallow in her chest.

Sliding above the wind and rain, she heard a voice. Not words. Not her friends talking to her – but music.

Beside her, Maggie had started to sing.

Eyes still closed, Joni listened. 'Under the Bridge' by the Red Hot Chili Peppers. A song they used to sing as teenagers, walking to lessons with their arms linked. She tried tuning in to the music to stop the terror dragging her far away.

A second voice joined the song. Loud and jaunty, hopelessly out of tune, but with a strong power. Helena.

Another crack of thunder. *One . . . T—*

Lightning danced outside, forks of it shooting to the ground, like a fireworks display. The storm was overhead. She tensed, waiting to feel it strike the cave . . .

Maggie and Helena, perched on lobster pots, continued to sing – and then Liz was joining in, too. Their three voices surrounding her, rising in volume, echoing in the dark chamber of the cave, singing louder than the rain and the waves and the wind.

Joni lifted her head. She opened her mouth. Began to sing.

Her voice came out shaky, thin, but as she used it, she began to feel the rhythm of the song move through her, strengthening.

Crouched low on the lobster pots, water dripping from the cave, the mountains steely beyond them, the four of them sang.

40

MAGGIE

The singing echoed beautifully in the hollow of the cave. She held on tight to Joni's small, cold hand, and in the other she held Helena's fingers.

They were together. Connected. Safe.

When the song ended, she chanced a look at Joni. Her expression had relaxed a little, her brow softening. The tautness around her mouth had eased.

Joni looked at each of her friends. Her eyes were misted with tears. She didn't say anything – she didn't need to.

Liz stood up, saying, 'I'm going to check the weather out there.'

They'd been sheltering in the cave for some time, and Maggie, exhausted and damp, was desperate to return to the tents to sleep.

A few moments later, she heard Liz's voice calling from the cave entrance. 'The storm is getting further away!'

'Thank God!' Maggie said. 'We can go back.'

'I don't know what's worse,' Helena said. 'A wet, dank cave, or a wet, dank tent.'

True. Maggie clambered from her perch on the lobster pots, knees stiff from sitting for so long. The heel of her hiking boot caught in the netting, and tugged over the pot, tumbling the stack. A mooring buoy rolled loose, clattering across the cave floor.

'You okay?' Helena asked, helping her upright.

'Fine,' she said, dusting off her knees.

She glanced at her hand, which still clasped Karin's bracelet and, without pausing to think about it, tucked the bracelet in her pocket.

Joni helped straighten the pots – but as she did so, her torch beam froze. 'That's odd.'

'What?' Liz asked.

Joni crouched lower. 'Something came out of the pot.'

'It's just the buoy—'

'No. There was something inside it.' She shone her torch on the orange mooring buoy. A clean line had opened across its centre and, from it, a brown package had fallen. As she reached to pick it up, a spill of white powder poured from a tear.

'Shit!' Joni whispered.

Maggie's breath caught in her throat. 'Is that . . . ?'

No one answered.

The four of them stared at the sugar-white powder glimmering under the torch beam.

Maggie could hear her pulse in her ears.

After a moment, Joni reached forward and dipped her forefinger into the powder. She held it up towards the light.

Then she brought it towards her mouth.

'Don't!' Maggie yelled, just as Joni dabbed the powder against her gum.

'Jesus! You don't know what that is!' Liz cried.

There was a pause.

Joni looked up, eyeing the others. 'Yes. I do.'

'Cocaine?' Maggie said.

Joni nodded.

'Why is there a bag of cocaine in this cave?' Helena whispered, glancing around, alarmed.

Joni examined the package, then the mooring buoy. 'It's been purposefully hidden inside the buoy.'

'We're in the middle of nowhere,' Helena said. 'Who is going to leave a bag of cocaine out here?'

'It must be a drop,' Joni said. Then she moved to the next pot, examining it. Every lobster pot had an orange mooring buoy attached to it. She reached for the next buoy, running her fingers over the hard, plastic surface.

'What are you doing?' Maggie asked.

'There'll be more.'

Almost as she said it, Joni found the crack in the buoy, twisted, and pulled it apart.

The beam of her torch bounced over the inside and there was a second bag of cocaine.

She let out a low whistle. 'Looks like they've been packed in kilos.'

Maggie had no idea how much a kilo of cocaine was worth, but she knew this was serious.

Helena straightened. 'Whoever left this here isn't going to take kindly to us blundering around their stock room.'

'Agreed,' Liz said. 'We need to get out of here.'

But Joni was already removing the buoy marker from the next pot. She held it close to her ear. Shook it once. She must have felt the dull thud of the package inside it as she said, 'There's more here, too.'

'Stop touching things! Please!' Maggie begged.

Joni set it back and surveyed the cave, hands on hips. 'There are over a dozen pots with mooring buoys,' she continued. 'If they've all got cocaine in them, then that's twelve kilos of coke. Right here.'

'How much is that worth?' Helena asked.

'I've no idea what the street value is in Norway – but back home, I'd guess it must be . . .' She paused, doing the maths. 'Over a million.'

Helena whistled. 'More profitable than netting lobsters.'

Joni said, 'We saw that fishing boat leaving the bay last night. D'you remember? Maybe they were delivering it.'

At the time, Maggie had thought how picturesque it looked – the red wooden boat motoring out of the empty bay. Now the image was recast with a dangerous edge. 'Do you think they saw us?'

Liz shook her head. 'No, they were at such a distance. We'd have been hard to notice against the mountainside.'

Joni said, 'If the boat left the cocaine here, then it's a drop. Someone else will be picking it up.'

'Another boat?' Helena asked.

'Could be,' Joni said, 'or someone on foot. If there are a dozen kilos here, then it'd be possible to hike it out.'

A cool feeling travelled over Maggie's skin. They could have passed the person who was coming for this. She thought of Erik, appearing from the shadows in the woods.

Her fingertips brushed the bracelet in her pocket. 'Do you think it's connected to the bracelet?'

Liz shrugged. 'All I know is we need to get out of here. Pack the tents. Go.'

'Agreed,' Helena said, lifting the pots back into position.

'What about the spilt stuff?' Maggie asked. 'What do we do with that?'

Everyone looked at the ripped bag of cocaine that was dusting the wet cave floor.

Liz said, 'We leave the lobster pot as it is on its side. Maybe it'll look like an animal disturbed it?'

'What animals have you seen around here?' Helena asked.

'I don't know!' Liz said. 'But we can't move it – the bag is ripped. It'd be obvious someone was trying to cover it up.'

'Our footprints will be all over the beach!' Maggie said. 'They'll see which way we've walked!'

'It's still raining out there. It'll wash them away,' Liz said. 'We need to go. Now.'

Maggie stole a final glance at the lobster pots. Then she followed the torch beam through the cavernous tunnel, her fingertips pushing into her jacket pocket, turning the letters of Karin's name.

41

HELENA

Helena trudged through the dunes behind Liz, sand sticking to her hiking boots in heavy clumps. The dune grass bowed in the wind, needle-sharp blades lashing at her waterproof trousers.

Rivers of water ran down the beach, flashing silver in her torchlight. Above the continuing rain, she could hear the rush of new waterfalls streaming down the mountain.

Maggie caught up, damp hair hanging limp around her face. 'I wish we'd never found the cocaine,' she said with a shudder. 'I've got a bad feeling about it.'

Helena agreed. It stained the clean purity of the wilderness and what this hike was about. 'I don't want to scatter Mum's ashes here now. Doesn't feel right anymore.'

'I'm sorry. I know this had felt like the place.'

Ahead of them, Liz suddenly halted. She ran her torch beam across the beach. 'Where are the tents?'

Helena looked across the sand towards the lower slopes of the mountainside where they'd hiked in. Oddly, she couldn't see their tents. She scanned her torch outward: mountain, beach, ocean.

No tents.

She squinted into the beam of light, confused. They must have lost their bearings in the darkness.

'They must be there,' Maggie said, rising panic in her voice.

Helena searched again, tracing the line of the white water until it met beach.

'Oh my God!' Joni said from the back of the group. 'Look!'

The four of them stood rooted to the spot. Joni's torch was directed up towards the path where, hours earlier, they'd hiked in.

The lower slope of the mountainside was now a river of mud and earth and rock.

'Landslide,' someone whispered.

Helena blinked slowly as the beam absorbed the devastation: a solid hill of earth and rock had settled where their tents had been pitched. An entire section of the mountain slope had crumbled.

'No . . . no . . .'

'Our tents . . .'

They spoke over one another, voices stretched with disbelief, torch beams scanning for a different outcome, but with each widening sweep of light, only more devastation was revealed.

A huge section of the mountainside had been lost, dragging loose boulders and trees and bushes that blocked the entrance to the beach like a muddy avalanche.

'I felt the ground tremble when we were in the cave . . .' Maggie said breathlessly. 'It was this. A landslide.'

'I can't believe this . . .' Liz said. 'The heavy rain must have dislodged the rocks and earth.'

As they surveyed the sheer scale of the landslide, a cold sensation spread through Helena's body. 'If we hadn't sheltered in the cave, we'd be . . .'

'Dead,' Maggie whispered, arms wrapped around herself.

The horror of that possibility silenced them all.

Helena imagined the rumbling of the ground, the awful noise

of the earth beginning to loosen, slide and crumble, the rush to get out of the tent, the crushing weight of thousands of tonnes of earth ploughing into them.

The relief of sheltering in the cave was short-lived. 'But . . . all our things were in the tents,' Liz said.

Helena let the seriousness of the situation settle.

No tents. No sleeping bags. No stove. No food. No water.

Panic rose, a dark tide of it washing over them as they stood soaked and scared, shock ricocheting.

A new thought screeched into Helena's brain – her mother's ashes! – and then she was running towards the crumbled earth.

'Helena! Stop!' Maggie cried.

But she stumbled on, clambering over the first heap of earth, boots sinking into mud.

She needed to find the tents! Get her mother's ashes! She couldn't leave her out here, buried in this terrifying mess of earth!

'Helena, no! It's too dangerous!' Liz shouted.

She scrambled on, using a boulder for purchase. The smell of wet mud was thick in her nostrils.

Her foot slipped deeper, mud climbing over her knees. She tried to push on but could feel the suction of the earth against her boots, trying to force them from her feet as she battled to pull out her legs.

She dragged her left boot out of the deep mud. Took another step – but sank even further this time, up to her thighs.

'Helena!' the others screamed.

She used her hands, digging into the soil, meeting hard fragments of stone.

Tears and mud streaked her face.

Then there were hands on her shoulders, pulling her back.

She tried to shake them off – but couldn't.

Maggie was talking to her, telling her it'd be all right. Promising her over and over again.

But it wouldn't be.

It couldn't be.

Her mother's ashes were gone.

42

LIZ

Helena leaned heavily against Maggie as she steered her away from the landslide. Their legs and boots were caked in mud, hair pasted to their heads.

When they were far enough away from the landslide, Helena collapsed onto the beach. Spine rounded, head hanging low, her ragged sobs echoed through the rain.

Maggie crouched beside her, rubbing her back in slow circles, talking in a low, steady voice.

'I'm so sorry,' Liz said, moving to Helena's other side. 'It's going to be okay.'

Locked deep in her own shock and grief, Helena didn't respond.

Liz felt helpless. There was nothing she – or any of them – could do to make this better. There was no way to retrieve the ashes. They were gone.

She also knew they had a more immediate problem to deal with. She straightened, scanning the mountainside steadily with her torch beam, searching each part of the landscape.

Joni glanced at her. 'Liz? What is it?'

'Our trail out of here. It's gone.'

Joni's eyes widened.

Maggie glanced over her shoulder. 'Gone?'

Liz nodded. She stared at the hundreds of tonnes of earth and rock, collapsed on the beach. There was no way they could scramble over it – the earth sinking and dangerous, loose rock unsettled. It would be impossible – deadly.

'There has to be another way out,' Joni said.

Liz answered, 'There is.' She turned, looking in the opposite direction to the far end of the beach. Then her gaze lifted to the huge beast of a mountain towering there.

'Blafjell,' Joni whispered. 'But . . . we can't do it. You said so yourself, Liz. It's too hard!'

'We have no choice. There's no other path.'

Joni's voice was wretched. 'It's a huge mountain. We've got no supplies – no water, no food, nothing.'

'There'll be streams and waterfall runoff,' Liz said. 'Water won't be a problem.'

'And food?'

'We'll be hungry. But we'll survive.' She could feel her heart racing in her chest, but she needed to keep her head. The others were relying on her. 'We're in weatherproof clothes and hiking boots. If we go carefully, we can do this.' Then she remembered: 'My map, I left it in the tent.'

'I've got my phone,' Joni said. 'I took a photo of the trail.'

'Let's see it,' Liz said, moving to Joni's shoulder.

The rain had thinned to a drizzle, which studded the flare of the screen as Joni thumbed to the image of the map.

As they huddled close, a message appeared. *Low battery 20%.*

Liz's insides tightened.

Joni swiped the notification aside and pinched the map wider with a damp forefinger and thumb.

'This is where we are now,' Liz said, indicating the beach. 'It'll be light soon. The trail up Blafjell should be well marked.'

205

She'd read about the climb and knew the conditions were tough, lots of scrambling and steep elevations. 'The first peak looks okay. But the challenge is crossing the ridge. It's half a kilometre long – and it's narrow, which means it's lethal if it's wet or windy or the visibility is bad.'

Joni's brow was pinched tight as she said, 'Even if we make it across the ridge, what then? Where do we sleep? We've no tent . . . No sleeping bags . . .'

'Here,' Liz said, pointing. 'There's a DNT hut.'

'What's that?' Joni asked.

'A mountain cabin. They're all over Norway. Little wooden huts that are left unlocked for hikers and mountaineers. Bit like a Scottish bothy. They have wood stoves. We'll be warm. Dry. If we're lucky there could be a food store.'

'Looks a long way. How high are we talking?'

'Over a thousand metres,' Liz said.

'Do you think Helena is going to be up to it?' Joni asked.

They both looked to where Helena remained huddled on the ground, being comforted by Maggie. Helena was shivering hard, arms hugged to her body, wet hair pasted to her scalp.

'She'll have to be.'

Joni, pinching her lip between her thumb and index finger, asked, 'What's the alternative?'

Liz looked at the map, studying it forensically, noting the undulations of the contour lines. She shook her head. 'There isn't one.'

DAY 3

THE SEARCH

Leif's radio buzzes. He snaps it from the waistband of his shorts without slowing his pace, answering as he jogs.

It's Knut from the rescue base. 'It's a mess over at Hyvik rock,' he says without preamble. 'The helicopter is still out. I've sent a second team your way by road, but the Hyvik Tunnel is shut. Damn repair work. Won't reach your lodge for another hour.'

Leif feels the adrenalin rip harder. He's out here on his own.

'Radio in when you get eyes on the hiker,' Knut says.

'Will do,' Leif confirms. Leif's father had worked alongside Knut plenty during the years he volunteered as a mountain rescue worker. His father used to say of Knut that he wasn't the sort of man you'd share your problems with over a beer – rather the sort you'd want at your side in a tough spot on a rescue mission: decisive, unemotional, prepared to make tough calls, fast.

'What are the weather conditions like out there?' Knut asks.

'Low cloud,' Leif answers, still jogging as he talks. 'Visibility moderate. If the wind drops, we could be in for fog.' That would be a problem. Without a GPS position he'd have almost no chance of locating the hiker. He's been out on the mountain when the fog rolls in, and you're lucky if you can see your own hand in front of your face. Scary as hell. You take a step in the wrong direction, and you go off the edge.

The weather up here this morning, though, has been mostly clear – or that's how it looked from the lodge. No fog to cause a misstep or accident. He doesn't understand it.

He's beginning to pant, but he works to keep his breath as steady as he can.

Knut says, 'Radio in with a location when you find her. If she's a long way down, no hero stuff. You wait for the team, okay?'

'Course,' he agrees, but Leif knows that every moment out here counts. And that the team will be several hours behind him. If it's safe and he can get to her, he will.

43

MAGGIE

They set out across the wet beach in silence. Dawn was washed grey, waves rolling blankly onto shore.

Maggie's shoulders felt disconcertingly empty – she longed for the weight of food, shelter, water carried in her pack. They had nothing but the clothes on their backs.

She'd grown used to her friends' gaits weighted beneath heavy packs. Liz looked strangely exposed without the map hanging at her neck and her technical backpack gone. Joni walked beside her, hands hanging heavy, gaze down, goosebumps specking her bare legs. Her bandana still held a damp pile of hair which had slipped to one side, throwing her off balance. But it was Helena who seemed most adrift. Her hiking trousers were caked in mud. Streaks of it ran across her face. No trace of make-up. Hair matted and kinked. She looked exhausted, too pale.

Maggie stepped over a pile of seaweed carried in by the storm, flies lifting briefly to investigate her muddy purple leggings, before resettling further along the beach.

She thought about how they'd wasted the fish that Vilhelm had left at their last camp. A hollow sensation was already spreading through her middle; she wished they'd been able to eat a proper meal last night.

When they reached the north end of the bay, they came to a standstill at the foot of Blafjell. She raised her head until her neck couldn't flex any further.

Her gaze mapped a wall of black, jagged rock. Its twin peaks rose into the morning clouds like a two-headed beast. Connecting the peaks was a narrow, sheer-sided ridge. The scratched path of their trail, visible at the bottom, looked narrow and steep, and was quickly lost to the folding layers of rock. A cold, uneasy sensation spread through her insides.

She turned, looking back, staring at the collapsed slope of the mountain they'd left behind. Hundreds of tonnes of earth and rock had fallen in a crush of debris. It had been her idea to camp there, refusing to walk a step further. It was her fault they were out here with no gear; that Helena's mother's ashes were lost; that they were about to attempt a mountain summit with no supplies.

Facing the looming presence of Blafjell, fear rode high in her chest. She wanted to turn, run. Make all of this disappear. She wasn't fit enough. Strong enough. Brave enough.

But there was no choice, except to climb. She *had* to do this.

She eyed the first faded red T-marker painted on a huge boulder. She stepped forward, placing her palm beside it, as if touching a holy object, asking for safe passage. Crescents of dirt were packed beneath her nails, and a bloody scratch ran across the back of her hand.

Joni came silently to her shoulder and laid her hand flat beside Maggie's.

Then Liz and Helena joined them, placing their palms on the boulder.

They were silent. Four hands pressed to stone.

Maggie looked steadily at each of them, eye to eye.

Right there, hands on the trail marker, she felt something strong and fierce being fired in the kiln of her heart: they could do this.

Maggie would climb this mountain. She would keep her friends safe. She would hike back to her daughter.

They were too exhausted to speak, slogging ever upward, legs like dead weights. An hour passed. Then another, and another.

Maggie was desperate to rest, but what was the point? The mountain would still be waiting for them. If they stopped, it only meant they would have to start again.

Up here, the air felt cooler, a sharpening wind licking the rockface and cooling the sweat on her back. 'It's so cold,' she said.

'For every hundred feet you climb, the temperature drops by a degree,' Liz explained.

Joni looked alarmed. She was the only one in the group wearing shorts. 'So by the time we reach the summit, it'll be ten degrees cooler than on the beach?'

Liz nodded.

Ahead of them, Helena stumbled, her toe snagging against rock. She tipped forward, landing hard on all fours. Maggie rushed to her side, taking her elbow and helping her up. 'You okay?'

'Just light-headed. I'm fine.'

'There's a waterfall up there,' Maggie said, pointing. 'Let's take a break.'

A sheer section of rockface ran white with rushing water. It streamed close to the rock, pouring over the ferns that grew in the cracks.

They picked their way off the trail, negotiating the loose scree which worked its way over the tops of her hiking boots, adding a gritty layer to her socks.

The rush of the waterfall filled her ears as she moved nearer. She cupped her hands – but the strength of the flow pounded against her palms, splashing icy water into her face.

She tried again, finding a lighter section of the flow, and managing to catch just enough in her hands to slurp. The water tasted of slate and earth, with a mineral bite, but she drank gratefully, filling her belly.

'Here,' she said, drawing Helena over. 'Drink.'

Helena did as instructed. She sipped a little, then sluiced the rest over her face, cleaning the mud from her temples and cheeks, dampening the dark hollows beneath her eyes.

Liz was sitting apart from the others, shoulders slumped. It worried Maggie to see her pep and energy gone, her face pale, eyes dull. 'Anyone got anything useful in their pockets?' she asked, turning out her own and laying a pack of tissues on a table-like rock along with her head torch.

Joni stretched forward and placed down her phone and half a packet of chewing gum.

Next, Helena took out her torch, then rooted around and discovered a lipstick. She eyed it for a moment, then twisted the tube and applied it, making a smooth sweep of her lips. Her eyes briefly fluttered closed, and Maggie imagined the scent of it transporting her away from the rocky mountainside. Her shoulders seemed to draw back a little as she opened her eyes and lifted her chin.

'She's back,' Maggie said, with a wink.

Helena managed a smile.

'Maggie, what have you got?' Liz asked.

She patted down her jacket, hoping to discover a mystery snack in one of the numerous hidden pockets – but all she found was a small heart-shaped shell, a hairband, and Karin's bracelet.

She ran a fingertip lightly across the silver letters, its presence feeling important somehow. 'Do you think,' she said quietly, voicing a thought that had been troubling her, 'that Karin found the cocaine in the cave? Maybe she was involved in it somehow?'

214

The others looked at her.

'Maybe that's why she disappeared . . .'

The rush of the waterfall was the only sound.

She wanted one of her friends to say, *Of course not! Don't be ridiculous!* But no one spoke.

A scattering noise caused them all to look up. Tiny stones rolled down the mountain face some distance from them. It was like a waterfall of rock – little stones skittering and bouncing down the steep side, gathering others as they fell.

Maggie froze, waiting for more earth to loosen, begin rumbling. For the mountainside to waver and tremble beneath her feet, to feel the first slide as the ground shifted.

But there was nothing more. The tiny rocks settled. Stilled.

No one passed comment. They all knew how precarious the terrain was. How careful they needed to be.

Maggie pushed to her feet and continued to climb.

44

HELENA

The trail cut steeply upwards, less hike, more scramble. Helena was climbing hand over hand, the trail studded with rock and boulder. In one particularly steep section, a chain had been drilled into the rock to help haul oneself upwards.

Helena was ravenous. She was craving salty, beige foods – dry-roasted peanuts or sea salt and cider vinegar crisps or a block of vintage cheddar. She wondered how much she'd pay, right now, for a hunk of cheese.

Thousands, she decided.

Ahead, Joni gripped the grey hide of a boulder, pushing herself up with a grunt. As she stretched, a bulge appeared in the deep pocket of her jacket.

Strange, Helena thought. The shape was too large to be a phone or a pack of chewing gum, which were the only items Joni had declared earlier.

'Joni?' she called, blowing hard through her cheeks as she caught up. 'What's that in your pocket?'

Joni's fingers immediately brushed the shape at her side. 'Tissues,' she said, without slowing her pace.

Her tone was too breezy, the answer too quick. Helena wondered if she was hiding food.

'Can I use one?'

A hesitation. 'What for?'

'I need a piss.'

'We should save them,' Joni said, not slowing.

As Joni continued to climb, Helena kept her gaze on the shape in her pocket. It was too large, too solid, to be tissues.

'Seriously,' Helena called again, trying to keep pace. 'What is in your pocket?'

Joni pretended not to hear.

Helena had to scramble to reach her side, panting hard. She put a hand on Joni's arm.

Joni span around, eyes narrowed. 'What?'

Helena snatched a breath. 'What have you got in there?'

Joni shook her off and tried to rejoin the trail.

Helena followed, fury making her fast. Then, just as suddenly, she stopped. She blinked, staring at the back of Joni as she realised. 'Oh God! You didn't?'

Ahead of her, Joni hesitated.

Maggie and Liz, catching up, asked, 'What's going on?'

Slowly, Joni turned and faced her friends. Her tanned skin had blanched.

Helena glared at her. 'You stole the fucking coke!'

Joni's expression was strange, eyes hard, but glistening. 'The bag was already ripped. What were they gonna do with it?'

'You went back for it?' Liz asked, aghast.

'So?'

Joni had been the last to leave the cave. She must have grabbed the bag and stuffed it in her jacket pocket.

'Why would you take it?' Liz asked. Her voice came out small, bewildered.

She shrugged. 'If our energy flags, it'll help us get through.'

Helena baulked. 'You want us to snort cocaine halfway up a bloody mountain? Are you insane? We're not at a music

217

festival! We're on a remote mountain face! If we don't keep our shit together, don't make it off the mountain, we will die out here!'

Maggie's voice was thin. 'You've put us all in danger!'

Joni was glaring at them like a cornered animal. When she was in the wrong, Joni fought.

'*I've* put us in danger? It wasn't my idea to peg our tents at the bottom of the mountain—'

Maggie looked mortified. 'I'm sorry. I never thought—'

'—And it wasn't my idea to hike out into the wilderness despite the storm warnings!'

It was Liz's turn to flush.

'If you're so worried about the cocaine,' Joni said, yanking the package free of her pocket and tossing it on a rock between them, 'then we ditch it.'

Helena stared at the package. Joni had managed to patch the split using a section of tape from the seal of the bag. 'We can't get rid of it! Someone is coming to collect the drugs – and when they find a bag is missing, they're not going to be happy.' She shook her head. 'You never think! That's your problem, Joni!'

'That's my problem?' Joni retorted, folding her arms.

'One of them.'

'When did you become so uptight?' Joni challenged. 'You used to be the first to step forward for a line.'

'Yeah. In a club. On a big weekend. In my twenties. Not during a hiking trip! I'm not in Norway to get high – I came out here to spend time with my friends and to spread my mother's ashes.' She felt the sharp ache of loss, thinking again of the ashes lost beneath thousands of tonnes of earth. Irretrievable. She looked at Joni, eyes narrowing. 'Not that *you* would give a shit about that.'

Joni blinked at the quicksilver switch of the argument. 'What does that mean?'

Maggie lifted her palms. 'Let's not—'

'You know exactly what it means!' Helena snapped. 'You weren't there when Mum was dying. You weren't there at her funeral. And you haven't been there since.'

Joni looked like she'd been slapped. She stood very still, just the shallow rise and fall of her chest as she breathed.

'Do you know what song Mum requested to open the funeral service?'

Joni swallowed.

'One of yours. "Rainbows". Mum wrote down her final wishes: *"Rainbows" sung by Joni.* Then, in brackets afterwards, she put, *Or on CD if Joni can't be there.*' Helena sucked in a breath. 'Broke my heart seeing that, because even Mum knew you wouldn't show up.'

Joni was blinking rapidly. 'I couldn't be there. I was on tour. I had a gig.'

'I checked your schedule,' Helena said, gaze still pinned to her. 'There was no gig.'

45

JONI

Shame infused Joni's skin. Helena was right: there had been no gig.

'I checked the tour dates,' Helena was saying, lips barely moving. 'You were in Madrid the night before the funeral, then your next gig was two days later in Prague. You could have flown back. There was time.' Her voice wavered as she asked, 'What were you doing that was more important than saying goodbye to my mother?'

Joni felt the collective gaze of her friends. She swallowed repeatedly, unsure how to explain.

When Helena had messaged her about the funeral, asking if she'd play, Joni was mid-tour. She knew it would be gruelling to fly there and back in forty-eight hours. Her schedule was so jammed – twenty-seven gigs in thirty-three days – that she needed that rare window to decompress.

Touring was impossible to explain. It was this crazy, messed-up, distorted reality. The drugs and alcohol. The haze of jetlag. The brutal insomnia. The adrenalin that never left her body or let her sleep. The screaming fans. The press following her every move. The cameras shoved in her face.

It was arriving at a different arena night after night, knowing you had nothing left to give. Looking through the wings at a sea of faces, fans screaming your name, expecting Joni Gold. Only it's not you. It's someone else pasting on a smile, stepping out into those dazzling lights, arms thrown wide – *Hello Brooklyn! Hello Sydney! Hello Tokyo!* – when all you want is to curl up tight, to stay in the dark, because that's where you belong. But you can't. You must pump out this energy, fill a whole stadium with it, and it's got to come from somewhere. But you don't have any left. You're a shell. An empty, broken shell! So, you get it on loan any way you can – caffeine, cocaine, anti-depressants, champagne, vodka, nicotine, ketamine – whatever you can get.

The idea of flying home, standing in a small, respectable church in the village where she'd grown up, seeing all those people who had known her, championed her, believed in her. She just . . . she couldn't do it.

She hadn't flown back and seen Helena's mother when she was sick. And now she was dead. She didn't feel worthy of turning up at the funeral, singing a song to the whole church and being praised for it. So she didn't fly home. She sat in a hotel room on her own and got blasted out of her skull.

'I . . . I didn't have it in me . . .' Joni tried. 'I was in a bad place. I didn't want that to be how I sent off your mum.'

'So you didn't send her off at all,' Helena said, eyes glistening with tears.

'I sent flowers—'

'A big, ostentatious bunch that your manager probably arranged. I wanted *you* there. Mum wanted *you* there. You didn't even call me in the weeks that followed. You just carried on living your big, beautiful life and abandoned me.' Helena's voice tripped over those last two words.

Tears stung Joni's eyes. Her throat felt like it was closing. The air on the mountain felt too thin, hard to breathe. Maggie

221

and Liz were hanging back, eyes wide. 'I'm sorry,' she said, eventually. 'I didn't know that's how it felt. I cared about your mum—'

Helena shook her head. 'You only care about yourself.'

'Helena . . .' Liz said, quietly.

'You don't get to jump in. Defend her,' Helena barked.

'I wasn't going—'

'Everyone fawns around Joni. Grateful for her scraps of attention. You do it, too, Maggie. She bowls into your wedding, all jet-set super stardom, does her thing on the mic and everyone thinks she's a hero. Then you don't see her again. Not when you go through the divorce, not when you're bringing up Phoebe alone. Tell me I'm wrong?'

Maggie looked pained as her gaze fell to her feet.

'All that glitters is not gold,' Helena said. 'To me, a friend is someone who is there when it counts: when a parent dies; when you're going through a divorce; when life isn't shiny and bright. Not for the holidays and the high days, or when you need a place to crash to try on a family Christmas for size.'

Joni felt like her chest was being crushed. 'You don't understand my life!'

'Quick! Grab your guitar! Catchy chorus line.'

'Fuck you,' Joni spat, the tears coming now. She turned away. Her mind raced, a flood of adrenalin washing away the tired muscles and exhaustion. She tipped forward into a run, ignoring Liz's shouts.

The wind was against her face. Into it she let out a huge explosion of noise, a scream of frustration, of hurt, of she-didn't-know-what! Just knew she wanted to be anywhere but this mountain trail.

She felt like her skin had been flayed right off. She wanted the cocaine. Wanted to disappear from herself.

'Just stop!' Liz yelled.

Joni turned back.

'What is it?' Maggie asked.

Liz's face was pinched. She was pointing towards the beach.
'Look! Someone's down there.'

46

LIZ

Below on the beach, Liz could just make out the shape of a person.

'Who is that?' Maggie whispered.

Liz squinted, trying to squeeze her vision into something sharper – but all she could make out was a figure moving across an otherwise still scene. 'Whoever it is, they're heading for the cave.'

A collective tension grew between them as they stood together, Joni and Helena's argument fading to a background hum.

Maggie shook her head, saying, 'The trail onto the beach was destroyed in the landslide. How have they got down there?'

Liz glanced towards the sea. 'There's no sign of a boat.'

'And we've not crossed anyone on the mountain trail,' Helena added.

'Unless . . .' Liz began, turning cold at the thought, '. . . the person was down there the whole time?'

'They're going inside!' Maggie said, hugging her arms to her body.

They fell silent, watching as the lone figure was swallowed by the mouth of the cave.

Liz imagined the person taking a torch from their pocket, its beam lighting the way towards the stack of lobster pots. Would they see the spill of powder on the floor and the tumbled pot? How long would it take them to notice that one of the packages was missing?

'They're going to find out, aren't they?' Maggie said, voice panicked. 'They'll know someone took their cocaine.'

'I'm sorry,' Joni said quietly, tone dejected. Her hands had dropped to her sides, her head was lowered. 'I've messed up. I shouldn't have taken it. I'm so sorry.'

No one said anything.

All eyes were on the cave.

'Who do you think is down there?' Maggie asked, her voice lowered.

'Could be anyone,' Liz said, pulling at the collar of her jacket. Whoever it was, Liz knew she didn't want to come face to face with them.

She glanced at the bag of cocaine still slumped on the rock in front of them. 'What do we do with this?'

'Chuck it over the mountainside!' Maggie said.

'No!' Joni said, stepping forward. 'If someone *does* come looking for it – better that we return it.' She picked up the cocaine and went to pocket it, but Liz stepped forward, opening her hand.

Joni's gaze fell on her palm. Her eyes were dull, deep shadows beneath them. Her fingers kept their grip on the cocaine. Liz wondered just how dark things had become. She'd thought Joni's drug use was social, for a buzz, to keep up the pace – because maybe that was what she'd wanted to see. But for Joni to take the risk of stealing cocaine – to even want it in these circumstances – it worried her.

She met Joni's gaze, waiting for her to hand it over.

A gust of wind wound up the mountainside, cool and sharp.

After a beat, Joni placed the cocaine in Liz's palm. Then she wrapped her arms tight around herself, as if she was suddenly chilled.

Liz forced the bag into the widest pocket of her jacket, zipping it shut.

When she turned, Helena was still squinting at the cave.

'What is it?' Maggie asked.

'Whoever is in that cave is going to discover some of the cocaine is missing. And then they're going to come looking for it.' She paused, turning to face the others. 'We're standing on the only trail out of Blafjell.'

The friends looked at each other.

Liz said, 'We need to move.'

THE SEARCH

Leif scrambles up the next section of mountain. The elevation has steepened, so he needs both hands to grab onto huge boulders and pull himself up. For speed, he's abandoned the trail, which rises more gradually up a series of switchbacks, taking the softer flank of the mountain. Leif's route will shave off half an hour – if he doesn't fall.

Every moment counts, he knows, thinking of the injured woman, unmoving on the ledge. At high elevation, being exposed to the elements for this length of time isn't good. If her injuries are serious, he may already be too late.

As he pushes on, he can feel the slick of sweat between his T-shirt and pack. He pulls himself up over a large boulder, his sight keen, looking around, keeping alert.

As a child, he'd often come out here with Erik. They had always been good climbers. It didn't feel learned, it was just part of their everyday, climbing the mountains because they were there. Flat ground didn't exist in their village. There was nowhere to play football except at the valley bottom, which was level, but dank and shaded most of the summer or covered in snow in winter. So instead, they climbed.

It was only when Leif was an adult and he visited other

places in Europe – taking in flat, square gardens and concrete and brick expanses – that he realised that he lived somewhere so beautiful.

He knows Erik set out on the Svelle trail three days earlier. Erik didn't tell him – just did it. Name in the logbook. Pack on his shoulders. Gone. Always flying low to the ground. Secretive. Never letting Leif in.

Maybe I'm no different, Leif thinks.

His gaze lifts to the mountain top, then he turns as he takes in the ridge, the second peak. He wonders where Erik is now. Recalls the description the German hikers gave. *A younger man . . . alone. Head in his hands.*

The image makes him recall their father's funeral – Erik walking out mid-hymn, kicking the door open with his foot. Leif had found him later, not in the burial ground, but down by the lodge lake where their father used to sit with his morning coffee watching the birds dive for insects. Erik had been slumped on the bank, head in his hands, fingers digging into his scalp. Leif had tried to talk, to tell him it would be okay, but he'd started to shout, mouthing off about tourists who had no right to be out there in the mountains, endangering the rescue teams' lives. He was angry, hurting, full of blame, wanting to lash out.

If Erik was on the Svelle trail, he should have been hiking out by now. They should've passed one another.

Leif scans the landscape once again.

No sign of his brother.

47

MAGGIE

Maggie had never felt more exhausted. Her leg muscles spiked with the burn of lactic acid; a deep pressure was throbbing at her temples; her breath came in uneven gasps.

Helena and Joni hadn't spoken a word to one another. The argument hung over them all, weighting the atmosphere. Helena marched at the front; Joni lagged at the rear. Sandwiched by their animosity, Liz and Maggie walked in silence, too.

Despite the strengthening wind, Maggie was hot beneath her jacket. She paused to unzip it, tying it around her waist. The freckled skin on her arms was flushed pink. She stretched one way and then the other, easing out her back.

Joni drew closer, gaze on the ground, expression bleak. Wisps of dark hair had escaped her headband. The verve and spark that she'd blazed with on stage at the lodge had burned out, and she looked tired and fragile now.

'You okay?' Maggie asked.

Joni shook her head. 'I'm a shit person.'

'Don't say that.'

'Everything Helena said about me – it's true. I wasn't there for her when her mum died. I should have been. And you,

229

Mags,' she said, eyes misting, 'she's right. After you and Aidan ended, I didn't check in enough. I let you down.'

Maybe there was some truth in that. At the time, Maggie had felt abandoned – but there was no point kicking someone when they were down. 'You were away. I understood.'

'But you shouldn't have to understand! I want to be the type of friend who you can rely on. Like Liz and Helena.'

She was right that Liz and Helena had been brilliant. It was Liz who'd found the house she was now renting, and who'd given up a weekend to help her move in. Helena had driven down too, arriving with food to stock her cupboards and two bottles of champagne, 'To toast your freedom!'

'I could have called you, messaged, sent something for Phoebe. But I didn't,' Joni said. 'There's something wrong with me. I think about doing something nice – and then I never follow through!'

Maggie knew that Joni lived so fully in the moment that sometimes she didn't pause to think outside of that reality. If she were out drinking, she'd never be the one to think ahead about the early start, or the hangover that would come. Maggie suspected that when Joni was apart from them, it was like they didn't exist. It wasn't Joni being callous or selfish – she was simply living in another moment, and they weren't part of it.

'You three – you're everything I have.' Joni's eyes were teary. 'And I just . . . I keep messing up.'

'We're always going to be here. We love you.'

'But I don't deserve you. Any of you. There are things I've done . . .' she said, looking ahead at Helena, then Liz. She shook her head, trailing off.

'Joni?'

'Sorry. I'm not good company. I think . . . I just need to be on my own for a bit.' Without waiting for a response, she picked up her pace, leaving Maggie alone on the trail.

The stony path continued to ascend steeply, weaving past boulders. The vegetation grew sparse, hard growing grasses and tough shrubs poking between rocks. She imagined that in a few more weeks, the trail they were walking on would be buried beneath snow.

Maggie slipped a hand into her pocket and felt the bracelet she'd tucked there. She pressed the cool silver between her fingertips, turning each letter of Karin's name like a rosary.

Her thoughts spun back to the moment in the woods when she'd stepped off the trail, separating from the others. She remembered the clean slice of fear when she realised that she was lost. A cold dread of being alone out there. Then she recalled Erik appearing from the shadows, staring right at her. Hooded eyes dark and disturbed. *Karin*, he'd whispered, turning her blood cold.

Maggie rotated the letters harder, feeling the press of each of them.

Had it been Erik they'd spotted on the beach entering the cave? She thought of the sagging backpack he'd been carrying in the woods. Plenty of space to fill it with bags of cocaine.

Soon Erik – or whoever was down there – would discover that some of the cocaine was missing. He'd follow the footprints. Would know what they'd done.

She checked over her shoulder. Her chest tightened as she wondered when he'd come for them. How long it would take for him to catch up. And what would happen when he did.

48

HELENA

Helena was striding ahead of the others. Bright spots were beginning to swim at the corners of her vision. She knew she was pushing herself too hard, but she didn't want to slow and allow the others to catch up with her. She needed space.

Her hiking boots pounded over stone and rock. The mud streaking her legs and caking her socks had dried and cracked, flakes of it falling into her boots. Thankfully her blisters were less painful, having managed to tape them last night.

She pushed on, aware that her heart was racing. Then a strange, boneless sensation followed in her legs.

Odd, she thought.

Without warning, a whoosh of heat moved through her body and her vision began to tunnel, while the ground seemed to lurch away from her.

Then black.

'Helena!' she heard Maggie calling distantly.

She blinked, opening her eyes slowly. She was lying down, cheek on the cold ground. Maggie was crouched beside her, a hand on her shoulder, eyes wide with worry.

'What happened?'

'You fainted,' Maggie said.

Had she? Helena pushed herself upright with the heels of her hands, head spinning.

The others were standing around her looking concerned. She pressed her lips together. Felt the grit of earth stuck to her lipstick. Wiped her mouth with the back of her hand.

Maggie was stroking her back. 'You need food. Your blood sugar can go nuts in pregnancy—'

Helena blinked.

She saw Joni and Liz's heads swivel to look at Maggie.

Maggie clamped a hand to her mouth. 'Sorry! I—'

'God's sake!' Helena said, pushing herself to her feet, the ground swaying a little.

'Go steady,' Maggie said. 'You need to rest.'

'If there's a service station coming up, do let me know,' Helena said, spikily. She dusted herself off while Liz and Joni just stared at her. 'What?' she said into their silence.

'You're pregnant . . .' Liz marvelled, eyes bright.

'Yes, I'm pregnant. No, I don't know who the father is. Yes, I'm still in shock. No, I haven't decided what I'm going to do. I think that answers all the main questions.' She moved to step past them, saying, 'As you were.'

'But – wait! Are you okay?' Liz asked, voice filled with concern. She was standing on the narrow trail, blocking Helena's path. 'This is a lot. How do you feel?'

'Like I've been walking for three days and am halfway up a mountain with no food or water.'

'I can't believe you didn't tell us before setting off!' Liz said. 'I would never have let you do this. Are you okay? Really?'

Helena wanted to say she was fine, but she could feel her throat thickening with emotion. 'Look, let's not. We've got bigger things to worry about right now.'

Maggie gave her a hard stare. '*You* are what matters right

now.' She asked, 'Have you thought more about what you want?'

Out here, Helena was so far away from normal life that she felt free of herself. She didn't know if that even made sense, she just knew that the image of who she was, and how her life should be, had blurred a little at the edges. Everything felt more possible. And into that space of possibility, there was space to feel what she wanted.

Maggie was watching her, waiting.

When she was a kid, she'd visited an older cousin, whose newborn was plonked in Helena's arms. The baby took one look at her and bawled. Helena remembered thinking that the baby must have sensed something off about her. Knew he wasn't safe with her. Other girls were always so eager to hold babies, but she hung back, said she wasn't a 'baby person', whatever that meant. She started to say she didn't want kids. It became a story she told herself so often that she believed it.

But now she wondered if she'd written that story because she was afraid that she wouldn't be any good at motherhood.

'I'm going to consider all options,' she said, aware she sounded like she was in a business meeting.

A tiny smile appeared on Liz's face.

'If you do have the baby, you know we'll be there for you, don't you?' Maggie said. 'You wouldn't have to do it alone.'

Joni was standing at the edge of the group. Quietly, she said, 'You would be an amazing mother.'

Helena blinked. Joni hadn't spoken a word to her since their argument, hanging back, eyes down, hands balled into fists. And now here she was, looking right at Helena, saying something so startling that it made Helena's breath catch in her throat.

Those words – *You. Amazing. Mother* – they cracked something open. They were the very words she needed to hear. 'You really think so?'

Joni continued to look at her – right at her – as if she could see exactly who Helena was. 'I know so.'

49

LIZ

The wind strengthened the higher they climbed. It moulded jackets to bodies, stole words from mouths, whipped hair across faces.

With each step, Liz could feel the weight of the cocaine bouncing against her hip. Every few minutes, one of them would pause, turning to look over a shoulder, peering further down the trail to see if they were being followed. There was no sign of anyone out here – yet she couldn't shake the feeling of being watched.

Maggie had put her jacket back on, tugging the sleeves over her hands to keep them warm. 'How much light do we have left?'

Helena, at the front of the group, checked her watch. 'An hour and a half until sunset.'

It wasn't long enough, Liz knew, looking up at the mountain trail, which stretched ever upwards. 'Joni, can I see the map?'

Joni, who was walking with her hood tightened beneath her chin, took out her phone, and passed it to Liz.

Liz ignored the low battery notification and concentrated squarely on locating themselves. She blinked, squinting at the map, and tried to focus. 'It looks like another kilometre to the

236

peak.' It was nothing in terms of distance – if you were on flat ground – but climbing up steep, strenuous sections was another thing entirely.

'After that,' Liz said, 'we need to cross the ridge top. The DNT cabin should be on the other side.' She could see it marked on the map as a red hut symbol.

'And if we don't find the cabin?' Maggie asked.

We'll be spending the night on the mountain top, without tents, sleeping bags, or a stove, Liz thought. Joni was already hunched within her jacket, legs bare and goose flecked, and she didn't like her chances of making it through the night without hypothermia setting in.

'We will find it,' Liz said decisively.

'This must be the mountain pass!' Helena called from up front, her cheeks red, blowing hard.

Joni stood with hands on hips, catching her breath. They'd pushed themselves to their limits to reach the pass by dusk, but now they fell quiet, silenced by the sight of what lay ahead.

'It's so narrow,' Maggie said, face white.

The peak they were standing on connected to Blafjell's highest peak, over five hundred metres away. The trail ran along the brow of a steep-sided ridge. From here, it appeared so narrow in places that Liz guessed one misstep could send any of them to their deaths.

A strange sensation travelled across Liz's shoulder blades. Not as clean as fear – something more shadowy. She stared at the black, rocky spine cutting across the dimming sky. Her insides tightened.

Wind gusted up the mountain side, flattening her jacket to her body, buffeting them all closer.

'There's no protection from the wind on the ridge, so stay low if you need to,' she said. 'And we all stick together.'

Liz tightened the hood of her jacket to protect against the battering wind. It was difficult to tell where the strongest gusts were coming from, the mountains creating their own weather system as cold air rolled in from the ocean, was drawn upwards, then circled and ran away.

Fear fizzed and spiked in Liz's veins as she began to lead Maggie, Joni and Helena across. Her legs trembled, muscles spent and overworked as she teetered forward, keeping low to the ground.

Daylight had faded into a darkening dusk, leaching the texture from the earth, making it hard to tell the depth of each footstep.

Forward was the only direction. A zipper on her coat swung and flapped in the wind. There was nowhere flat to set her gaze, just sheer drops on either side of the ridge. She dragged in a breath, the air cold.

Without warning, the ground seemed to shift from under her, as if it were moving. A dizzying rush filled her head as she crouched to the earth, hands digging at the stony path. She broke out in a sweat. Her breath turned rapid and shallow as she lay flattened to the ground, cheek pressing into the dirt.

'What is it?' Maggie cried.

She'd never experienced it before – but knew instinctively what this was. 'Vertigo . . .'

A terrifying, plunging sensation had overtaken her body, as if she were tipping, the axis of the world spinning around her. Even though she could feel the earth hard beneath her, it was as if the ground were turning, sliding out from under her, intent on shaking her over the edge.

Vertigo wasn't a fear of heights. It was a scrambling of messages to the brain when the ground wasn't level so it couldn't process all the sensory information. Liz lay flattened to the cold ridge, frozen, not trusting herself – or the ground – not to spin away. She felt nauseous, a hot liquid sensation rising into her throat.

Maggie pressed her hands over Liz's. 'You're safe. Just breathe.'

Liz sucked air in and out of her chest. Behind her she could hear Joni and Helena asking if she was okay – but she couldn't risk looking around, terrified to see the drop off the ridge.

She tried to set her gaze on Maggie, but around her the landscape swirled and shifted. She screwed her eyes closed. Felt saliva fill her mouth.

'Open your eyes!' Maggie instructed.

Liz did as she was told.

'Just focus on me and it'll pass, okay?'

Liz nodded, keeping her gaze glued to Maggie's. She took in the auburn tips of her eyelashes, the spray of freckles across the bridge of her nose, her cracked lips as Maggie pasted on a smile. 'It'll pass and, when it does, we're going to keep on going.'

'I can't.'

'If you can't walk, we'll do this on our hands and knees, okay? We're almost halfway. The cabin will be waiting on the other side. We'll get warm. Rest. We can do this.'

Liz heaved in another breath.

'I promise I won't let anything happen to you.'

The world had eased its lurching. She could focus on Maggie's face a little better. She managed a nod.

'We crawl, okay?'

Liz pushed herself up to her hands and knees, stones digging into the taut fabric of her hiking trousers. She made herself move forward, inch by inch, following Maggie.

Gradually, the dizzying sensation faded, along with the light, until the four of them were crawling in the dark, knees raw, palms grazed, just the sound of wind and breath and earth.

THE SEARCH

Leif pauses for a drink. Cold liquid running down his throat. He can feel his heart beating hard in his chest, blood pumping. He likes the feeling of being fully in his body, alive.

He's almost at the top of Blafjell now. The landscape is grey and barren. Rock, earth, lichen-stained rock. The wind is brutal up here, buffeting him from switching directions.

He's never felt comfortable on Blafjell. There are other peaks that he loves – where he's slept in his bivvy beneath the stars and felt like he was soaring – but up here, there's a desolate feeling. The mountain lures the clouds, which huddle so close they shoulder out any view.

A gust of wind sheets across the mountain like a shove. The hairs stand up on the backs of Leif's arms – not from the cold.

He remembers his father talking about Blafjell. *Thin places. Elementals*. Words spoken in a lowered voice.

When Leif was just a boy, his father knew a teacher who used to bring his sixth-form class up into the mountains each summer.

One year, there was a seventeen-year-old boy in the group who was known to be able to sense things. His teacher wasn't a man who gave much heed to *sensing things* – but afterwards, he wished he had.

This boy – he climbed halfway up Blafjell and then stopped dead. Apparently, he just stood there, middle of the trail, staring up at the peak, refusing to go further. Said there was something wrong about the place. Told the teacher they should all turn back.

The teacher wasn't having it. Tried to make him hike on. Threatened all manner of trouble if he didn't – but the boy refused. Bar dragging him, the teacher was out of options. He couldn't leave the boy to walk back alone, so a second teacher descended with him. The boy pleaded with her, begged her to stop the others from continuing – but the remaining group went on.

Knut took the emergency call. A freak snowstorm had blown in. Four feet of snow in as many hours. It was July. Not a hint of it on the forecast.

The teacher and his students were stranded on the summit of Blafjell, the trail markers swallowed, a total whiteout.

Rescue teams dug them out the following morning – Leif's father among them. The teacher and his students had survived. They'd done all the right things – built a snow shelter, huddled tight, talked and sung to stay awake – but they were terrorised. Kept saying that when the first snowflakes fell, they had been not white, but black.

Leif's father wasn't a man easily spooked, but Leif had seen it in his face that summer. There was a new wariness. Fear had got to him.

He glances at the goosebumps trailing his arms. Clenches his fists. Pushes on.

50

MAGGIE

They made it across the mountain pass, knees scraped and bloody, breath coming in short draws.

Maggie glanced back to check on Liz, who was sitting down, head tipped up to the night, the beam of her torch disappearing into blackness. 'You okay?' Maggie called.

'Yes . . . I think so . . . You got me across. I couldn't have done it without you . . .'

Maggie felt a swell of pride rising through the exhaustion. She would never have believed herself capable of crossing that mountain pass – but she had done it. And she'd led the others, too.

'Where's the cabin?' Joni asked, who was standing with her arms wrapped around herself, moving from foot to foot to keep warm.

Liz pushed to her feet, saying, 'I thought it would be right here.' She scanned the beam of her torch across the empty trail ahead.

Maggie heard an eerie groaning behind her – a faint wailing that was there, then gone. The wind felt alive up here – twisting at her hair, seeping through her clothes, scaling down her neck. 'What was that?'

The others inched closer. 'I don't know,' Helena said, her voice edged with fear.

The noise came again, like a low growl.

Maggie swung her torch around – but the beam met nothing but blackness.

'Let's check for signal again,' Helena said.

Joni took out her phone, hands trembling and bloodless.

As the screen flared to life, Maggie could see the battery was down to ten per cent and there were no bars of signal. Joni dialled anyway, holding the phone tight to her ear to block out the wind.

The rest of them waited, listening to the howl of wind against rock.

Maggie's toes were numb in her hiking boots, and she curled and released them to try to keep the blood moving.

'No connection,' Joni said flatly. She turned off the phone and that tiny flame of hope was snuffed.

Liz, rubbing her hands together, said, 'We need to keep moving. The cabin's got to be close.'

They trudged on, Maggie scanning the trail with her torch. With no ceiling or walls to protect them, the dark wind felt ravenous, reaching for them. She had the ominous sensation that something was lurking nearby. She kept the torch trained to the ground in front of her feet, and then would occasionally lift it, streaking the beam through the night, as if she'd catch something stalking them.

At the rear, Helena used her torch to scan over the mountain peak, hunting for a sign of the cabin. There were no stars or moon to help navigate, thick layers of cloud closing out the light.

Maggie pushed a cold hand into her coat pocket and felt the cool slip of Karin's bracelet. She remembered Vilhelm telling them that Blafjell was where Karin had last been seen. He'd described it as a thin place. *Something beyond the limit of our understanding. That feeling of unease, of not being alone, that isn't immediately explicable.*

Again, a faint moaning noise lifted from the mountain, the wind turning ever colder. Goosebumps rose across her arms and spread down the back of her neck. It was as if she could feel someone watching them.

She was so focused on the sensation that she must have failed to look where she was putting her feet. Rock moved beneath her, a sudden destabilising lurch as solid ground began to shift. She felt a strange, cold grip around her ankle, as if an icy hand had yanked her off balance. The thick soles of her hiking boots made it hard to feel the ground, to grip for purchase, and her ankle turned.

She felt it – the stretch and ping of something in her ankle. She screamed at the piercing, sheer pain.

The torch flew from her grip as she put out her hands. Then she was down on the ground, landing hard. She lay there, the wind knocked out of her.

Liz was at her side. 'Maggie?'

'My ankle!' she gasped. 'I went over on it.' The pain crashed over her in intense waves.

'What happened?' Helena asked, crouching beside her.

'Must have tripped . . .' Maggie turned to shine her head torch back and look for the offending rock or stone, but when she looked – there was nothing there. She recalled the feeling of something tugging hard at her ankle. She swallowed back her fear. Said, 'We need to get to the cabin . . .' Sucked in another breath. 'Help me up.'

Joni took one arm, Helena the other, and they hauled Maggie to her feet.

Liz took the torch beam and directed it at Maggie's ankle. 'Can you put any weight on it?'

She tested, but a shock of pain ripped through her ankle. Even the weight of her hiking boot felt awful. 'None!'

'Just lean on us,' Joni said, through chattering teeth. 'We must be close.'

Arms hooked around Joni and Liz, she lurched on, teeth gritted against the pain.

A gust of wind wheeled over the mountain, shouldering into them. They clung close, muscles clenched.

Liz raised the torch beam, which travelled further down the rocky path, revealing only blackness.

They were all silent, watching as she swept the light again down the length of the trail, travelling over huge rocky boulders.

'Wait! Stop!' Joni cried. 'There! Go back!'

Slowly, Liz drew the beam back towards them.

'Oh!' Maggie heard herself cry. There, only fifty metres away now, was a small wooden cabin, clinging to the edge of the mountain.

51

JONI

'Thank God!' Joni said, as the torch beam illuminated a small timber building perched on an exposed outcrop of rock. Two square windows reflected the harsh beam of their torchlight.

Joni moved her torch beam over a slim wooden door, which had a red sign beside it, reading: DNT BLAFJELL. 'We made it!'

'What if it's locked?' Helena said from behind the others.

Liz said, 'It shouldn't be. The cabins are left open so they can be accessed by anyone on the mountain.'

Pressing her palm flat to the cold wood, Joni made a silent prayer that Liz was correct.

She pushed.

The door creaked open, and she took a tentative step inside, breathing in a dank, woody smell. 'Hello?' she called, instinctively.

No answer.

She shone the torch around the wood-clad space, illuminating four bunks, a small table and chairs, and a log burner. A nook branched off from the main room, where a sideboard was set up with a two-ringed camping hob, metal sink, and cupboards.

'It's open! Come in!' she called to the others, holding the

door wide so that Liz could support Maggie as she hobbled inside.

The door clanked shut behind them and the wind died. There was quiet, apart from the creaking of floorboards beneath their boots, the rustle of their jackets. The air was icy cold, but at least they were out of the wind.

'We made it!' Helena said, relief thickening her tone.

It was so strange to be inside after days of walking through the ferocity of the elements. She pressed her filthy palms gratefully to the wooden walls, marvelling that they had a ceiling above them, a firm floor beneath their feet.

Liz pulled out a chair for Maggie, helping her to sit. Then she dragged a second chair closer to settle Maggie's raised foot on it. While Liz was assessing her ankle, Joni searched through the cupboards by torchlight.

'Candles!' she said, finding half a dozen used candles wedged into holders, beside a box of matches. With numbed fingers, she lit each of the blackened wicks with a single match, the flame burning down to her fingertips.

She set out the candles – two on the table beside Maggie, another on the windowsill, more by the wood stove and hob – and their warming glow was an instant comfort.

'There's food! And water!' Helena cried, lifting her torch to one of the cupboards. She pulled out bottles of water, packs of noodles, tins of beans, and canned meat.

'There's more here,' Joni said, opening the next cupboard and finding sachets of coffee and hot chocolate and powdered milk. A note explained that the cupboard was kept stocked with dry goods and you paid via an honesty box.

'Can you fetch Maggie some water?' Liz called, who'd located a first-aid kit and was cleaning the cut on Maggie's knee where she'd gone over.

Joni delivered it to Maggie, asking, 'How's the ankle feeling?'

'It'll be fine. We made it to the cabin. That's the main thing,' Maggie answered, smiling bravely.

'You were my hero on the ridge top,' Liz said. 'I wouldn't have made it across without you.'

Joni squeezed Maggie's hand once. 'I'm going to get the woodstove lit.'

She found a basket filled with dry logs and kindling, and beside it there was a box full of Norwegian newspapers. She knelt, bare knees on the cold wooden floor, scrunching the paper into balls with icy fingers. She laid the kindling on top, remembering all the times as a child that she'd laid the fire for her grandmother before school.

She struck a match and held it to the paper, watching as it began to light and flame, licking at the dry wood.

In the kitchen area, Helena had found a camping stove and had now set a pan of water to boil ready for noodles.

With the candles lit and the fire beginning to kick out a little heat, Joni felt her shoulders soften. They were safe.

The smell of warming noodles filled the cabin. They'd pulled their chairs close to the woodstove, and all that could be heard was the clink of forks against enamel bowls, steam rising in the candlelight.

Joni burned her tongue, too hungry and impatient to wait for the noodles to cool.

'This is the most delicious thing I've ever tasted,' Maggie said, the bowl lifted close to her mouth.

'Have you warmed up now?' Helena asked Joni.

She nodded. 'I don't know if I'd have made it through the night if we hadn't found the cabin.' It must have been close to zero out on the mountain now, with the wind chill.

'Thank God we did,' Maggie said, her expression serious. Everyone knew the stakes if they hadn't managed to locate the cabin.

No one wanted to think about what tomorrow would bring – how they would get Maggie down the mountain. They ate the rest of their meal quietly, exhaustion washing over them.

When Joni was finished, she gathered the empty bowls and stacked them by the hob. Warmed up finally, she unzipped her jacket and hung it over the back of her chair. As she did so, she noticed Liz's hanging there – the bulge of the cocaine visible in her pocket.

An instant kick of longing filled her.

She dragged her gaze away, wishing she'd chucked the stuff while she'd had chance. Knowing it was right there, in the cabin with her, was messing with her head. It would be so easy to do a quick line.

A dark, sticky feeling of loathing squirmed through her insides. She disgusted herself. They'd found the cabin; they were safe – but still it wasn't enough.

She stretched across the table, reaching for the notebook that had been left there. DNT LOGGBOK was printed on the front and a biro was attached to the spine by string. She opened it, flicking through pages of handwritten names, dates, notations. She drew the candle closer, then searched for today's date and saw it was empty. She travelled back a few lines and realised no one had stopped at this cabin in ten days.

Pulling the logbook closer, she clicked the biro and committed their names beneath today's date. Her writing was small, shaky. Seeing the four of them on the page felt meaningful in a way she couldn't put her finger on.

Joni looked up towards the window: the night was black and starless, ravaged by wind.

She could see her own reflection in the glass, hair in a ragged topknot, loose strands falling over her twisted headscarf. The reflection of the candle burned at the edge of her face, and she focused on it, letting the flame distort her image, burning away the mask of who the world saw, melting her, feature by feature, until only something twisted and horror-struck was left.

She blinked. Pulled her gaze away, disturbed by the dark places her thoughts travelled.

She drummed her fingers on the table. Thought once more about the coke. Just a hit, that's all she needed.

She forced the thought away, instead returning her attention to the logbook. She flicked through it, reading lists of names and nationalities. In the winter months the cabin was mostly empty, but throughout summer, there were entries most weeks.

Joni found herself pausing on today's date one year earlier, reading down and seeing only two names. 'On this day a year ago,' she said quietly, 'Erik was staying in the cabin.'

Opposite her, Maggie's brow dipped. 'Who was he with?'

Joni read the scrawled handwriting beneath his name. 'Karin.'

52

HELENA

Helena peered at Erik and Karin's names in the logbook. It was unsettling to think they had been here exactly a year before, like an ominous echo lingering in the cabin.

A gust of wind breathed into the chimney flue, making the fire roar. Maggie shuddered. 'Is it just me, or does it feel like the mountain is trying to get in?'

The night seemed to press up against the windows, the breeze working its way through gaps in the panes. She could feel other draughts rising through the floorboards. Outside, the cabin had been bolted to the rock with two wire struts, and the wind hummed around them, making a cold, keening noise.

'I keep thinking about that person we saw on the beach – going into the cave,' Helena said, fingering the horseshoe necklace she wore at her throat.

'Me, too,' Liz said, shuffling closer to the fire. 'It was the way they crossed the beach. Went directly to the cave. They knew what was inside, didn't they?'

Joni stared into the flames, firelight dancing across her pupils. 'I shouldn't have taken the cocaine. I'm sorry . . .'

In the shadows of the cabin, Joni seemed smaller, sitting cross-legged on the floor, gaze on her lap. Watching her, Helena realised that Joni hadn't stolen the cocaine just for the laugh of getting high. Maybe once, way back when, but not here, on the mountain, with them. She'd taken it because she wanted to escape herself.

Helena could have reached out and asked what was troubling her. She could've stepped up as a friend, but she was too exhausted. Or maybe there was just too much history to stretch an olive branch that far.

Maggie said hopefully, 'It's possible that whoever was walking into that cave to collect the cocaine didn't notice any was missing.'

Helena raised an eyebrow at that. 'Think I'm going to crash,' she said, getting to her feet. Exhaustion was a wall and there was no pushing through it.

'Me, too,' Liz agreed.

As she crossed the cabin towards the bunks, she glanced beyond the window and thought she caught a flash of light. At first, Helena assumed it could only be the reflection of one of the candles, but when she looked again, the light was moving.

It wasn't a reflection. It was coming from outside.

'Did anyone see that?'

'What is it?' Liz asked, crossing the cabin towards the window.

Helena pressed her face closer to the pane, her breath leaving a circle of condensation. Then she realised what she was looking at. 'Torchlight.'

There was silence in the cabin, except for another gust of wind breathing at the door.

They all watched as the torchlight travelled across the mountain pass.

'Someone is out there,' Helena said, 'and they are heading this way.'

53

JONI

'Come away from the window!' Joni said. 'Whoever is out there will be able to see you.'

Helena snapped back, pressing herself against the cabin wall.

'Should we blow out the candles?' Maggie asked.

Liz shook her head. 'They'll still smell the smoke from the chimney. They know we're inside.'

A flash of torchlight passed the window, driving across the walls of the cabin.

Helena whispered, 'They're getting closer.'

Joni recalled the lone figure they'd seen earlier crossing the beach, heading for the cave. 'They're coming for the cocaine . . .' she whispered to herself, a slick of sweat building under her arms. She had set something in motion that she was unable to stop.

Liz snatched a breath, her expression pinched in the flickering light. 'We say nothing, okay? Stick together. There are four of us.'

Outside, they heard the tread of approaching footsteps. They were heavy, slow. The trudge of boots on stone.

Instinctively, the four of them gathered closer, bunching around Maggie who was still seated, injured ankle raised.

The footsteps drew nearer, following the perimeter of the cabin, making their way steadily towards the door.

Then they stopped.

Joni held her breath. She glanced at her friends. In the candle-light she could see the furrow of Liz's brow, and the clench of Helena's knuckles as she held her hands in fists at her sides.

'What are they doing out there?' Maggie whispered.

Whoever was out there must have been waiting on the other side of the door.

Joni picked up the iron poker lying beside the fire, feeling its reassuring weight in her hands. She held it at her side, realising too late that they should have locked the door.

The cabin door swung wide. A blast of cold wind gusted in from the mountain, blowing out the candles. The icy wind lifted the curtains, flicked through the leaves of the logbook, rattled an open cupboard – and then stopped as the stranger stepped inside, the door clanking shut behind them.

Joni raised her free hand in front of her face as a dazzling beam of torchlight blazed into the cabin. The stranger flicked off their head torch and, for a moment, there was only darkness and the roar of blood in Joni's ears.

Gradually, her eyesight adjusted to the low light from the wood-stove, and she could make out a dark figure blocking the exit.

The shape of the man's face emerged: a shadow of dark stubble, an angular nose balancing a lean face, an orange beanie pulled low.

She heard Maggie's swallow. 'Erik.'

In the glow of the woodstove, Joni watched as Erik stared at Maggie, unblinking. After several long seconds, he ran a hand over his face, as if wiping away a thought that wasn't welcome.

He cleared his throat. Took in the others. 'Hello,' he said, voice gruff.

Liz hurried to relight the candles, fumbling in the semi-darkness with the matches.

'Sorry I disturb you,' he said, gaze lowering, a strange formality to his statement.

'It's late to be out hiking,' Joni said, keeping the poker flush to her thigh, out of his eyeline.

'Yes,' he agreed and said no more.

There was silence in the cabin, gazes searching, feet shifting.

'Can I . . . come in?'

The friends looked at one another. What could they say? It wasn't their cabin. She remembered Liz explaining that the philosophy behind the DNT cabins was that they never turned anyone away.

Eventually Joni nodded.

Erik took off his backpack, which thumped to the ground. Hadn't Maggie said it had been half-full when she'd come across him in the woods? Now it looked bulging, buckles pulled tight.

He took off his jacket and unlaced his boots, setting them together neatly by the door. He crossed the cabin towards the kitchen area, socked feet leaving a trail of damp condensation marks on the wooden floorboards. She could smell something animal breathing from his skin.

There were dark shadows beneath his eyes, and he looked as if he hadn't slept properly in days. A restless energy burned off him as he shifted his weight from foot to foot, searching in the cupboards. He glanced sideways over his shoulder, looking at Maggie then quickly away.

He rummaged in one of the drawers and pulled from it a pan and wooden spoon. From the next, he took a can of something meaty, snapping back the ring pull and tipping its contents into the pan.

There was a strange tension brimming in the cabin. She felt

alert, on edge, trying to gauge Erik's sudden appearance. Had he come for the cocaine? Or was he simply out hiking? He'd posed no immediate threat to them, yet Joni's heart rate was rocketing, as if she were in danger. She turned the poker in her hand, uncertain.

'Where have you come from?' she asked.

'The mountain.'

Joni glanced at her friends, trying to read what the others were thinking. She wanted to get Erik talking, to try and unpiece what he was about, and why he was here. 'You and Leif are brothers, right?'

He lit the hob and set the pan on the flame. 'Yes.'

'He said you've been away for a while.'

He nodded. 'Moving around.'

'It must be nice to see each other again,' Joni said, a forced note to her tone.

He shrugged his shoulders. 'It is easier when I am away.'

Maggie caught her eye, looking as uncertain as Joni felt.

Erik pushed a hand beneath his orange beanie, resettling it over his dark hair. Joni could see the similarity between the brothers in their bone structure, but where Leif had a solid, calming presence, Erik seemed twitchy, making small, jerky movements, eyes lowered.

While he waited for his food to warm, he took out a hip flask and drank from it. 'Are you going to stoke the fire, then?' he said to Joni, his gaze flicking briefly to the poker in her grip.

She felt heat in her cheeks. 'Sure.' She knelt in front of the woodstove, making a show of adding another log and using the poker to adjust its position.

Beside her, Helena, arms folded, said, 'I hear you came across Maggie when she was lost in the woods.'

Erik's dark gaze shifted briefly to Maggie. 'Yes.'

'We were surprised to find her so far off the path,' Helena

said, a clear challenge in her tone. 'You were supposed to be leading her back to the coast.'

Erik's eyes narrowed the smallest amount. 'I was – but I took a detour to avoid a river crossing.'

Helena looked unconvinced. 'You disappeared in a hurry when the rest of us arrived.'

Maggie shot her a warning glance.

There was silence. Into it, Erik said, 'I came out here to be alone.'

Helena glanced around the cabin and said, 'And yet, here you are.'

Erik's mouth tightened. He said nothing further. He didn't mention Karin, just like he didn't mention the cocaine. It was the absence of words that felt unnerving.

Joni could hear the first bubbles of the wet meat warming in the pan.

There was a disconcerting sense of waiting for something to happen – but what, she didn't know.

54

MAGGIE

Maggie's injured ankle was throbbing hotly, the skin swollen and puffy to the touch.

The woodstove kicked out a thick, dry heat. The air had become heavy with the smell of unwashed bodies and damp socks. The cabin felt claustrophobic with its cramped space, candlelight creating shadows where she needed light.

All she wanted was to be at home with her daughter. She imagined the warmth of Phoebe in her arms, the soft weight of her, the smell of her neck, the perfect smoothness of her cheek.

Tears threatened at her lower lids. She looked up at the ceiling, blinking them back.

There was a clatter as Erik snatched the pan off the hob, and carried it to the small table, the wooden spindles of a chair complaining as he slumped down. He spooned forkfuls of meat into his mouth, an elbow on the table. He ate hurriedly, as if it had been a long time since he'd had a meal.

Joni, who'd moved to the table, picked up the logbook. 'You've been up at the DNT cabin before?'

He answered with a faint nod of his head.

'You stayed this time last year.'

Erik turned slowly, eyes falling on the logbook, and then lifting to Joni. 'That's right.'

'You were here with Karin, it says.'

He put down his fork. Glared at Joni. 'Karin was my girl-friend.'

Maggie noted the use of *was*.

As he raised his spoon again, Erik suddenly froze. His eyes widened, while the rest of his face fell completely still.

He was staring at something at the far end of the table.

Maggie turned to follow his gaze and realised with a lurch what he'd seen. She had left Karin's bracelet on the table.

Erik pushed his dinner aside and, slowly, reached out a hand and drew the bracelet across the table towards him.

He angled it towards the candlelight, and Maggie watched the way his brow furrowed. He blinked again, a hand running over the back of his skull, massaging the place where the tattoo of the black mountains was inked to his neck.

He stood up, his knee knocking the table – candlelight wavering. The colour in Erik's face had drained away. He swung around, eyes shining. 'Where has this come from?'

Maggie looked at the others.

No one spoke.

'Where!' he demanded with such aggression that they all jumped. 'I gave this to Karin! Right here! In the DNT cabin! I put it on her wrist. She went to sleep wearing the bracelet!' He squeezed a hand to his brow. 'The police searched the cabin. There was nothing of hers left behind. Nothing!' Erik glared at them. 'One of you put it here, didn't you?'

Maggie shook her head. 'No! I found it.'

He took a lurching step towards her. 'Where? Tell me where you found it!'

'It was last night. We camped at the beach. It was in the cave.'

Erik's eyes widened.

As soon as she'd said it, she realised her mistake.

A hot flush of panic swept through Maggie: she'd given away their whereabouts.

'The cave?' Erik repeated, blinking.

Slowly, she nodded.

'But . . . Karin never went to the cave. We were up here. In the DNT. We were going to hike out the next day, down Blafjell, back to the lodge . . . I don't understand . . . How could it be there?'

He'd begun to pace, his footsteps hurried.

He stopped by Maggie. His voice was quieter. 'Tell me how you found it?'

She felt herself leaning away from him, her chair creaking. 'It was caught on a ledge. Covered in cobwebs. I think it'd been there a while.'

'Was there anything else in the cave?'

She glanced down at her lap. Shook her head.

He eyed her narrowly. 'You are certain?'

Helena stepped forward, voice authoritative as she said, 'Yes. We were all there. We checked the cave. There was nothing else, just some lobster pots stored there.' There was something provocative in her tone, as if she were testing him.

Erik gave no reaction to the remark, simply lowered his head, looking again at the bracelet, transfixed.

'What happened to Karin?' Maggie asked. 'You called me by her name when we were in the woods.'

He looked anguished, his mouth peeling back over his teeth. 'She disappeared.'

He slumped down in a chair, running the bracelet across his palm. 'We came out here for Karin's birthday. It is today. She should be twenty-six,' he said, head lowered, shoulders rounded.

'The bracelet was my birthday gift. We spent the night here and were supposed to hike out the next day. But . . . we argued.'

'About what?' Helena asked.

He bunched his lips towards his nose as if the memory was painful. 'About nothing that mattered.' He dragged the heel of his hand across his chest, then said, 'Karin told me she'd applied for a job in Bergen. She loved art – and there was a brilliant gallery there where a job came up. I should have told her to accept it. But I got scared. Said it was selfish, leaving.' He shook his head. 'I got angry. Walked out. Pounded the trails for a while. When I finally cooled off and came back here, Karin had packed up and gone.'

Into his silence, the wind funnelled into the flue of the wood-stove, making the flames dance.

'I thought she'd walked back to the lodge – but she never turned up. No one knows why not. She just . . . disappeared.'

'No one saw her again?'

'There was a sighting . . . it gave us hope for a time . . . but it was nothing.'

A log in the fire disintegrated, red embers resettling.

'I'm sorry,' Maggie said quietly.

'Me, too,' Erik said, closing his fingers around the delicate silver bracelet, sealing it within his fist.

55

LIZ

The atmosphere in the cabin remained taut following Erik's admission.

'I need to get some sleep,' Helena said through a yawn.

Liz could see she was exhausted from the slump of her posture. Her lipstick had long since rubbed off, and there were puffy circles beneath her eyes.

There were only four bunks in the small cabin, so Erik took out his roll mat and laid it by the fire. 'I'll sleep down here.' Before he settled, he pushed his feet back into his boots and went outside.

The moment the door closed behind him, Liz huddled close to the others. 'What do you think? Are we safe to all go to sleep with Erik here?'

Helena shook her head. 'You saw the reaction in the lodge when Erik walked in. His own brother looked wary.'

Liz nodded, remembering how he'd argued with Karin's parents down by the lake. 'Then we sleep in shifts. I'll stay awake to begin.'

Maggie looked towards the door, her brow creased. 'Do you think he's connected to the cocaine?'

Liz lifted her shoulders. 'Wouldn't he have questioned us? Wanted to know more about the caves?'

'There's one way to find out,' Joni said, pointing to his backpack. 'If he was going to the caves to collect it, then it'd be stuffed in there.'

'You think we should look?' Maggie said.

Joni nodded. 'I'll do it. Keep an ear out for when he's coming—'

Before Joni could finish her sentence, the door was pushed open – candles dancing – and Erik returned, zipping up his fly. Then he set to unrolling his sleeping bag and settling himself on the floor.

With nothing to be done, the women found a bunk each and Maggie handed out blankets that she'd found in a cupboard.

Liz checked the fire and candles, then climbed onto the top bunk. Her teeth were furred and icky and she would have loved to brush them clean, or change into fresh clothes, but all she could do was lie on the lumpy mattress and listen to the wind outside battering against the cabin.

From their breathing, Joni was the first to fall asleep, then after a time Maggie, and finally Helena. As all fell quiet, she could hear logs shifting in the woodstove, crumbling to ash.

Lying there, Liz felt a sharp pang of loneliness. She missed Patrick with an ache that hollowed her. She thought of him right now, at home in their king-sized bed, in a T-shirt and pants, just like every other night – and wondered if he'd reached over to her side of the bed, forgetting she wasn't there. Or whether he'd spread out, enjoying the extra space.

What if Patrick *liked* the trial separation? Wanted it to be permanent?

Liz had to hope there was a path back to how they used to be together. She wasn't a fool: she knew no couples could maintain that stomach-dropping, butterfly sensation of being in love year after year. But moments of it? Yes, they could still reach for that.

Maybe that's what this trip was about, Liz thought as she lay still watching shadows dancing over the cabin walls: Liz had come out here looking for the girl she used to be. The one Patrick had fallen in love with.

Liz rolled onto her back. Her eyes stung hotly from the woodsmoke. The heat in the cabin was too much. She was so tired her eyelids could barely stay open.

She caught the shifting sound of a sleeping bag on the floor and knew without looking that Erik was still awake.

She checked her watch. Another forty minutes until she could wake Joni for her shift.

She listened closely to her friends' snores, a low wave of inhales and exhales, soporific in their rhythm.

Liz tried to keep herself awake – she really did – but the fading candlelight, the soft sound of slowed breathing, and the heat of the fire gradually lulled her eyelids closed.

DAY 4

56

JONI

Joni woke. She could hear the light snores of the others in the dim. A deep gloom had settled over her, like a heavy weight pressing against her chest. A feeling of dread suffused her.

Her first clear thought was: *I need the cocaine.*

She hated herself for it. Hated the magnetic pull, her blood hot and desperate, craving the hit. When she was on tour, it was easier to call this feeling by another name: partying, getting high, life on the road.

Out here, in the clarity of the mountains, it had only one: addiction.

She stole silently out of the lower bunk. Her calves were tight and knotted from yesterday's ascent as she tiptoed stiffly across the icy floorboards. She'd slept in her shorts and fleece but now, with the woodstove out, the cabin was frigid. Her bare legs pricked with goosebumps, and she could see her breath in small, shallow clouds.

She crept through the dim towards the chair where Liz had draped her jacket. Carefully, she picked her way around Erik, who lay on his roll mat, sleeping bag pulled to his chin. Reaching the jacket, she slipped her hand into the pocket. Empty.

Her heart kicked between her ribs. She needed the cocaine!

Behind her, Erik stirred. She froze, hearing him rolling onto his side, pulling the sleeping bag tighter.

Joni waited, barely breathing. After a few moments, once she was certain he'd settled, she slid her hand into the second pocket of Liz's coat.

There! The familiar shape of the bag, the weight of it in her fingertips. The relief was golden.

She grabbed her own jacket, pushed the cocaine into its deepest pocket, and made for the door, grabbing her hiking boots as she went.

She stole out into the early dawn, taking a full breath as her feet met the damp ground and the cabin door closed quietly behind her.

Joni walked a little way, bare toes clinging to the rocky path. The morning was cool, mist thickening the air with tiny particles of moisture.

She moved quickly, wanting to put space between her and the cabin, so she could do this in private. The path was stone and earth, descending gradually along the edge of the mountain.

She glanced over her shoulder but could still see the cabin. She needed to be out of sight.

Joni must have been walking for about fifteen minutes when she noticed a smooth outcrop of rock overhanging the mountain edge. It looked like a platform suspended above the clouded mountain valley.

Drawn towards it, Joni left the trail and moved closer. The platform was only a couple of metres wide and hung – seemingly impossibly – above air.

One day, this rocky pinnacle would snap, tumble down the mountain face.

What day would it choose?

Three decades' time?

Tomorrow?

Now?

She stepped onto it.

She looked out over the wide-open landscape, taking in the undulating mountains, the coast in the far distance, revealed in glimmers by drifting bands of cloud and, below her, a deep river snaking far, far down.

Breeze against her face, cocaine heavy in her pocket, a slow dawning arrived. This was the spot, she realised. The front cover of the geography project she'd made with Liz. They'd known it was somewhere on the Svelle route, but here it was.

Joni didn't feel any sense of elation because this moment was supposed to be for the two of them – fulfilling their childhood promise together. Forged in innocence. Yet the reality was something darker: here she was, alone, a bag of stolen coke stuffed in her jacket. That's who Joni Gold had become. The sort of person who went through her friends' things. Who'd walk out on her band. Who didn't show up when it counted. Who lied. Cheated.

Yesterday, Helena's words had hit bone. Everything she'd said was true. Instead of going to the funeral, Joni had stayed on tour, gotten out of her mind. Hadn't even raised a glass to Helena's mother. Hadn't even known what day of the week it was.

That's who she was.

Someone who'd do that to a friend.

Someone who'd do worse.

She wondered what it would feel like to take one more step. Right off the edge. That moment of weightlessness. The plunge downward, the breath of cloud against her face.

She moved forward a touch – and waited to feel something.

Her heart rate didn't change. Low, steady. She waited to feel a burst of fear – of something stronger than the loathing. But there was nothing.

She eased her feet further forward.

There was no one to stop her except herself.

THE SEARCH

Leif lays the map over the rocky ground, using a knee and palm to pin it flat.

He squints at the wavering paper. Yes. Just up ahead is the spot the German hikers had described. There's a platform of rock that juts out from the mountainside, fairly near the DNT cabin.

He folds up the map as best he can, slotting it into his pack, and then continues.

A fierce wind pushes into his face, makes his breath harder to exhale. It cools the sweat on his back, and he feels himself leaning into it, a sensation as if it is bearing some of his weight.

On a clear day, you can see miles and miles into the distant peaks in the east, and right out over the ocean in the west. But this afternoon, the cloud is billowing fast, pouring over the mountains, like white smoke.

He walks hesitantly towards the pinnacle and, when he reaches it, his stomach tightens. He wants it to be a mistake, for those German women to have somehow got it wrong. They were a good distance away, down on the lower path. They'd thought they'd seen a woman, but maybe it was no more than a loose tarp. They wouldn't be the first ones to see something that wasn't there in the wilderness.

He takes a breath, then steps out onto the table of rock, hands instinctively rising for balance. He can feel the wind lifting over the mountain face, sharp against his skin.

Why would a hiker be out here alone? Why would no one have called it in? That's what troubles him.

He puts his feet to the very edge – and then he looks down.

57

LIZ

The moment Liz had seen Joni's bunk was empty, she'd known.

She hadn't needed to pat down the pockets of her jacket to realise that the cocaine would be missing. Stupid to leave it there! Liz had been short-sighted, or maybe she just hadn't been ready to admit how bad things were for Joni.

Now her boots pounded the hard, rocky earth as she searched the mountain top. It was cold out here and she pulled down the sleeves of her jacket.

Glancing left, the ridge top appeared empty as far as she could see, although a low mist hung in patches, obscuring sections. Joni must have been on the trail headed in the other direction, which descended from the peak towards forest.

'Joni?' she called into the still air.

She pushed on, her muscles stiff and unyielding. She felt unrested and dehydrated – she'd rather have been in the cabin, stoking the fire, opening a sachet of coffee while the kettle boiled, waking up gradually and forming a plan for the day.

Not this.

She rubbed her eyelids with a knuckle. They felt dry and irritated from the wood-smoke and . . . had she been crying in her sleep? There was a raw puffiness to them, and she'd woken with a heavy feeling, Patrick deeply on her mind. This wasn't the time to pick through the carcass of her marriage. She needed to find Joni. Help her. Think of a way to get them all safely off the mountain.

She strode on, knees complaining, feeling rock and earth turn beneath her boots.

She rounded a large boulder marked with a red T-marker, the sight faintly reassuring. If they could support Maggie, perhaps it was possible for them to follow the trail down before the next nightfall.

In the distance, Liz noticed a pinnacle jutting from the mountainside, a platform of rock suspended from its edge. And there – standing on top, was Joni. With a rush of pleasure, she realised that this was it – the pinnacle from their school project!

Then an icy coolness flooded her body as she absorbed the scene. Joni was standing at the edge, her head tilted downward as she assessed the drop beneath her feet. One moment's lapse in concentration – that was all it'd take.

Liz wanted to call out – tell her to step back – but she couldn't risk startling her.

Then, suddenly, Joni moved, taking something from her pocket and turning it through her fingers. Then she raised her hand and let the object slip from her grasp, dropping it over the side of the pinnacle into the emptiness.

58

JONI

Joni stepped away from the edge. As she turned, she saw Liz was coming towards her, cheeks pink, hair loose around her face, her expression tight with worry.

Liz stopped, not placing a foot on the rock. She reached out a hand. 'You're too close to the edge!'

Yes, Joni thought. She stared at Liz's proffered hand, aware of the empty drop at her back and Liz there in front of her. Her heart squeezed tight. Liz. Liz. Liz. Always coming after her.

She stepped away from the edge, taking Liz's hand, letting herself be drawn into the warmth of her embrace.

'Are you okay?' Liz asked, holding Joni by the tops of her arms, and looking right at her.

Liz's skin was so fresh, her eyes sparkling. Joni wondered what it'd be like to live in her world. To have two children who orbit you. To have a husband who grows the vegetables he serves you for dinner. To have a job where you make a difference in people's lives. To have a home to return to, filled with people you love. Liz's life had been built on level, fertile ground, and all good things would grow.

Into Joni's silence, Liz said, 'Please, talk to me.'

Oh Liz, she thought. She could picture her in the GP surgery, hands on the desk, listening so intently, a V of concentration squeezed between her brows as she searched for a solution.

Liz wanted to solve everyone's problems – but some people couldn't be fixed.

'I want you to know,' Joni said, 'that I love you. I know I can be a shit friend and that my life is chaotic, and I don't manage things well, but I do love you.'

Liz held her tight. 'I know you do.'

'I took the cocaine from your pocket,' Joni said quietly.

She nodded. 'It's okay—'

'But I didn't snort it. Look,' Joni said, turning and pointing. She'd thrown the coke off the edge in what was meant to be a symbolic gesture of her starting fresh, getting clean. Disappointingly, the bag had caught on a ledge about twenty metres down, but still, it was the gesture that was important.

Liz's face broke into a smile. 'Well done!'

She loved Liz for that – her honest, open praise. It would always feel an impossible feat for Joni to juggle two worlds – the band and music and touring and drugs, with Liz, Maggie and Helena's settled, full lives. But all Joni knew was that she wanted to try.

'I want to sort myself out. Get clean. Get clear-headed again. Have some time out. Start making good decisions, y'know?'

Liz nodded. 'You've just started.'

She smiled, the gloom lifting a fraction.

Liz turned towards the view. 'We're at our spot. The geography project.'

'I know!' Joni said, hooking an arm around Liz's waist.

'The hike might not have worked out as we'd hoped. But we are here. I'm proud of that.'

'Me, too.'

Together, they absorbed the soaring view. The mist had started drawing in closer, thick bands of it partially obscuring the river below. It seemed to rise, cold and dense, curling over the mountain face.

Joni realised that – in the time she'd been up here – the visibility had decreased rapidly. 'I don't like the look of that mist. It's thickening into fog. What's our plan for getting down the mountain? You think Maggie can hike out of here?'

'Unless we find a phone signal, she hasn't got a choice,' Liz said.

'Could Erik help? Do we trust him?'

Liz shrugged her shoulders uncertainly.

Joni slipped her phone from her pocket but, turning it on, the battery symbol flashed to red. One per cent remaining – and still not a bar of signal.

'Let's check the map quickly. See how far the lodge is,' Liz said.

She passed the phone to Liz, who went to open the map, but her thumb knocked the icon beside it: *Messages*.

Liz went to swipe back – but hesitated.

'Patrick?' she said.

Joni's attention snapped to the screen. 'What?'

'What was Patrick messaging you about . . .' she peered at the screen, eyeing the time stamp, '. . . three days ago?'

Her blood ran cool. 'Oh. He was . . . just saying he'd heard I'd joined the hike.'

Liz was watching her, a small crease between her brows deepening. 'But I've not spoken to him. He doesn't know that.'

Joni's mouth turned dry.

She could see Liz about to click on the message.

'Don't!'

'Don't?' Liz said, bemused. 'Don't look at a message my husband sent you?'

'It's . . . just . . .'

279

Liz was staring at her, head tipped to one side.

'Please, Liz. Don't.'

It was too late. Liz had already opened the message and begun to read.

Joni felt the blood drain from her face. She went completely still, frozen with dread. She watched Liz reading the messages on her phone – a dozen tiny missives that should've been deleted, but that she'd wanted to keep – to give her what? Proof it had happened?

Now she saw how stupid she'd been.

Patrick Wallace. Her first crush at school with his easy, slow smile that took over his face. A laugh that tipped his head back when it rumbled out. A way of listening, really listening, with his whole body.

She had seen the way Patrick looked at her – but Liz was besotted with him. Liz had spent so many hours talking about Patrick, that when Joni finally talked to him herself, she already knew that his favourite band was Green Day, that he liked to run and skate, that he was happiest outdoors.

The summer she and Liz turned eighteen, Liz's older brother threw a party – and Patrick was there. He'd been searching for Joni all evening and found her in the garden, smoking alone. They'd hung out and she remembered he had smelt so clean and fresh – of toothpaste and soap and good laundry detergent. She knew that you don't poach your best friend's crush. She knew it. But when he leaned towards her, his hand so light on the base of her spine, all her reservation melted beneath the heat of her desire.

Afterwards, Maggie had found Joni in tears.

When Joni explained, saying she didn't know what to do, Maggie had squeezed her hand and said, 'You're going travelling next month. There'll be hundreds of guys.'

Maggie was right. There were. Patrick was just a boy – and there were so many more out there. It shamed her that she'd needed someone else to tell her to do the right thing.

So she had left, gone travelling.

And when she'd returned, two years later, Liz and Patrick had been a couple.

She used to watch the two of them together and think: *This is right*. They fit. Patrick with his toothpaste smile, and Liz with her good sleep habits and focus and work.

But occasionally, when she and Patrick were alone, there was something there – an energy that she didn't want to name. She pretended to herself there wasn't. And for years it was fine. He and Liz married and had the twins, and she could see the pride and adoration in his face when he looked at their family. He loved Liz with every fibre of his being, and so Joni snuffed out that flame with other men, her music, the bright lights of fame.

Until, one day, she realised it was still burning.

Liz had finished reading the messages. She looked up.

Her expression wasn't steely or furious. She looked scared.

59

LIZ

Liz could hear nothing but the rush of blood in her ears. She had read each of the messages, eyes widening, as words like *Dublin . . . hotel room . . . Liz can never find out . . .* danced across the screen.

She blinked. Shook her head.

No.

Please . . . Oh god. No!

Patrick had known Joni for almost as long as he'd known Liz. He respected Joni, made her laugh, was protective of her, would stand up for her – but Liz had always told herself that he wasn't attracted to her.

Why had she chosen to believe that? Last summer a women's magazine had crowned Joni 'The Sexiest Woman on the Planet'. She and Patrick had laughed about the article in the kitchen while making quesadillas.

Now she lifted her gaze to Joni, whose face was white, lips dry.

'Dublin,' Liz whispered, understanding. 'When I went back to the hotel with a migraine, you two . . .' she couldn't finish the sentence.

She remembered being backstage, her migraine already sending lights dancing in front of her eyes, as she'd told Joni she couldn't come to the after-party. Joni had looked crestfallen, so Liz had said, 'Patrick will party with you!' She'd offered him up like a consolation prize.

Patrick had turned to Liz, 'Sure you don't want me to come back with you?'

'I'll get a taxi. Stay! Party! Please. You can tell me all about it tomorrow.'

It hadn't taken Patrick much persuasion. He'd always liked to party. She was happy for him to roll in late, then wake hungover and affectionate the morning after. So she had sent the two of them off, Joni glimmering in her gown and stage make-up, Patrick so solid and handsome at her side. And she – stupid, naïve Liz – had taken a taxi back to the hotel, with no idea that she was holding a lit match to her marriage.

60

JONI

A deep pressure was building in Joni's chest. Liz was standing in front of her, and behind there was nothing but cloud, air, and a sheer, plummeting drop.

Liz's voice was thin, ragged with emotion. 'Did you have sex with Patrick?'

Joni swallowed repetitively, eyes down. She noticed the goose-bumps on her bare legs; that one of her laces had come undone. Wind licked at her neck.

Dublin. That gig had been a beacon, knowing Liz and Patrick would be there. She'd been losing her head on that tour. She needed them. Backstage, after the gig, when Liz said she had a migraine, had to go, Joni thought she'd buckle with disappointment. Everything was spinning out of control – her life, her thoughts, the drugs; all of it. Liz was her anchor.

And then Liz had said, 'Patrick will party with you!' and Joni had gripped his arm like a lifeline.

She'd taken Patrick to the after-party, introducing him to the band, proud to say, 'This is one of my oldest friends, Patrick Wallace.' Her manager, Kai, who she was already sleeping with, tried to extract her to do a line of coke, but she wanted a clear head. She wanted to be with Patrick and enjoy his company. So she'd told Kai *no*.

'I didn't think you could say no,' Kai had whispered without breaking his smile. 'I'll put a line on your bedside table for later.'

That's when she knew she needed to leave the party. 'Let's go somewhere else,' she'd said to Patrick, taking him by the hand.

So they'd found themselves in a dark hotel bar, where no one would recognise her, on cold leather sofas, drinking Guinness. She'd left in her sequined gown, so he'd wrapped his big coat around her shoulders, and she had breathed in that clean soaped smell of his and Liz's home. It had smelt like safety and she'd curled into it, bare feet tucked beneath her.

'How are you, Joni?' he'd asked in the quiet of the bar, and the way he'd said it, looking her right in the eye, it was as if he saw exactly how she was.

She'd talked with honesty about the exhaustion of touring, how her songwriting was drying up, that she wasn't happy. He'd held her hands in his. As they'd talked, she'd become aware of the heat in their fingers, connected, palm to palm. Patrick had looked down at their linked hands. Swallowed. 'I'm not sure,' he said, very slowly, 'that I should be holding your hand.'

She felt an electric charge so strong that she couldn't stop herself from leaning into it – into him. They kissed.

It was an explosion. Like the best hit of any drug she'd taken, the feeling of it lighting up her whole body, electric and delicious and soft and vibrant and so utterly, utterly addictive that her body ached and quivered with its demand for more – because she never wanted the gloriousness of that feeling to end.

'I'm sorry . . .' Patrick said. He tucked his hands under his arms, as if he needed to physically clamp them down. 'I can't—'

'I know,' she said, because she did. Liz and Patrick were the two people on earth Joni loved the most, and she couldn't lose either of them.

And yet, somehow those thoughts were obliterated by the richness of desire and need and wanting . . . and without thought, there was only body, and their bodies were leaning in, kissing, and she knew he wanted her. And it was the best high of her life. And if there was one thing Joni Gold liked, it was to get fucking high.

They were already in a hotel. All they needed was a room. Who says no when the drink is poured and already on its way to your lips?

Now Joni expelled an audible breath.

Liz was staring at her, waiting for her question to be answered: *Did you have sex with Patrick?*

61

LIZ

'Yes,' Joni admitted at last. 'I did.'

Liz covered her face with her hands. Her chest felt like it was caving in.

Joni was talking, apologising, but Liz wasn't listening, because all she could picture was Joni fucking her husband.

Her brain lurched. *The trial separation: it was my idea. I wanted it. Suggested it.* She had thought it was on her terms. That it was a good idea. She had diagnosed a problem in their marriage, so she'd put on her GP hat and – after much talking, because good communication was part of their strength – she'd suggested a trial separation.

When he'd said it sounded like a good idea, she'd experienced a deep, profound ache in her heart, as if something were tearing.

She told herself that it would be fine. It could be a good thing, in fact, because once they were apart, he'd be forced to imagine his life without her – and then they could come back together stronger, prepared to fight.

But now everything looked different.

Joni Gold.

On their first night at the lodge, she'd come across Joni on the phone down by the lake. She'd been speaking in a low

287

voice, and when she'd seen Liz, her face had paled and she'd whispered to the caller, 'I need to go.'

She'd told Liz it was Kai.

But it had been Patrick.

Liz started to shake. She could feel a tingling in her fingertips. She suddenly felt deeply exposed, separated physically from her family. She'd left them – and a wolf had got in.

She imagined Joni sitting at her breakfast bar, the twins grinning at her, Patrick smiling by the stove, waiting for the coffee to brew.

'What do you want? My husband? My family?'

'No! I'd never do that to you!'

'Yet you'd sleep with Patrick! Send him messages when we're on a trial separation!'

Joni pressed her teeth into her lower lip.

'Of all the men, Joni. Of all the men!' Throughout their school years, Liz had watched in awe as the boys gravitated towards Joni. She radiated magnetism with her infectious, deep laugh, and the way she'd say something completely surprising that caught you off guard, or how she dressed without a care for what anyone thought. Liz was familiar with the feeling of being passed over, so when Patrick kissed her – chose her! – Liz realised that the other boys no longer mattered because she had Patrick.

Liz said, 'You can have anyone you want, Joni. Anyone! Why Patrick?'

Joni took a breath. 'I thought I was in love with him.'

'Love?' Liz hissed through her teeth. 'Don't you dare use that word! It's not some song, Joni! This is my life!'

Liz took a step closer to her. A visceral, muscular rage made her body quiver. She saw the whites of Joni's eyes, the way she widened them with the shock of realising how near the edge she was.

288

Liz thought of her husband, of her children, of how their family would be ripped apart. Red-hot fury heated her blood. Her hands shook as she raised them.

Her fingers gripped the fabric of Joni's coat. Her rage turned blinding-white and, in that moment, there were no thoughts, just a soaring, scorching fury, and she leaned in.

THE SEARCH

Leif stands with his hiking boots planted on the pinnacle edge. The wind snakes around his bare calves, pushes down the neckline of his T-shirt, cooling the sweat on his back.

This is the location.

Feet on the edge, he looks down.

So far down.

No!

The German hikers were right: there is a woman down there. Lying still. It's as if someone has attempted to put her in the recovery position – legs bent, on her side, an arm winged tight to her body.

Ever since he'd heard the report from the German hikers, there has been a dark whisper in his ear: *Don't let it be her.*

Even now, he tells himself, I can't be sure. He can't see her face, hidden by her hair. She must be twenty metres down, caught on a ledge that sticks out before the full descent into the river below.

He shouts, 'Hey! Hey! Are you okay?'

The question feels crass. Nothing about what he sees is okay.

He takes out the radio and calls it in. His hand is trembling. 'Found her,' he tells Knut. He gives him the GPS position. 'I'm on the pinnacle. I've called to her. No response. She's not moving.'

'You think we're dealing with a body removal?'

Leif swallows. Feels the cutting wind in his mouth as he answers. 'Maybe.' Eyes still on her, he asks, 'How far away are the team?'

'The guys on the truck are trying to get down the logging track, bring them in deeper.' It's taken Leif three hours at a run to get out here. Even if they shave off a few kilometres by using the logging track, it'll still be two hours. It's no good.

'And the helicopter?' he asks, hopefully.

'Could be as little as an hour – or as much as three. I'll keep you posted. Anyone with you?'

'No. I'm alone,' Leif answers. His gaze is still on the woman, assessing the descent. It would be possible to abseil to her. He's visually mapping areas he could set up. Thinks he spots a possibility.

'What are you going to do, Leif?' Knut asks.

'Abseil down. Take a look.'

He expects Knut to try to stop him. It goes against every rescue protocol. No heroics. Everything measured and checked and partnered.

After a moment, he hears Knut say, 'Good man.'

62

HELENA

Helena woke to an eerie calm in the cabin. She lay still with her eyes closed, listening. The wind had died in the night, and all was quiet. From the icy temperature, the fire must have burned out, but the smell of wood-smoke lingered.

She felt a faint stirring of nausea low in her throat – a wavering sensation, as if she were a little travel sick. Her eyes flicked open, remembering: the baby.

She blinked. Wait. *Baby*, not foetus.

Oddly, the word didn't spike her with panic. It just popped into her head. *Baby.*

She felt another nauseous swim of her stomach and thought: *Okay, so here you are, making yourself known.* Clearly things were happening in her body – hormones releasing, chemicals firing, extra blood circulating – regardless of what she wanted.

She wished she could call her mother. Say, *Mum! I'm pregnant!* She wanted to hear her mother's voice. Oh god, she so, so desperately wanted to hear her voice, because her mother would say exactly the right thing – and Helena needed to hear that right thing, because she didn't know what it was.

Her mother knew Helena better than anyone. Across a phone line, a hundred miles apart, she could sense Helena's mood

293

from the simple greeting, *It's me*. She knew her in ways that no one else would, like when she was run-down, two dry patches of skin framed the bridge of her nose, or how she was self-conscious of her knees, and always preferred to wear trousers. They were tiny things. Nothing things. But they were also everything.

Loneliness wasn't the absence of people, she realised. It was the absence of people who understood you.

Her mother had loved her harder and more fiercely and fully than any other human ever would. To lose her was like losing a part of Helena's self. The well of grief opened right there in her chest, waiting for her to fall into all that empty darkness. She could feel the teetering, tipping sensation, and braced, ready to be swallowed.

But then another wave of nausea roiled through her body, her mouth turning slick with saliva. The sensation was so strong and sudden that she snapped upright, concentrating only on breathing.

She remained like that for some time, waiting for the nausea to pass, yet distantly aware that she'd been pulled back into the present by the new life growing inside her.

Eventually she climbed from her bunk, the skin of her blistered heels pulling tight as she stood. She rubbed her eyes, taking in the dim cabin. The adjacent bunks where Joni and Liz had slept were empty. She blinked, pushing a hand over her face, suddenly uncertain.

Erik's pack was propped against the table, but his roll mat was empty on the cabin floor.

Where was everyone?

Then she heard a faint murmur and looked around. Maggie! She was still here, stirring in the lower bunk, face down in her pillow.

'Mags, where are the others?'

She lifted her head. Murmured that she didn't know.

Helena moved to the window, drawing back the thin curtain, disturbing a moth. Outside, she looked for the ridge. It wasn't there. Billowing cloud had swallowed it whole, obscuring the entire mountain range. Below the cabin, there was nothing but a sea of cloud, dense as smoke.

It was like waking in a different world. She felt cut off. Trapped.

She crossed the cabin and pushed open the door onto daylight. The wind had dropped in the night, but so had the temperature. Her skin turned to goose flesh, and she reached for her jacket.

She noticed Liz's and Joni's hiking boots were gone. Erik's, too. Helena didn't bother jamming her feet into her own, so stepped out barefoot, the stone path cold beneath her feet.

Her eyes adjusted slowly to the hazy daylight as she walked a few paces, scanning the landscape for signs of her friends.

Behind her, the cabin door opened, and she turned to see Maggie hobbling out. She'd grabbed a broom and used it as a crutch as she stepped carefully onto the path, moving to Helena's side.

Voice thick with sleep, Maggie asked, 'Do you think Erik is with them?'

'His pack is still inside,' Helena said, feeling a low, thudding sensation in her chest. She couldn't tell whether it was anxiety at simply waking on a mountain – or whether it was an instinct that something was wrong.

Maggie lowered her voice and leaned closer to Helena. 'We should check Erik's pack.'

'For the cocaine? You still think he's in on it?' Helena whispered.

Maggie shrugged. 'It'd be one way of ruling it out.'

Helena glanced towards the cabin. 'We'll need to be quick.'

They turned and picked their way back to the cabin, Helena supporting Maggie as she helped her across the threshold.

Inside, Helena glanced once over her shoulder, then moved toward Erik's pack. Crouching, she unclipped the buckles, pulled open the drawstring and peered into the dark belly of the bag.

'Oh! God!' she said.

Maggie looked up. 'What?'

Helena's heart was beating so hard, her concentration so fierce, that she didn't hear the cabin door quietly opening, Erik stepping inside.

63

LIZ

Liz ran from the pinnacle, feet pounding. Rock and boulder and earth and stone. Breath ragged, mouth slack.

Her thoughts were burning, too hot to touch. Her hair had come loose from its ponytail, swinging and tangling at her shoulders. Cold sweat cloaked her skin.

She was sweat and rage and the pulse of blood.

She didn't know where she was going – just kept running. Mist had thickened into fog, concealing the mountain. But it was there – brutal and impersonal.

'FUCK YOU!' she screamed into the fog, throat raw, lips cracking. She wanted rocks to teeter, the earth beneath her to rumble, splinter, fall away.

Everything she'd believed was solid and stable and true was a lie! She lurched on, feeling the heat of her own breath as she panted. She gouged her fingers into her hairline.

Love, Joni had said.

The word on her lips had been a blade.

Tears rolled down Liz's face. She heard herself sobbing, the sound so distant and strange, a wailing misery echoing through the mountain.

Everything that she'd held in – all those emotions and worries that she'd neatly filed, telling herself instead to focus on the positives. Be grateful. Remain polite. Never offend. Stay calm and supportive and strong and busy. Because that is who you are, Liz Wallace. You help others. You lead. You can be relied upon. Trusted.

She made a strange, barking sound, half laugh, half choked sob. That Liz was gone!

When she'd stepped forward on that pinnacle, hands reaching for Joni, the old Liz Wallace would have shown discipline. Stopped herself. Taken a step back. Allowed Joni to apologise, speak, explain.

But this Liz – she'd seen the widening of Joni's eyes, registered the first flicker of fear as Joni realised she was so close to the edge – had wanted it. Wanted Joni to be afraid.

You can't go into the wilderness without uncovering your wild self.

She had squeezed harder, feeling the bones of Joni's shoulders beneath her grip, pushing her thumbs into her collarbone. She'd stared into her face, at those deep brown eyes with their thick, dark lashes – and had seen nothing she recognised. Their noses almost touched as Liz hissed, 'Helena was right. We mean nothing to you. Because you are empty.'

Joni had blinked, eyes swimming with tears.

Liz had felt the wild race of her heartbeat and the heat of Joni's body beneath her hands.

Behind her, only the mountain had watched.

THE SEARCH

Working fast, Leif secures the belay, then threads the rope through the abseil device on his harness and pulls it tight.

Then he lowers himself carefully over the edge. He's not wearing climbing shoes and his hiking boots feel thick-toed and cumbersome. He uses one hand to control the rope flow, the other on the taut rope above. His feet brace against the rock, attempting to keep his descent steady.

There's a bulge in the rockface, and he has to swing out to get around it. He uses too much force, and when he swings back, his feet clatter into the wall, loosening rock. He sees it teetering.

Don't fall.

But it does.

It rumbles down the almost-sheer mountain face, dropping and hitting the ledge where she lies. For one awful moment, he thinks it's going to connect with her head – but the stone rides right past her, only inches away, and crashes further down the mountain, plummeting into the river far below.

He takes a breath. Forces his heart rate to settle. Then he begins to descend again, with more care as to where he places his feet.

When he finally reaches the ledge, he secures himself to the rock with a belay.

The ledge is only a few metres wide, with a sheer drop below. There is a moment – just a moment – when Leif thinks: *I could leave.*

He doesn't want to be here – because now it is down to him. He must go to her. He must know.

But of course, he already knows.

He knew when he saw the names in the logbook.

He knew when the German hikers described a man with his head in his hands, a tattoo of the mountain on his neck.

And he knows now as he moves towards the woman who lies still.

He crouches by her. Says, 'I'm here. I'm going to help you.' Words that come out flat and lifeless and fake because he is scared and he's trying to sound like he's in control. He can tell now, this close, from the shape of her body, from the colour of her hair, from the slenderness of her wrists.

He knows.

He brushes her hair aside.

He's always known.

He sees her face, perfectly still, eyes unmoving. The woman who was out on the mountain with his brother.

He says, 'I'm here now, Karin.'

64

HELENA

Erik was standing in the doorway of the cabin, arms loose at his sides, jaw clenched. His orange beanie was pushed back on his head, the ends of his dark hair curling from beneath it. 'What are you doing?'

Helena lurched away from his backpack, raising her hands.

Erik took a step further into the cabin. The door swung shut behind him, and he stayed there, blocking their exit.

Maggie was staring at her, silently asking: *What did you see?*

Helena wanted to pull her to one side – tell her what she'd discovered in Erik's pack – but there was no time.

'I asked, what are you doing?' Erik demanded.

'Sorry, I was just . . . looking . . .' Helena stalled to a halt.

Erik strode across the cabin in two steps, snatched up his backpack, and pulled it to him. He looked into the main pocket, then turned to Helena. 'You saw them?'

She shook her head. 'No! I didn't see anything!'

Only she had.

It wasn't cocaine that Helena had found in his backpack. It was a bundle of letters – dozens of them – all with one hand-written name on the front.

Karin.

Erik glared at her, eyes dark. He shook his head once, sadly, like he was disappointed that she was lying to him. Then he reached into his backpack and pulled out the stack of envelopes, tied together with an elastic band. She saw the swallow of his Adam's apple.

'I write to Karin,' he said, eventually.

Helena glanced at Maggie, whose brow was furrowed as she stared at the clutch of letters.

Erik moved his thumb slowly across Karin's name on the top envelope. 'It's hard . . .' he began, voice quiet, '. . . to let go when there are no answers.'

Helena said nothing.

'So I write.'

'Why did you bring them up here?' Maggie asked, her voice gentle.

'To burn them. Here. In the cabin. On the anniversary.' He looked at them both.

'But we were here,' Helena said, realising why he'd looked so affronted to discover them in the cabin last night. He would have imagined that the cabin would be empty at this time of year.

Maggie, weight resting on her good leg, asked gently, 'What do the letters say?'

Erik shrugged. 'The things I can't tell her.'

Helena thought she understood. In the early weeks after losing her mother, she would call her mother and leave an answerphone message, which she knew would never be played. But she needed that connection – somewhere to put her thoughts. 'I'm sorry,' Helena said eventually. 'For going through your things. It was wrong.'

He returned the letters to his backpack. 'What were you looking for?'

She glanced at Maggie, who lifted her shoulders as if to say, *What choice do we have?*

302

Helena said, 'Cocaine.'

Erik blinked. 'Cocaine? Why?'

Helena was watching him closely. 'Yesterday we stumbled across something we shouldn't have. Several kilos of cocaine.'

His eyes widened. 'What? Out here?'

She nodded. 'We were camping on the beach and, when the storm came, we sheltered in the cave. That's where we saw it. Hidden in lobster pots.'

'Wait,' he said, brow furrowing. 'The same cave where you found Karin's bracelet?'

Maggie nodded.

Erik ran a hand across the back of his skull, adjusting his orange beanie. 'Why did you think the cocaine belonged to me?'

Warily, Maggie answered, 'We thought, maybe, that you were on the trail to collect the cocaine. It's just, when I saw you in the woods, your pack looked half empty. And then, last night . . . you turned up with a full pack.'

'When I saw you, I'd already set up camp for the night. Left my bivouac and sleeping bag set up before trying to help you back to your friends.'

'Oh, I see,' Maggie said, cheeks pinkening.

Erik's brow was creased as he asked, 'Who left the cocaine there? Did you see anyone?'

Helena answered, 'We saw a fishing boat leaving the bay – but we didn't get a look at anyone on board.'

'What did the boat look like?'

She thought back to that early evening when they'd arrived at the beach. 'It was red.'

'With a white wheelhouse,' Maggie added, pushing her hair behind her ears.

Erik's expression darkened. 'It's Bjørn's boat. Karin's father.'

Helena thought of the slim man she'd seen in the lodge, him

holding tight to his wife, his face a mask of sadness. 'You think *Bjørn's* smuggling drugs?'

'No. Bjørn ran that boat for twenty years. Supplied all the local fish and lobster in the village. But his back got bad. He needed help with the pots. He was hoping to take someone on, an apprentice. But a local man in the village – Austin – offered to buy the boat outright, take over.'

'Austin?' Maggie said. 'Isn't that the guy you . . . ?' she began, turning to Helena.

Helena nodded. She thought of Austin walking into the bar, the faint smell of something briny about him. Then later, legs wrapped around him, his rough, calloused hands on her breasts. The expensive watch on his wrist. The way he'd stared after her when she'd left.

'We met him at the lodge,' Helena said to Erik. 'White-blond hair shaved close?'

'That's him,' Erik confirmed. 'Karin thought there was some-thing suspect about him buying the boat. Her father never brought in much money, yet Austin paid over the odds for it. He barely seemed to take it out – yet was never short of money.'

Erik removed Karin's bracelet from his pocket. It looked so delicate in his large palm.

'We saw someone going into the cave yesterday,' Maggie said, 'but we were too far away to see clearly.'

'You think they saw you?'

She shook her head. 'No – but they'll have realised someone had been in there. Joni took a bag of the cocaine.'

'Shit,' Erik said.

'Because of the landslide,' Maggie said, explaining what had happened to their tents, 'our only route back to the lodge is over Blafjell. Whoever went into that cave will know that.'

'You think they're trailing you?'

'We don't know,' Helena said.

304

Erik looked again at Karin's bracelet. After a moment he said, 'Everyone assumed Karin hiked out the way I had. Down Blafjell, through the forest, back towards the lodge. But what if she didn't? What if she walked in the opposite direction – to the beach?'

He crossed the cabin, moving to the window.

'What if she saw Austin unloading the pots? Maybe she followed him into the cave.'

'You think Karin discovered the cocaine?' Helena asked.

After a moment, Erik nodded.

The cabin felt airless and warm. 'I have never believed that Karin just disappeared. She knew these mountains as well as anybody. She was experienced, smart.'

Erik dragged his gaze away from the window and turned to face them.

'You met the locals. It's clear they all think I killed Karin.'

Helena took in his defeated posture, eyes full of sorrow.

'They're right in a way: someone did kill Karin. But if it wasn't me, then who?'

THE SEARCH

Leif stares at Karin.

Her body lies broken on the mountainside. It rests on a bed of dark rock, a thin pillow of green lichen beneath her cracked skull.

Her irises hold the reflection of the sky, clouds travelling across unseeing pupils. Her face is undamaged – almost unnervingly so – her skin pale and clear. The breeze carries the scent of earth, salt, blood. It toys with a wisp of hair at her temple, then worries the collar of her top. Other than that, she is still.

He can hear the crash of his own heartbeat, his pulse loud and forceful in his throat. He thinks of Karin as a child, snow-shoes on, a pink glow to her cheeks as she'd called to him across the frozen lake.

Leif knows that Karin had set out from the lodge three days ago to hike with Erik. His brother had looked so buoyed as he'd prepared for the hike, checking the forecast, packing candles, good food, and a bottle of wine despite the extra weight. It was nice to see him happy for a change.

But now Karin is lying here.

Erik gone.

He registers something odd: where is her pack? He looks about. Maybe it went off the ledge, down into the river? If she'd rolled from the edge, there would be no trace she was ever here.

Alert to something being off, he examines her more closely now. A cold sensation spreads through his stomach as he notices the four heart-like bruises kissing the top of her left arm. His mouth feels papery as, next, he spots the crescents of dried blood beneath her fingernails.

His radio buzzes, startling him. He snaps it from his buckle, ready to speak to Knut. To tell him what he sees, what he hopes he is desperately wrong about: *This doesn't look like an accident.*

65

LIZ

Liz lurched on, currents of thought fizzing and jolting. A dizzying – almost vertiginous – sensation overtook her, as if the ground were shifting, loosening, sliding away.

She managed to stumble onward, legs trembling. Her breath was high and shallow in her chest.

She'd come so close to pushing Joni. There had been a beat where Liz's hands gripped her shoulders, and she'd wanted it – she'd wanted to see the moment Joni's feet left solid ground. Her stunned surprise, the windmill of her arms, the whoosh of air as she dropped.

Somehow, Liz had lowered her hands, stepped back. But it had been there – the fierce instinct to destroy.

The two women had stared at one another. Then Liz had said simply, 'We are done,' then turned and walked away.

She'd no idea how long she'd been walking – just feet pounding earth, blood pumping through her body – but now she finally ground to a stop. She planted her hands on her hips, her breath frayed.

She glanced around, turning on the spot. The damp breath of mist had thickened into fog. It made the world feel dreamlike and surreal, blurring the edges of the landscape, clouding the view. Visibility was down to only a few metres. She rubbed her brow, trying to get her bearings.

She searched for a red trail marker – but there were none. Had she come off the trail? She'd stormed away from Joni, not even thinking about the direction she was going in, and now the path had been swallowed.

Liz turned again, sweeping her gaze across the landscape. No sign of the cabin. All she could see was rock and boulder and earth and fog.

Her heart rate sped into a new, more urgent rhythm.

She stood very still, letting the situation digest. She had no phone, no food, no water – and had told no one where she was. Sit tight, she told herself, trying to quell the panic. Let the weather pass. Then the landscape would be revealed once again.

She lowered herself onto a boulder – then stood again, too agitated to be still. As she did, Liz thought she heard something.

Footsteps?

She listened closely.

Could hear the rhythmic tread of boots against earth.

'Hello!' she called instinctively into the fog.

The footsteps stopped.

'Hello?' she said again, tentative this time.

Then ahead of her, she could see the shape of someone emerging through the fog. As they approached, she recognised the gait, the shoulders, the thick legs pushed into boots. She lifted her hand, waved.

THE SEARCH

The call on the radio ends. Leif remains crouched on the mountain ledge, harness cutting into his thighs, staring at the radio. His heart thunders. His skin is cloaked in sweat.

He glances down at Karin, scared now. She is still, skin as pale as cloud.

Tension grinds through his jaw.

Erik, he thinks. *Oh, no. Erik.*

He pictures their mother, alone at the lodge, in poor health, waiting for her sons to return.

He tips his head back, teeth bared, wanting to yell until the mountain shakes. But there is no space for emotion here.

He drags in a breath, then he carefully manoeuvres himself closer to Karin. He places his hands beneath Karin's body, sliding one beneath her shoulders, the other beneath her thighs.

He tries not to breathe in the smell of her hair, or notice the softness of her skin.

His heart is pounding. His thoughts race and scream, but the one that cuts through is: *There's no choice.*

Then, with a surge of force, he heaves. His muscles strain, his core locks, he hears the grunt of exertion as he rolls Karin off the ledge, until there is nothing beneath his arms, except air.

311

He watches as her body falls. Tendrils of auburn hair flying in the wind. Arms opening as if she is waving a last goodbye. It is so long, and time has slowed, and he sees every detail acutely – the awful weightlessness of her body, the way she drops and drops. The silver river that lies below. He watches as her body hits the water and is swallowed whole. It is so far down that there is no sound. No splash. No ripple.

Leif stays very still, heart racing, wind licking at his neck.

He could take a step away to safety, but he remains on the edge, wind flattening his T-shirt against his chest.

The thoughts are slow to come. He's all body. Heart rate erratic, beating at the cage of his ribs. Hands trembling. Skin pulsing with energy and a strange cold heat.

He keeps staring, eyes wide and dry. There is nothing to see. She is gone.

He wants to cut the last sixty seconds out of his life, make a clean incision like a surgeon might remove a tumour.

But the thoughts start to rush in. Bjørn and Brit at home, glancing to the clock above their farmhouse table, wondering when Karin will be back.

Knut's team arriving on the mountainside soon.

The search beginning.

Every footstep to come, a lie.

66

LIZ

'Leif!' Liz called, the relief almost buckling her. 'Thank God! It is you!'

He appeared through the fog, pack on his shoulders, expression focused. He was wearing shorts, muscular legs pushed into hiking boots.

'You found us,' she said, voice shaken with disbelief. 'We didn't know anyone was looking! We lost everything in the landslide! And Maggie . . . she's hurt. We don't know how we'll get off the mountain.' She dragged in a breath, aware she was speaking too rapidly.

'It's okay,' Leif said, moving towards her. 'We will work it out, *ja*?'

She could feel herself on the edge of tears. She knew how she must look – hair wild and lank, face tear-stained, dirt beneath her nails. 'I can't find the cabin. The fog came in . . . I lost my bearings.'

'Where are the others?' Leif cut in. He shifted his weight from foot to foot. There was something distracted – almost edgy – about him that she'd missed at first.

'Joni's out here, somewhere. We . . . we . . . argued . . . I don't know where she is—'

'And the other two?' he asked, eyes darting around.

'Maggie and Helena – they were in the DNT cabin when I left. Still asleep. Your brother is there, too.'

His gaze shot to her face. 'Erik?'

She nodded.

His expression had changed, the skin around his mouth tightening, his eyes darting, unable to stay still.

'What's wrong?'

Leif glanced over his shoulder, and she saw a muscle working at his jaw. 'Where did Erik hike from? The beach? With you?'

She shook her head. 'No. He arrived late, after dark. I don't know where he came from. I think he was already on the mountain.'

He was silent, a sheen of sweat appearing on his forehead.

'Leif, what is it? Are my friends safe?'

His jaw sawed from side to side. He didn't answer.

Liz felt the damp press of the fog around her, chilling her skin.

Something wasn't right. The warm, friendly Leif she remembered when he'd joined them in the lodge bar was gone. Now there was something wary and unsettled about him that was beginning to scare her.

She needed to find her way back to the cabin; be with her friends.

Something electronic buzzed – and she watched Leif produce a radio from the outer pocket of his pack.

He answered it in Norwegian, turning away.

The person on the other end of the radio spoke in rapid fire, a sharpness to their tone.

'*Ja. Det er greit,*' Leif responded, glancing sideways at Liz.

A chill spread down her back.

'Who was that?' she asked, as Leif returned the radio to his pack.

'The rescue base.'

'Did you tell them you'd found me?'

He looked agitated, blinking rapidly. 'Yes,' he said, but there was something in his expression that told her he was lying.

'I want to get back to the cabin now.'

But Leif only stared at her, any final traces of warmth washing away.

She thought of Erik at the cabin with Helena and Maggie – and her out here, alone with Leif. Suddenly Liz didn't know if she was more afraid for her friends – or herself.

67

MAGGIE

Maggie peered through the cabin window. Outside, the fog had swallowed the visibility. She could no longer see the mountain peaks or ridge. It felt as if the cabin were floating in cloud, unanchored.

'They've been gone too long,' Maggie said.

'Something isn't right,' Helena agreed. 'I need to go and look for them.'

'No!' Maggie said, turning too quickly, a bolt of pain shooting down her ankle. 'Not on your own. It's too dangerous.'

From the corner of the cabin, Erik lifted his head, 'I'll go with you.'

Maggie and Helena looked at one another, both silently communicating the same question: *Can we trust Erik?*

A whole village didn't – and yet, his reaction to Karin's bracelet and the cocaine seemed genuine. She wanted to believe that he would help. She *needed* to believe it.

His dark eyes flicked between them, fingers moving to the tattoo on his neck, which he scratched distractedly.

Helena looked at him for a long moment, then nodded. 'Okay. Let's go then.'

'Are you sure?' Maggie asked, her head swimming with misgivings.

She nodded. Then Helena crossed to the cabin door, wincing as she pushed her feet into her hiking boots.

Erik, who'd been rummaging in his backpack, pulled something from it and tucked it within the pocket of his jacket.

'What was that?' Maggie asked, glimpsing something metal.

'Penknife,' he said. 'Better to be ready.'

For what? she thought, catching Helena's eye.

Helena moved towards Maggie, giving her a quick hug. 'We'll be back soon.'

Face pressed into Helena's hair, she whispered, 'Are you sure we can trust Erik?'

Helena, lips close to Maggie's ear, said, 'We only trust each other.' As Helena pulled away, she instructed in a normal voice, 'Lock the door behind us, okay?'

Maggie nodded.

She watched from the doorway as they walked away from the cabin, Erik's bare calves lean and muscular, Helena trying to keep stride, her trousers mud-streaked from the day before. The fog was so thick that it was only a matter of metres before their outlines grew fainter, eventually disappearing like spectres.

Maggie pulled the cabin door shut.

The silence was complete, disconcerting. She could hear nothing except her own heartbeat and the light mountain wind whispering outside.

She slid the bolt into place with a clunk.

68

JONI

Joni sat with her arms hugged to her knees, chin resting on them. She let the tears pour hot and salty down her cheeks.

Her bare legs were studded with goosebumps, but she didn't feel cold. She didn't feel anything except shame. It suffused her body, made her feel dirty from inside to out.

She replayed Liz's expression, wracked with pain, like Joni's admission had torn her open.

Liz, who she loved. Who was the one person who'd been there throughout everything. Who'd never abandoned her. Who was as solid as the rock she was sitting on.

And Joni had done that to her.

For what?

She pushed forward onto her hands and knees, crawling to the edge of the rock platform.

She peered over the edge and saw it down there – the bag of cocaine caught on the ledge. An hour earlier she'd tossed it away, feeling empowered and bold. Now she wanted it in her bloodstream, to blast far away from herself.

Could she climb down to the ledge? It looked almost vertical in places – but perhaps there were enough handholds and nooks.

And if she slipped?

Then it would all be over.

Her head spun as she looked down into nothingness. Hadn't she already lost it all?

Her best friend.

Patrick.

Helena and Maggie.

Her band.

Her career.

She'd made bad decision after bad decision. She pictured her own face glittering on screen, people cheering and hollering and wanting to be her.

But *she* didn't want to be her.

It was a mistake, Dublin. She knew it and Patrick knew it. He'd been released from family life for a night, and she represented all the things he'd missed: freedom and music and novelty and sex. And for Joni – who'd been living in a world of chaos and flux – being in Patrick's company was like finding land after being at sea.

Joni and Patrick . . . it wasn't love. Maybe she'd thought it had been, once. Not now. Joni cared about him deeply – loved him as a friend – but they both knew it would never be more than that. She'd called him when she'd arrived in Norway to say as much. Sleeping together was about trying on a life to see if it would fit. It wasn't Patrick she wanted – it was someone to love her the way he loved Liz.

She just wanted to be loved.

There it was. The raw, pathetic truth that ran beneath everything else.

She saw herself with a startling clarity. That wanting ran like a river beneath everything in her life. Her need to perform for people. To be seen on stage. Her name cheered. The applause and adulation were just another addiction.

319

Lucy Clarke

Tears dripped down her face as she pushed to her feet. She turned away from the edge, and began to walk, lost in her own wilderness.

69

LIZ

A cool, prickling sensation travelled across Liz's skin. As she stared at Leif's masked expression, it was like looking at a stranger.

'What's going on, Leif? Who was on the radio?'

He looked agitated, gaze jumping about. He ignored her question and asked his own. 'When you were on the beach sheltering from the storm, where did you go?'

'The caves,' she answered.

There was a tightening in Leif's jaw, a flicker of something travelling across his face.

A dawning, cold and stark, spread like a shiver across Liz's body: Leif was here for the cocaine.

She swallowed. Her expression must have given her away, as Leif's eyes narrowed. 'Where's the cocaine?' he demanded.

She thought of his kind, helpful manner at the lodge, how he'd sat with them and talked about their route. 'You?' she said, appalled.

He glanced over his shoulder. 'You weren't meant to get involved. No one was.'

'But you run the lodge. We trusted you—'

'Where is it?' he cut across her.

'If you didn't want us out on the trail, you could have told us to change routes!'

'The drop wasn't meant to happen when you were out here. You should've been safely back. No one should've been on the trail.' He rubbed the back of his neck. 'Where is the cocaine you stole?'

She shook her head. 'It's gone.'

He stepped closer. He was broad-chested, a head taller than her. His eyes were bright and dancing. She could see the similarity between Leif and Erik.

'Is Erik in on this? The two of you?'

Leif didn't answer. 'A kilo is missing. I need it back.'

Her thoughts felt scrambled and disorientated. If she tried to run, which direction would she go? Leif was fit, strong, fast. He knew these mountains. He'd be on her in a flash.

'We got rid of it,' she admitted.

His hands clenched into fists. 'Where?'

She thought of Joni throwing the cocaine from the pinnacle – the bag catching on a ledge. If she led Leif to it, would he let her go?

'Where?' he demanded, voice louder.

'There's a pinnacle near here. A few minutes' walk. A platform of rock sticks out. Joni threw the cocaine off there – but . . . but it snagged on a ledge below. You could climb down.'

He looked at her, fingers flexing at his sides as he came to a decision. 'Let's go.'

Leif moved silently at Liz's side. He was light-footed on the mountain terrain, only speaking to give a command as to the right direction.

The air felt heavy with moisture, her coat beaded silver, a fine mist caught in her loose hair.

He knew the pinnacle she was talking about – but once they

found it, then what? Would he try to climb down and retrieve the cocaine? He had a rope lashed to his pack and she guessed he was capable. Would that be her chance to run? The cabin wasn't far from there – but then what? Would he come after them?

Her head swam with uncertainties. And beneath all the clamour and fear, there was Patrick. Their children. Everything they'd grown over the years – a marriage, children, a life as a family; she could lose it all.

She swallowed, throat tight with emotion.

'There?' Leif barked. He was pointing to a jutting rock. Beneath it, the fog had swallowed the drop that fell away hundreds of metres into a river. 'This the place?'

She nodded. It was the same spot where she and Joni had been standing earlier.

'Show me,' he demanded.

Liz moved gingerly towards the rocky platform.

'It's down there,' she said, pointing. 'The fog! I can't see it now! But it's there. A ledge juts out . . . and it got caught.'

She felt the steely grip of Leif's fingers on her upper arm. 'Don't mess me around. People will get hurt unless I get that cocaine.'

'It's there, I promise you.'

He glared at her. His face was so unlike that of the man she'd met at the lodge, hard lines between his brows.

'Then,' he said, taking the ropes from his bag, 'you can climb down and fetch it.'

Leif pulled the rope tight around her waist, knotting it securely. 'There.'

Liz's legs were trembling. She shook her head. 'I can't do it! I've never climbed before!'

Leif ignored her.

'Crossing the ridge, I got vertigo. I can't do this! You . . . you could climb. I'll hold the rope.'

He shook his head. 'You'll run.'

He was right. She would. And they both knew it. The moment he went over that ledge, she'd be out of here.

'The rope will keep you secure. You just need to climb down. Start on this section here. It is not as steep.'

'What if I fall?'

'I'll have hold of the rope.' Leif was wearing a harness and he'd made a belay, attaching himself to the rock with a sling. 'You're secure. Now move.'

Blood crashed in her ears, thoughts splintering. She didn't want to go over that edge. 'If I get the cocaine,' she said, looking him directly in the eye, 'then what?'

Leif held her gaze. 'You walk out of here.'

She had no idea if he'd keep his word – but what choice did she have? She gulped down a breath, then began to move to the edge of the rocky platform. 'I don't know what I'm doing.'

'Turn around. Put your foot over the edge and find a hold. Then you start climbing down.'

She was shaking all over, pulse rocketing. She didn't want to take her feet off firm ground. He could untie the rope. He could leave her dangling there. She could get vertigo. Freeze.

'Now!' he instructed.

She moved to the edge, lowering onto her hands and knees. The rock was cold beneath her palms. She felt her stomach lift into her mouth as she eased her foot over the lip of the mountain.

70

LIZ

The rope tied at Liz's waist bit into her lower ribs. Panic roiled through her body as she descended. She could feel saliva slick in her throat.

The fog stole the view below, so it was as if she were going down into nothingness.

Her fingers were working hard, gripping onto nooks and edges to keep herself steady. She lowered her left foot, finding a strong hold for it, then her right. The tendons in her hands fired and strained, lactic acid building in her muscles.

Finding a secure spot to pause, she glanced up. My god! She couldn't even see Leif through the fog!

She felt as if she'd entered a terrifying, other realm – only connected to reality by the lifeline of a rope. She wanted to feel level ground beneath her. Panic was building hotly in her body. She fought to hold back its rising tide.

Her breath was coming too fast.

'Keep moving!' Leif shouted from somewhere above.

His instruction made her rush, and she was too hurried searching for the next place to put her feet; the spot she found wasn't secure enough. Standing only on the tips of her toes, she was taking too much weight in her hands. They were curled tight around a good hold, but she could feel them beginning to seize. She couldn't keep her grip!

She cried out as her fingers unpeeled from the rock.

The rope swung her sideways. Momentum propelled her into a steep section and she didn't have time to put out her hands fully – and her knee smashed into rock. She cried out at the burst of pain that bloomed, hot and instant.

The rock had caught her on the side of the knee, slicing into the soft part of the kneecap. Warm blood trailed down her shin, sliding into her hiking socks.

'What's happening?' Leif yelled.

She was clinging to the rope, dangling above her death. 'Pull me up!'

'Reach for the rock!' Leif yelled.

This is how I die, she thought. *This is it.*

Her mind was blank with terror.

'Reach for it, Liz!' he bellowed.

Both hands were clinging to the rope, but she was too terrified to let it go and trust in the knot at her waist.

'Do it! The rope is secure. You are safe,' he yelled, tugging at the rope, which jerked a little, shocking her out of her frozen fear.

She stretched out a hand and reached for the rocky wall, finding a solid nook to grip with her right hand. Then she reached with her left. There was a shallow step in the rockface, and she managed to place both boots on it. Her legs were trembling wildly, and her body was cloaked in cold sweat.

'Okay?' he called.

She flattened herself to the rockface, her breathing ragged, mind racing.

'Can you see it yet?'

He wouldn't let her up until she had the cocaine, she knew that. She took a breath and forced herself to look down.

The Hike

The bag of cocaine was caught on a prominent ledge just below where she was now standing. All she needed to do was take a sidestep, then somehow crouch down and pick it up.

'I can see it!' She dragged in a deep breath. 'Hold me steady.'

She waited for the swaying of the rope to settle. Her palms were sweating, muscles trembling. She set her toes against the rockface, then she stretched to her right. She could feel the side of her body elongating, ribs expanding, fingertips outstretched. Shit! She couldn't reach!

She tried again, grimacing as she stretched, the pain in her knee hot and throbbing.

'Got it?'

'Almost!'

She kept her feet against the rockface as she lowered another few centimetres. This time, when she stretched for it, her fingers met the bag.

There! As she lifted it, the weight in her already exhausted fingertips was too much. She could feel the bag beginning to slip.

She tightened her grip, making a fist of her hand around the top portion of the plastic, but her fingers were damp, the purchase too weak.

There was nothing she could do: the bag slid out of her grasp.

No . . . She watched as the cocaine fell, disappearing into the fog.

There was no sound of it landing. Just emptiness.

She clung onto the ledge. Hands empty.

Her breath fizzed in her chest.

From up above came Leif's voice. 'Got it?'

Her mouth turned dry. She looked at her empty hands.

What would Leif do now?

Would he let her back up? Or untie her rope?

Panic built again, tightening her throat.

Stay calm. Think.

'Liz?' he yelled. 'What's going on down there?'

Her hands moved frantically across the rockface, searching. She needed something large. Sharp.

Wedged into the wall, she found a hand-sized piece of rock, one of its edges sharpened into a point. With a surge of effort, she pulled it free.

'Got the cocaine?' he called again.

She pushed the rock deep into her jacket pocket.

'Yes!' she shouted.

Then she felt the tug of the rope, and Liz began the climb up.

71

HELENA

Erik led the way; Helena followed. They walked in silence. Her energy levels were sapped, but adrenalin kept her moving. The fog was thick and cold on the mountain top, and she zipped her coat to her chin.

She watched Erik, the placing of his boots, the tanned skin at the back of his calves, the dark tattoo at his neck. With every step she was hiking further from the safety of the cabin, from Maggie. But fear for Liz and Joni's whereabouts kept her moving.

She glanced over her shoulder, eager to keep the DNT cabin in sight, but it had already been lost to the fog. She returned her gaze to the trail, searching for landmarks to help her remember the route back, but all she could see was earth and rock and huge grey boulders.

They'd not gone far, when Erik put up a hand, stopping her.

She froze, listening.

For a moment, she could only hear the quiet breath of the breeze. Then came the scuff of a boot over earth, the lightest movement of rock.

They held still, listening.

There it was again. Another footstep.

Joni's? Liz's?

She opened her mouth to call for her friends, but Erik waved his hand, silencing her.

He was right: they didn't know who was out there.

They inched forward, peering ahead into the fog, waiting for their eyes to land on something familiar.

Gradually, a figure emerged on the mountain edge. Male. Wearing shorts and hiking boots. A backpack slouched on the floor beside him. He was holding a rope, paying it out slowly through his hands.

'Leif?' Erik said.

Leif's head snapped around.

Helena's first thought was – thank God! It's Leif! But immediately her senses grew alert. There was something startled and tense about his expression – the rapid blink, the way he looked down over the mountain, and then away.

Helena knew nothing about climbing – but she could guess that these weren't the conditions someone would favour. So what was Leif doing out here?

She glanced to Erik, assessing what he made of the situation.

His brow was furrowed as he stared right at Leif.

Then Helena stepped forward, peering into the misted abyss, asking, 'Who is down there?'

Leif didn't answer. He was wearing a harness, a rope in each hand, knees bent, braced, holding the rope steady in his hands.

'Leif?' Erik prompted.

His jaw was working hard, gaze flicking agitatedly between them and the mountain.

Helena leaned further over the edge, but still, the fog revealed nothing. 'Hello?' she shouted.

There was silence.

'Who is down there?' she called louder.

Then her name was returned to her: 'Helena? Is that you?'

Her stomach lurched. 'Liz! Oh my god! Are you hurt?

What's happened?' She swung around to face Leif. 'Pull her up!'

Leif didn't move.

Erik's eyes were wide, pinned to his brother.

Helena could hear a high, panicked sob coming from the end of the rope. Through the billowing fog, she briefly saw the top of Liz's head.

'I'm here!' Helena reassured her. 'We'll get you up!'

She turned to Leif. 'Pull Liz up – NOW!'

'I cannot!' Leif shouted, showing that he held the rope firm, but that it was not possible for him to heave her up with muscle power alone. 'She must climb!'

'Liz!' she called. 'You need to keep climbing, okay? I'm right here! Waiting for you! Just keep going!'

Slowly, Liz's form began to emerge. Her face was corpse-white, eyes wide with fear. A river of blood ran down one of her legs, soaking into her hiking sock.

'Not far now,' Helena said, encouraging her onward. 'Take it steady.'

Liz reached for another section. Helena could see the tremble in her arms as she pulled herself upwards, the rope only there as a safety line.

Liz was almost in reaching distance now.

Helena stretched an arm towards her. 'Here! Grab on!'

Liz adjusted her feet, pushing herself higher, her fingers letting go of the rock and reaching for Helena.

Their hands met. Liz gripped on tight as Helena helped guide her back onto the mountain top, while Leif held the rope steady.

'Thank God!' Helena said, the moment Liz was on firm ground.

Liz clung to her, her whole body shaking.

'You're safe now. I've got you.'

Liz's body shuddered in her grasp.

331

'It's okay, it's okay . . .' she repeated. She helped Liz untie the knotted rope at her waist, telling her, 'It's over now.'

Behind them, Erik was talking to his brother in rapid Norwegian, hands gesticulating wildly.

Leif didn't answer him – just stepped towards Liz and demanded, 'Where's the cocaine?'

She hunched into herself.

'Where is it, Liz?' Louder.

She shook her head. 'I don't have it.'

'You must!'

'I dropped it! I'm sorry—'

Erik was staring at his brother. His face had lost all its colour. '*Du?*' he said, voice quiet, laced with disbelief.

Leif looked back at him, blinking rapidly.

'No . . .' Erik said, hands rising, clasping the back of his orange beanie, elbows tight to his temples.

'Austin's been dropping drugs in the lobster pots,' Helena said, mind racing, 'and *you* have been picking them up, haven't you?'

'I didn't know about the cocaine. Not to start with,' Leif said. 'I was just helping Austin . . . with something.'

Erik's face was white. 'With what?'

'Austin wanted me to clean some money through the lodge. He needed a cash business. The lodge made sense – hikers and tourists passing through wanting rooms, food, drink. We needed the money. You know what the trade is like – slow as hell. Mum and Dad had run it into the ground. We needed the extra money to pay for the renovations. How else do you think I've afforded to keep it going? I couldn't let it go to ruin! It's our home!'

Helena remembered the way Leif had talked about the lodge in the bar on that first night. There'd been an intensity about him as he'd explained that it was everything to him.

Leif continued. 'The laundering was meant to be a one-off – but they wouldn't let me out, Erik. They keep wanting more and more from me. Not just the laundering – but getting involved in the cocaine.' His voice sounded desperate, weak enough to crack. 'They threatened me. Said they'd come after Mum.'

Erik's eyes widened. 'Austin threatened her?'

Leif shook his head. 'He's not the one running things.' He looked at Erik. 'It's his father.'

Erik blinked, a hand running over his face. 'Vilhelm?'

72

MAGGIE

Alone in the cabin, Maggie waited at the window. There was still no sign of her friends. The thickening fog snaked across the mountain, its damp breath pressing against the glass pane.

Hugging her arms to her chest, she worried about Helena. She was pregnant, without a phone or map, and with a man she didn't know if they could trust. The fast beat of her heart pushed adrenalin through her body, and she felt wired, alert.

She turned in her seat, glancing around the cabin. Yesterday evening, it had felt like a refuge, with the warmth of the fire, the flickering candlelight, the noodles eaten by the woodstove. But in the grey daylight, the cabin looked shabby, ash dusting the floor, the smeared window letting in little light, drifts of dead insects on the windowsill.

Her gaze fixed on the bolted door. She didn't want to go out there – but she'd been putting it off and now she needed to pee. Her ankle was throbbing dully, and each time she tested putting a little weight on it, a stabbing pain bit through her nerve endings, causing her to suck in a sharp breath.

She reached for the broom she'd been using as a makeshift crutch and pushed from her seat, hobbling across the cabin.

She listened at the door – and heard only the sound of her own breath. She unbolted it, and pulled it open a crack.

Fog curled around the cabin, obscuring the territory it stalked through, whole shoulders of mountain disappearing beneath white smoke.

Vilhelm's description of Blafjell as a *thin place* came to mind again. She limped through the fog, thinking about the divide between this world and another at its thinnest. She could feel a coldness in the air that had nothing to do with temperature.

She looked about her, suddenly uncertain that she was alone. Her head twisted left to right – but she could see no one.

'Hello?' she called tentatively into the fog.

There was only silence.

She turned and looked back over her shoulder. The fog was so thick now that if she walked another few metres, the cabin would be swallowed.

One by one her friends had left the cabin – and none of them had returned.

And now she was out here. Alone.

She couldn't lose sight of the cabin. She wanted to get back inside, lock the door. She'd light the fire, get it roaring – use the smoke as a signal to lead her friends back to her.

She pulled down her trousers and squatted awkwardly, her ankle unable to bear much weight. From the corner of her eye, she glimpsed a shadow moving in the distance.

Her skin chilled as she felt a shifting, dark energy close by. She heard a whisper of wind. She resettled her trousers hurriedly.

Through the fog, a shape emerged. It was too low to be human. She felt a scream stifled in her throat.

She began to move, rushing and hobbling towards the cabin, using the broom for support. Pain shot through her ankle.

She burst into the cabin, heart thumping.

335

The door swung closed behind her, and she bolted the lock with a loud clang. Then she stood there, palms pressed against the wooden door, panting.

A few moments passed – the silence of the cabin holding her in its spell so that all she could hear was the rise and fall of her own breath.

Then a cool, prickling sensation travelled across the back of her neck, spreading down her spine. For a moment, she held her breath, listening.

But the sound of an exhale, then inhale, continued.

Maggie turned.

Sitting in her seat beside the window was Vilhelm.

73

JONI

Joni stumbled on, exhausted. She was shivering hard, her teeth chattering with cold.

When she raised her head, she saw a solid structure emerging in the distance. At first, she thought it was just another boulder, large and square, but as the fog billowed, she made out the shape of the DNT cabin.

She imagined Liz was already inside, telling the others about what she'd done. She pictured Maggie's shock. Helena's outrage. They would band together, arms around Liz, protecting her.

There were a thousand things Joni needed to say to Liz – and they all began with the word *sorry*. The worst truth was that Joni's mistake didn't only affect Liz, and her marriage, but it would affect her children, too. The twins would feel the shock-waves because it would linger in the fabric of their home – and that would haunt Joni.

She wanted to turn, leave, but some deep instinct told her that alone she'd never make it off the mountain alive. She needed water, food, but mostly, she needed *them*.

As she sat there, sheltered in the lee of a boulder, she had to decide whether to keep walking or face them.

All Joni knew was, without her friends, she had nothing.

74

LIZ

The knowledge settled, slow and cool: Vilhelm was Austin's father, and he was running things.

It all made a terrible sort of sense. She began piecing it together, remembering Vilhelm sitting in the lodge on that first day when she'd walked in – not just a local watching the comings and goings of lodge life, but watching *Leif*. He'd been in the reception office, talking with Austin, his expression tense and preoccupied when he emerged.

She thought of Vilhelm warning them off Blafjell then, later still in the woods, trying to encourage them to turn back.

'Vilhelm's got a brother in Antwerp,' Leif said. 'He's been running an operation there for years. Vilhelm covers the transport into Norway, with Austin's help. That's why they bought Bjørn's boat. They wanted an established fishing outfit so that it didn't look suspicious – and needed Bjørn out of the way so that the bay was theirs.'

Erik stood mute, his thumb knuckle kneading his chin.

'I never wanted anything to do with the cocaine, I promise,' Leif said. 'But they won't let me walk.'

'If you've got nothing to do with the cocaine,' Liz said, 'why force me to climb down after it?'

Leif turned and met her gaze. 'Vilhelm radioed to say a kilo of cocaine had been taken by your group. He said I had to find it . . . before he found you.'

She saw the slow swallow of his throat and slight flare of his nostrils. Leif was afraid.

'Are Austin and Vilhelm out here, looking for us?' Liz asked.

'Not Austin – he's still on the boat making another delivery up the coast.'

'But Vilhelm?' Liz prompted.

Slowly, Leif nodded. His gaze lifted, scanning the mountain. 'He's out there.'

'Oh God,' Helena said, hands rising to her mouth. 'Maggie's at the cabin. Alone.'

75

MAGGIE

Maggie faced Vilhelm. The cabin was dim and airless. The faint scent of ash lingered, along with the smell of something animal brought in on his clothes.

Vilhelm was sitting with his arms folded across his chest, plaid shirt buttoned to his neck. He watched her with interest, the faintest smile on thin lips.

Maggie could feel the tick of her pulse in her throat. Even before he spoke, she understood. She could see his backpack at his feet – knew that it was bags of cocaine that caused it to strain at the buckles.

He unfolded his arms, setting his wide, filthy hands on his thighs. The wooden chair complained as he leaned forward. 'I told you to turn back,' Vilhelm said, tone disappointed. 'But you didn't listen.'

Her muscles stiffened.

'I even warned you about Blafjell.'

'Thin places . . . elementals . . .' she whispered. 'A lie.'

A cold smile. 'Maybe. Maybe not. Doesn't hurt for people to be unsure about what they see up here.'

All the time he had been playing them . . .

'But you ignored my warnings. You got involved in something

you shouldn't.' He shook his head, sighing a cold *tsk*. He pushed to his feet, unfolding the full height of him. 'Just like Karin did.'

Her blood ran cool.

'Now you and your friends have left a mess for me to clean up.'

Her scalp prickled. 'I don't have the cocaine. It's gone.'

He adjusted the peak of his cap. 'Now, that is a problem.'

76

HELENA

'I left Maggie in the cabin alone. Told her to lock the doors,' Helena said.

Liz's face was ashen. 'Joni's out on the trail, too.'

Turning to Leif, who had a radio clipped to the front of his pack, Helena said, 'You need to radio in. Call for help.'

Leif paused from undoing his harness. 'No.'

Helena baulked. 'Our friends are in danger!'

Erik's brow dipped. 'Leif? Give them the radio.'

'I cannot.'

'This is crazy!' Helena snapped. There was no time for bullshit – they needed to get back to Maggie and Joni. She snatched the radio from Leif's pack.

'Hey!' Leif lunged for it – but his climbing harness was still attached to the belay, and held him back. 'Give that to me!' he said, fighting to undo his harness.

Helena knew she needed to act fast. 'Liz!' she called. 'Run!'

Liz was on her feet in a flash.

'Stop!' Leif yelled after them.

Gripping the radio tightly, Helena's feet pounded the stony ground as she raced alongside Liz.

The cabin couldn't be far. If they could just get inside – lock the door – then they could figure out how to use the radio. Call for help.

Muscles burning, breath ragged, Helena drove herself forwards, trying to keep pace with Liz. Behind them, she could hear Leif's footsteps covering the ground at speed. She chanced a backwards glance.

He was coming!

'Hurry!' Liz yelled, grabbing Helena by the hand – and pulling her to keep up.

'Stop!' Leif yelled.

Fear ripped through her body, heart pounding wildly.

He was gaining on them! She caught the ragged draw of his breath.

Then she felt it: fingers against the collar of her jacket. They scraped – missed.

She took a step, and another, and then his hand reached again, this time gripping tight to the scruff of her jacket, yanking her backwards.

She tossed the radio to Liz. 'Run!' she yelled.

Liz caught the radio – and continued to run.

Leif looked as if he were going to give chase – but then changed his strategy. In a single movement, he manoeuvred his right arm around Helena's throat and, with his left hand, pulled a knife from his pocket.

Cold terror gripped her. 'Liz!'

Liz glanced back and – seeing the scene – stumbled to a stop, her face blanching.

Leif held Helena pinned to him, knife at her throat.

'Give me the radio,' Leif demanded of Liz.

'Don't!' Helena cried. 'Call mountain rescue! Get help.'

'Quiet!' Leif yelled, pressing the knife lightly to her throat so she could feel its cool blade.

Erik crashed forward, reaching them now. His eyes grew

wide at the sight of the knife. He yelled something in Nor-wegian, face tight with shock.

Leif ignored him. 'Give me the radio, Liz. Then I'll let her go.'

Liz stared back, blinking.

'Leif, this isn't you!' Erik protested, incredulous. 'What are you doing? Just let them use the radio.'

Helena could feel the heat of Leif's body against hers, the weight of muscle and contained energy. 'Mountain rescue won't send help,' Leif said breathlessly, his mouth hot at her ear. 'This thing – it is far bigger than you think.'

Erik's brow furrowed. 'What do you mean?' He pulled off his orange beanie, running an agitated hand over his scalp, before resettling the hat.

Helena sensed a quiver in Leif's hand as he held the knife to her skin: he was afraid.

Leif said, 'You call on that radio and you'll be put through to Knut – the rescue coordinator. He's in on it.'

Erik shook his head. 'What?'

'Knut's been working with Vilhelm for years. They used to move cocaine across the border from Sweden, but land patrols tightened. So now they use the sea – and the caves. It was only meant to be for a couple of drops – out of season when hikers weren't on the trail – but now they're scaling things up. If you radio in, Knut won't send a rescue team: he'll give your location to Vilhelm. Or the others. I don't know how far this thing stretches, or who we can trust.'

Helena could still feel the knife at her throat – the blade resting against the delicate gold chain of her horseshoe neck-lace.

Liz said, 'Then I won't radio Knut. I'll call someone else.'

'It's not a satellite phone. It's a mountain rescue radio. There is no one else.'

Liz glanced at the radio in her shaking hand, uncertain.

Leif shook his head. 'You should never have gone into the cave, taken their cocaine!'

'The cave,' Erik said, head snapping up. 'Cocaine wasn't the only thing in there. So was this.' He pulled something from his pocket. Karin's bracelet glittered as he held it up.

Leif stared at the bracelet, blinking.

Erik must have registered something in his brother's expression, as he said, 'Wait – you already knew?'

'No . . . I . . . well, I . . .' Leif stammered.

'You're lying!' Erik said, lunging towards Leif.

Leif took a small step back, dragging Helena with him, the knife pressing sharply against her neck.

Liz was glancing warily between the brothers, reading the escalating tension. Perhaps to keep Leif talking, she addressed him, saying, 'We're the ones who found Karin's bracelet in the cave. Did she know about the cocaine, too?'

'Yes. Karin found the cocaine,' he said, voice hoarse. 'Vilhelm realised – and went after her. Followed her up to Blafjell.'

Like us, Helena thought darkly. It must have been Vilhelm they'd seen going into the cave when they were ascending Blafjell.

'He found Karin out by the pinnacle. She'd taken off her pack and was sitting up there.' He paused. 'There's the river below. Vilhelm knew that.'

Erik's face turned pale. 'So her body would not be found.'

Leif nodded slowly.

'Did he push her?'

Helena heard Leif swallow.

Silence. And then: '*Ja.*'

Erik's hands shot to the back of his skull. His fingertips turned white with the pressure. He was gripping so hard, the skin stretched around his mountain tattoo, distorting it into broken peaks.

'I'm sorry,' Leif said.

Erik's head was shaking from side to side, energy burning off him. 'But . . . but those German hikers. They reported that they'd seen a woman out here – on the ledge below the pinnacle. They ran to the lodge, told you and others about what they'd seen. And you . . . you went out looking for her.'

'I didn't know it was Karin. Not when I went out searching.'

'You said you hiked to the pinnacle. Looked at the spot where they described seeing someone. You . . . you said the German hikers must have made a mistake. That it was just tarpaulin trapped between the rocks. That from a distance it could have looked like a woman.' His voice sounded small, vulnerable – a younger brother wanting to believe in his older brother. 'That's what you told me.'

A heavy, anguished silence ripped between them.

Erik was blinking rapidly. 'But it wasn't a mistake, was it? It was Karin!'

Leif dragged in a breath. 'Yes. It was Karin. When she fell, her body caught on a ledge. I abseiled down to her – but she was dead, Erik. It was too great a fall to survive.'

Erik was shaking his head in disbelief. 'You didn't tell me . . .'

'I couldn't . . .'

'Why not?' Erik demanded.

'While I was down there, Knut radioed.'

There was a quake in Leif's tone and Helena could feel his grip slackening. *Keep talking*, she thought.

Leif went on. 'Knut said that the rescue team were an hour away – and when they arrived, they mustn't find Karin's body.'

Erik turned completely still. He was staring at Leif, eyes narrowing. 'What did you do?'

'They would have killed me. Killed Mum! Come after you!' Leif's breathing was rapid, shallow.

Helena felt the pressure on her throat release further. His hand holding the knife lowered.

She waited a beat, then took a small, careful step to the side. She glanced back at Leif, but his attention was squarely on Erik. 'She was dead, Erik! She was already dead!' He gulped.

'What did you do?' Erik repeated more loudly, taking a step closer.

'I . . . I had no choice . . .' Leif said, holding up his palms. He let the knife drop from them, falling to the ground.

Erik grabbed Leif by the shoulders. 'What did you do?' he screamed into his face. He was shaking Leif now, as if trying to dislodge the answer.

Leif stumbled backwards, falling to the ground, Erik landing hard on top of him. 'I'm sorry . . .'

'Tell me!' Erik yelled, spittle flying from his mouth. From the corner of his eye, he spotted the discarded knife in the dirt. He grabbed it, holding it above Leif. 'What did you do to Karin!' he seethed between gritted teeth.

Lying in the dirt, tears leaked from Leif's eyes. He didn't try to fight.

Erik brought the knife blade slowly down, pressing the tip against Leif's chest, directly above his heart.

Leif dragged in a breath. He held Erik's gaze as he finally admitted, 'I . . . I pushed her body over the edge!'

Teeth bared, Erik let out a wild animal sound of despair and rage.

His hand holding the knife was shaking. 'Everyone thought you were the hero, going out there, searching for Karin. But you pushed her! You let everyone blame me for Karin's disappearance. The whole village. Everyone thinks I killed her!' His head was shaking rapidly from side to side. 'And *you* – my own brother – let them!'

Erik raised the knife.

347

Leif looked at Erik, then the knife, which was hovering above his heart. He swallowed. 'Do it,' he said, voice low, trembling.

Erik, mouth twisted into a howl of pain, plunged the knife downward.

Leif's eyes widened.

Erik slammed the blade deep into the earth, an inch from Leif's neck.

Slowly, Leif blinked.

No one spoke. The breeze curled around them, puffs of cold mist swirling and dispersing.

Erik dragged himself off his brother. He crawled towards a boulder and sat slumped against it, legs drawn towards his chest.

Leif pushed himself up to sitting. He was gulping in air, his face wet with tears. 'Erik, please . . . I'm so sorry.' His features had turned slack, as if the weight of what he'd done pulled them down, his face crumbling. 'I wanted to tell you . . . It has been killing me. I'm sorry for everything.' Leif crawled towards Erik, clamping his hands around Erik's head, pulling him close until their foreheads were touching. He held him firmly, looking his brother in the eye. 'I'm sorry, Erik. I will make this right.'

There was nothing but silence from Erik.

Helena glanced at Liz.

They both understood: they needed to get back to the others.

Together, they turned and ran.

77

MAGGIE

Vilhelm watched Maggie, a thin smile on his lips.

'Let's take a walk.'

Fear sliced through her, rooting her to the spot. Her pulse roared in her ears. No way of running. All she had was her voice. 'No.'

With a sigh, Vilhelm moved a hand to his waistband and withdrew a gun. He pointed it at her almost wearily, as if it saddened him that it had come to this. 'I said, walk.'

Maggie stared at the gun, blinking. *This can't be happening.*

Vilhelm raised the gun until it was level with her forehead.

She let out a whimpering sound, instinctively lifting her hands.

'Turn around and WALK.'

She did as he said, moving towards the door. 'My ankle . . .' she began, but was silenced by the cool nose of the gun pressing against the back of her skull.

She exited the cabin, hobbling. Each step was agony. Her vision wavered from the pain. The fog was beginning to thin, feathering away in places, so rising boulders punctured the scene.

'Move,' he commanded.

She heard her own whimpered cry as another bolt of pain burst down her ankle.

Dragging herself forward, Maggie noticed the same low, black shape emerging from the mist, which she'd seen earlier. It moved steadily towards them and, for a moment, she allowed herself to hope.

But it was only Vilhelm's dog, Runa, coat matted, pink tongue lolling. It came to her side, brushing close to her legs. Instinctively she lowered the back of her hand, feeling the dog's fur against it.

Vilhelm cussed at the dog, sending it away. It slunk low to its belly, ears flattening.

Maggie swallowed down her fear, senses fizzing and acute. She knew the course Vilhelm was setting: the mountain edge.

The gun nosed the back of her head.

'You're going to kill me?'

She heard the smile in Vilhelm's voice as he said, 'You're already dead.'

Her skin prickled icily.

'There will be reports of the landslide soon. Four British women buried alive as they slept. A tragedy.'

A cold, chilling sensation shivered across her neck, down the backs of her arms. Her stomach tightened; everyone would think they had been crushed beneath hundreds of tonnes of earth and rock.

No one would be looking for them.

Vilhelm could make them all disappear.

She swallowed the saliva pooling in her throat. He would push her over the edge, her body disappearing into the river below.

No evidence. No witnesses.

Just like he did to Karin. The thought landed like an echo.

'You killed Karin, didn't you?' she said.

'I did what I had to.'

350

She swallowed. 'You could have let her go!'

'Impossible. She would have talked. Austin, my son, he is a good boy – not the brightest, perhaps – but I couldn't have her ruining his life.'

'So you pushed her,' she whispered, desolate at the thought of Karin's body lost down there, undiscovered.

A quaking began deep within her body.

Behind them somewhere, she heard the low whine of Runa, a plaintive sound that swirled with the mist.

Her brain scrambled for what to do. There was a gun at her back, a mountain edge ahead, her ankle too damaged to run.

For a beat, everything stood still. She was no longer walking or thinking. There was another sense that she had no words for. It was a feeling that rose beyond the clamour of her fear, drew her out of her body, as if she'd stepped apart from herself and were watching.

She could see herself on the mountain edge – waves of auburn hair tangled over her shoulders, gaze lifted to the mist. Her hands were loose at her sides, freckles dusting the skin of her bare forearms. There was a silver bracelet on her wrist, beaded with letters. She looked down at it.

K-A-R-I-N.

Maggie wasn't seeing herself, but Karin. It was an echo. A palpitating, living memory that was here. Too ethereal to understand, so it could only be felt.

Thin places, she thought distantly. The narrow divide between this world and another.

She wasn't scared. She was comforted.

Then she felt Karin's voice deep within her body – as if Karin were speaking within her.

Fight, Maggie.

The words breathed steel into her muscles. She thought of Phoebe waiting for her at Aidan's. Of the long life they'd planned

351

together, filled with puddles and sunflowers and reading dens and sleep-warmed cheeks.

Then Karin was gone and it was just Maggie on the mountain edge.

She took another jerky step forward. As her strong leg set down on the ground, she swung around with unexpected ferocity – and roared. The sound was an explosion from deep in her body. Violent. Surging. Not fear, but rage and anger and violence and instinct. Her wolf-self rising, howling, roaring into Vilhelm's astonished face.

She harnessed the element of surprise, knocking the gun from his hand. She heard the clank of metal against stone as it landed. And then she was on him, using her fists, the hook of her thumbs, the claw of her fingernails.

The rush of noise and movement gave her an advantage. She gouged her thumbs into his eye sockets, and still she roared, lips peeled back, teeth bared. She brought her knee up hard and swift to his groin.

Vilhelm doubled over. She landed a punch on the side of his neck – and he fell to the ground with a grunt.

But he wasn't done. Vilhelm was crawling forward to where the gun lay.

She couldn't let him reach it! She tried to kick it further away – but as her foot connected, her bad ankle gave out and she stumbled, landing hard on her knees.

Vilhelm seized the advantage, scrambling to his feet. He snatched up the gun and, a moment later, there was a sudden burning pain at her scalp as he grabbed a fistful of hair, snapping her head up.

She scrabbled frantically, kicking, screaming.

Somewhere, the dog was barking.

Vilhelm booted her in the ribs, steel caps shocking the air from her lungs. He released her hair and she fell onto the earth, gasping.

352

The dog was frantic now, making high-pitched yelps.

Vilhelm yelled at it.

There was blood in her mouth. Dust in her nostrils. She curled into a ball to protect herself from the next blows, but they came anyway, another violent kick to her side that flipped her, rolling her closer to the mountain edge.

Above her, his rasped breathing.

She lay still, curled at his feet.

A gurgled whimper left her lungs. The fight gone.

78

JONI

Joni stared at the cabin. She couldn't do it. Couldn't go in there and face her friends.

She dropped her head, turned, began walking away.

Then, behind her, she heard the cabin door open. She halted, glancing over her shoulder.

Maggie stepped out, Vilhelm behind her.

It took Joni several long moments to understand what she was seeing: the gun at Maggie's head, Vilhelm directing her towards the mountain edge.

Then it all began to make an awful, sudden sense: it had been Vilhelm who'd been out here to collect the cocaine; Vilhelm who'd found some missing from the cave; Vilhelm who'd been tracking them, hunting them.

Pulse racing, Joni ducked behind a boulder, keeping out of sight. If she yelled for him to let Maggie go, Vilhelm would turn the gun on her. She needed to think. Be smart.

Her mouth was dry. She could hear the thunder of blood in her ears.

Think!

She glanced about frantically, thoughts ricocheting in desperation. Then she looked towards the cabin . . . an idea emerging.

She'd need to be fast.

Staying low, she began to move, keeping obscured behind boulders where possible. She crept silently towards the cabin, Vilhelm moving in the opposite direction.

Damn! His dog had seen her! Runa came loping towards her, tail wagging.

Vilhelm hadn't noticed – kept leading Maggie towards the mountain edge. Joni rubbed the dog briefly behind the ears to keep him quiet, then made for the cabin.

She pushed open the door and it took her eyes a moment to adjust to the dimness.

Where is it?

She scanned the space, heartbeat racing.

Then her gaze landed on it: Vilhelm's pack.

She rushed forward, unclipping the buckles.

There! Just as she'd hoped, she saw bag upon bag of cocaine.

From outside, there came a sudden burst of noise. A wild roar, feral and rageful.

Maggie?

Without hesitating, Joni swung the heavy pack onto her shoulder – and then she was running, pushing out of the cabin, following the sound, feet pounding earth.

She could see Maggie and Vilhelm on the mountain edge. Maggie was reaching for something – the gun? – and then just as suddenly she was no longer upright but crashing to the ground. The dog had run towards them and was barking, frantic now.

She heard the blow of a boot connecting with a body.

A cry of pain.

Then she saw Vilhelm's tall, rangy frame, towering over Maggie.

Maggie was curled into herself. She was so close to the edge. One more kick could send her over.

Joni thundered towards them, sliding to a halt a few paces away. 'Don't touch her!' she screamed.

The barking stopped.

Vilhelm turned, startled. The gun swung to her.

With both hands she raised his pack high into the air, holding it above the drop.

'Bitch!'

Maggie lifted her head an inch, looking at Joni through a curtain of tangled hair. There was blood dripping from her lip. When her gaze managed to focus on Joni, her eyes crinkled with hope.

Maggie trusted her. Believed in her.

Vilhelm, head jerking towards Joni, snarled, 'Put the bag down, or I kill her!'

Joni knew how to command attention. How to make sure everyone in the room kept their eyes on her. How to be the star of the show. Chin lifted, voice drawn deep from her diaphragm, she told him, 'Touch her again and the cocaine goes!'

'You know I could shoot you?' Vilhelm growled.

Joni nodded. 'And then the cocaine goes over with me.'

He pushed his tongue between his top teeth and lip.

From the west of the mountain, she saw two figures emerging in the mist. They were rushing along the trail, shoulder to shoulder. Liz and Helena.

Liz looked pale and shaken, blood staining her lower leg, Helena at her side, face flushed. Their eyes widened as they absorbed the sight of Vilhelm on the mountain top, gun in hand, Maggie curled at his feet.

'My god! Maggie!' Helena said, rushing forward.

Vilhelm spun around, redirecting the gun at Helena. 'Don't move! Any of you!'

Helena stopped, hands raised.

Vilhelm was blinking quickly, his mouth hanging open, losing control of the situation. Joni needed him to remain calm – not do anything rash.

She was still holding the backpack above the drop into nothingness. The weight was causing her muscles to tremble. She couldn't hold it like this for much longer.

'Step back from Maggie,' Joni commanded Vilhelm. 'Then throw the gun over the edge – and you can have your cocaine.'

He turned, glaring at her, gun swinging in her direction. His finger was on the trigger. He pulled his lips over his teeth, thinking. Then he looked down at Maggie. After several long seconds, he grunted in concession – and took a step away from her.

'Maggie,' she said calmly. 'Crawl away from the edge, okay? Go to Liz and Helena.'

Maggie's head lifted fractionally, and then she heaved onto all fours, dragging herself towards the other two. Vilhelm's dog slunk on its belly towards Maggie, nosing her gently. When she reached Liz and Helena, they helped Maggie to her feet, holding her close.

'Now toss the gun,' Joni instructed.

Vilhelm looked at her narrowly, gun still pointed at her face. His finger twitched on the trigger.

The mountain top was silent.

She felt the burn of lactic acid in her muscles, arms shaking. She was going to drop the cocaine.

Finally, Vilhelm lowered the gun, muttering something beneath his breath, before tossing it over the edge. She watched the black weapon spin through the air, before dropping into nothingness.

'Now give me the cocaine!' Vilhelm yelled.

'I will, and when I do, you will leave this mountain. You will not harm any of us. You will pretend we have never met. We will do the same.' She was staring hard at him. 'Okay?'

His eyes were on the pack, not her. 'Fine,' he agreed. But she saw it in the slight curl of his lip, the narrowing of his gaze – and knew he was lying. The moment Vilhelm had the cocaine, he would turn, come for them. She would fight hard. Maybe she could land a few punches, get lucky, take him. Maybe not. And if not, then he'd go after the others. Maggie was badly injured, couldn't run. Helena was pregnant and she couldn't risk a blow to her middle. Liz looked exhausted, deeply shaken.

Vilhelm took a step towards her. 'Hand it to me.'

Her arms jerked beneath the weight of the pack. Kilos of cocaine – all that powdered glitter that was never gold but rot, pulling people out of themselves, promising something better that was only ever an illusion.

In her peripheral vision, she could see her friends huddled together, watching.

Then Joni noticed what she'd missed: there was a knife pressed into Vilhelm's trouser pocket. She could see the dark handle of it exposed at the top. All it would take was one quick movement.

Vilhelm took another step closer.

In a song, the most powerful note is silence. That moment of pause is when the meaning is communicated. She felt it now in the silence as she turned her gaze fully to meet Liz's. Joni was silently communicating – apologising for all the ways she'd failed her, telling her all the ways she'd loved her.

Then her gaze was back on Vilhelm as the music in her head began to play.

Vilhelm reached for the pack and, as he did so, with a surge of force, Joni launched it over the edge. In that moment – as Vilhelm's fingers were outstretched for the pack – that's when Joni took her chance.

She shoved Vilhelm hard in the side. Her palms met rib and flesh. She slammed the full weight of herself against him, and felt him starting to unbalance, to tip towards the edge.

As he staggered, he twisted, arms flailing desperately. He reached out, fingertips opening – and then sealing around Joni's wrist.

She felt the jolt in her shoulder socket as her arm was yanked hard, feet unbalancing, weight shifting, body tipping.

She heard her own gasp.

She had known the risk. By taking out Vilhelm, she was keeping her friends safe. They had families. Lives to go home to. They had each other. Joni wouldn't let all that be destroyed.

The wheel of time ran slow.

She felt her feet unpeeling from the edge, the burn of hard, bony fingers against her wrist, the brush of wind filling her jacket as she went over the edge.

There was mist and the wild drop beneath.

She closed her eyes. She was on stage, the crowd waiting below, eyes on her, a sea of hands raised to catch her.

She heard her name being screamed for the final time.

79

LIZ

'Joni!' Liz screamed.

She ran towards the space where Joni had been standing, an explosion of adrenalin ripping through her.

Sliding to a halt on the mountain edge, she stared into the emptiness below. Just rock and a silver stretch of water too distant to ripple.

'No! No! No!' she wailed, head shaking from side to side.

This can't be happening.

She jammed a fist against her mouth, backing away.

Helena was standing near her shoulder, face white, mouth slack.

Liz clutched her arm. 'Where is she?' Liz begged. 'Where's Joni?'

Helena blinked rapidly.

'WHERE IS JONI?' Liz yelled again.

'She . . . went over the edge,' Helena said, voice grated by disbelief.

'We need to get to her! Help her!' Liz was shouting, pacing the edge, looking for a route.

'There's no way down,' Helena said.

'We need to do something! Call someone!' She was desperate,

her voice unspooling. A deep, cold pressure was expanding inside her. 'Joni is down there!'

Helena looked Liz in the eye, head shaking slowly. 'No one could survive that.'

She thought of her and Joni's last conversation, hours earlier, standing on a rocky platform, her hands gripped to Joni's shoulders. She'd wanted to push her – wanted her out of her life.

And now she . . . she was . . .

'Joni's dead . . .' Liz gasped at last, understanding.

Her stomach pitched, hot and liquid. She leaned forward, hands braced on her thighs as she vomited across the hard earth.

She crouched there, heaving breath in and out of her body. Wretched, broken. Tears streaming down her face.

Helena moved to her side, a hand on her back.

Maggie dragged herself towards them. Her hair was tangled and wild. Her right eye was already beginning to swell. Her lip had split, the blood drying down her chin. She stood on the other side of Liz, holding her tight.

Bleeding and battered, faces streaked with salt and blood and earth, they clung together.

Three where there should be four.

AFTERWARDS

80

HELENA

Helena strode out in front, hiking boots beating a clean route on the clifftop trail. The sun glimmered off a flat sea, the ground soft and covered with the purple tips of heather.

A light sheen of sweat cloaked her forehead, and she hooked her thumbs beneath the straps of her pack, adjusting them to release the full weight for a moment.

She reached a widening in the trail and paused, waiting for the others. She took a moment to drink in the view. The South West Coast Path had none of the mountainous peaks of Norway, but there was a wild beauty to the rolling hills and soaring cliffs, the sea always at her shoulder.

She'd discovered an uncomplicated pleasure in walking. It took her out of her own head, made her look up from a screen and, in the weeks after losing Joni, it was the only thing that seemed to make any sense.

Liz had tried explaining the science of why walking healed – something to do with decreasing activity in the part of the brain responsible for negative thoughts and rumination, instead activating a rest and digest mode – but Helena didn't need to understand the science. She just needed to walk.

So that's what they did. The three of them. They met whenever they could and, walk by walk, they were weaving their way along the South West Coast Path. It seemed fitting – a tribute to Joni – that they would do this together, step by step.

The media had gone crazy when the news of Joni's death broke. All over the world, Joni Gold fans mourned. There was a shrine at her favourite concert hall in London. People posted tributes across social media. Her face seemed to be on every other magazine cover. Her latest album stayed at number one for seven weeks. Kai, her manager, who'd conveniently forgotten about his vengeful attitude to Joni, told the world that she was the love of his life. The video that Helena had recorded at the lodge was the final live recording of Joni, and now had over twenty million views.

For a time, Helena didn't turn on the news or radio or buy a magazine – everything too much of a trigger. She stayed home from work. She kept herself closed off, experiencing a cruel double slam of grief as she mourned Joni's death, and her mother's death afresh, like one grief had unearthed the other.

It had been hard for all of them leaving Joni's body behind on Blafjell. With Maggie supported between her and Liz, they'd struggled down the mountain, Runa following at their heels. They'd barely spoken on the descent, the horror too fresh, or the words too many to know which to reach for first. She recalled her relief as the mountain finally softened into forest, and then came the first glimpse of the lake – wide and still; a blue gem in a clasp of trees – with the lodge waiting at its end.

Now Liz and Maggie reached her side. Liz looked brighter this weekend, a little fuller in the face. She'd taken Joni's death the hardest, her grief wrapped so tightly around Patrick and Joni's betrayal that it was hard to separate one from the other.

Helena asked, 'What's Patrick up to this weekend?'

'Planting fruit trees with the twins.'

'Course he is,' she said with warmth. 'You two still doing your date walks?'

Liz nodded. 'It's easier to talk when we're out of the house. Moving.' She had explained before that date walks were like date nights, except on foot: a bottle of wine shared as they meandered along the banks of the Stour, or a moonlit hike across the hills around their village.

'How are things?' Helena asked.

Liz lifted and dropped her shoulders. 'There are rough days when I still feel so mad at him. But we have good days too, when we're happy, really happy – like we know how close we came to losing each other and it's made everything more present. Anyway,' she said, rolling back her shoulders to signal a subject change, 'how's your new backpack?'

'Best one I've ever carried,' Helena answered with a grin, reaching a hand behind her and feeling along the base of the pack until her fingers met with a tiny, warm foot. 'Still sleeping?'

Maggie, who was wearing red leggings with sunflower-yellow socks pulled above her boots, pushed onto her tiptoes to peer into the backpack carrier. 'Yup, he is.'

Freddie was seven months old now, a placid little being born with a shock of dark hair, and bright green eyes that were a gift from his grandmother. There was a calming, quiet wisdom about his features, and some days Helena would lie beside him, staring into those glittering eyes like he held the answer to every question she'd ever had.

Other days there wasn't much lying down at all. There was sterilising bottles, lugging car seats, pureeing food, and trying to remember to eat something herself. And somewhere – skirting the edges of her days as a mother – there was her work. She was still adjusting to the rhythm and demands of motherhood and this new version of herself, but she was enjoying the journey.

She remembered waking in the mountain cabin all those

months ago, nauseous and grief-stricken, consumed by the knowledge that she'd never again be loved the way her mother had once loved her.

Now she understood that her mother's love didn't end with her death. She felt the evidence each day – when she sang to Freddie, discovering the words of a lullaby she didn't realise she knew, or the way she'd cradle him to her body, making a low shushing sound, like her mother must have once done to her.

Losing her mother – and then Joni – forced Helena to see that life was short. As she stood beside Liz and Maggie, the warm weight of her son on her back, she knew it was time to start living.

81

MAGGIE

Maggie strode along the clifftop path, pleased to notice that she wasn't out of breath. She felt fitter than she had done in years.

Phoebe was staying with Aidan for the weekend. A monthly two-night visit was the routine they'd settled upon and, although Maggie still dreaded their goodbyes, she was also enjoying having some time for herself.

She'd finally cleared out the shed, painting it a bright pop of cobalt blue, throwing down a hessian mat, adding pot plants, and tacking favourite prints and postcards to the walls. She'd bought an old wooden desk where her flower presses and canvases were set up. Her Etsy shop was thriving and, when she wasn't fulfilling orders, she managed to carve out a little space simply to paint. Last month, on one of Aidan's weekends, she'd finally opened the beautiful set of acrylics Joni had gifted her. As she'd lifted her brush to the fresh white space of her canvas, she could hear Joni's voice: *Stay you. Always create.*

Ahead on the trail, two young men were walking in the opposite direction, climbing ropes lashed to their packs. They waved in greeting as they passed, and the sight of them drew Maggie's thoughts to Blafjell.

'I heard from Erik earlier this week,' she told the others.

They emailed one another occasionally. It was an unexpected, gentle friendship, that had surprised them both. It had begun when Maggie had been in touch to find out who was caring for Vilhelm's dog. *I'm looking after Runa for now*, Erik had emailed back. *He's the lodge dog, happy to be fed twice what he ought to be by my mother*. Then, gradually, they'd begun communicating about other things, too. Erik often wanted to write about Karin – and Maggie was happy to respond, feeling a connection to her that was hard to articulate to anyone else.

'How is he?' Helena asked.

'He said the snows have arrived early this year. The lodge has been quiet – but they're getting by.' He was running the place in Leif's absence, and also looking after his mother. 'He said Leif gets out of prison soon.'

Leif had been given a reduced sentence for his role in things. Devastated by what he'd done, and how Vilhelm's hold had been rotting their community, Leif handed himself in and provided the police with evidence that had led to one of the largest seizures of cocaine in Norway's history, and the dismantling of a drugs ring that had a decade-long reign.

'Do you think Leif will return to the lodge?' Liz asked.

Maggie had wondered that, too. 'It's home. I don't think he can lose it.'

Helena asked, 'Did Erik mention Austin?'

'Not this time.' Austin had been sent to a prison in Oslo. Apparently he had been shown some leniency by the judge because of the years of systematic coercive control he'd suffered from Vilhelm.

So much darkness hidden within all that wild beauty, Maggie thought as they walked quietly, each lost to her own thoughts.

After a time, Liz turned towards the water and said, 'Look!' She was pointing towards the faint scratch of a path cutting down towards the sea.

The Hike

Maggie turned, remembering that first glimpse of the crystal-clear bay in Norway, glistening between the mountains. Joni had bounded down the switchbacks, whooping and hooting, peeling off her clothes, and rushing straight for the icy kiss of the sea. She had always lived hard and fast and boldly.

Warmed by the memory, Maggie said to the others: 'Let's go down!'

She led the way and when her hiking boots met the sand, she helped Helena take the carrier off her shoulders, Freddie still fast asleep as they propped him carefully in the shade.

Maggie remembered hesitating on that Norwegian beach, worrying about her stretchmarks and the extra weight at her middle, while the others called to her from the water. But those worries felt distant, because what did any of it matter? She had new scars now – some you could see, others you couldn't – but she had survived. She was here. Alive.

She felt a fizz of adrenalin in her body as she began to unlace her boots. She peeled off her leggings, stripped off her underwear, and, without a beat of pause, ran towards the sea.

82

LIZ

Liz hadn't joined the others for a swim. She paddled barefoot in the shallows, alone, salt water lapping coolly at her ankles.

The last time she'd swum in the sea, Joni had been with her. She pictured the arctic blue waters, Joni swimming over to her, dark hair slicked back, eyes glittering. She had reached for Liz's hand, their wet fingers entwining, as she'd thanked her for organising the hike, saying, 'We came for this.' Joni's *this* had been that golden moment: the four of them, together, in the ocean.

Liz dipped her hand into the clear water, reaching for a shell. She turned it over in her palm, examining the sunburst of ridges and smooth interior. Then she carried it to the shoreline, carefully placing the shell in the pattern she'd created, pressing its salt-damp surface into the sand.

'You didn't fancy the swim?' Maggie asked, approaching, wet hair dripping down her shoulders.

Helena had reinstated Freddie on her back and joined them, too.

'Not this time,' Liz said, quietly.

Maggie looked down, her gaze registering the pattern of shells and pebbles that Liz had arranged. Cockles, razor clams, and limpet shells weaved together to form letters that stretched across a metre of beach.

J O N I   G O L D

Maggie smiled, eyes misting. 'It's beautiful.'

'I dreamed about her last night,' Helena said quietly. 'I often do. The mountain. That night in the cabin. Walking over the ridge. The thunderstorm. All of it.' She rubbed her arms as if she were cold.

Liz dreamt about her, too. Sometimes she'd wake in a cold sweat from a recurring nightmare. In it, she was standing on that pinnacle edge, heart splintered with rage, hands gripping Joni's shoulders. Only, in the nightmare, Liz didn't step back: she pushed. And as Joni fell, eyes widening with terror, Joni cried out, 'You wanted me dead!' That's when Liz would wake, breathless, disorientated – reaching for Patrick, the light.

Other times though, the dreams were good. That was what she tried to hold onto. Joni singing to a beaming crowd in the lodge. Chocolate shared around a campfire. The lush green grass at her ankles as she strode out beneath a blue sky.

Tears leaked from her eyes.

'Liz?' Maggie asked, placing a hand on her arm.

'I still can't get my head around it. How are we here, and she's not?'

'I know . . .' Maggie said gently.

'The hike – it was my idea. If I hadn't suggested it, Joni would still be alive. I feel so guilty.' She shook her head. Swallowed. 'But . . . but I also feel angry! So fucking furious with her! She did the very worst thing to me – *she slept with Patrick!*' Liz kicked the display of shells, scattering them across the shore, leaving a darkened gouge in the sand.

'But then she followed it by doing the most selfless thing of all.' She looked at her friends. 'Joni died for us. And I don't know how I'm meant to feel.'

After a time, Maggie said quietly, 'There is no *meant to* when it comes to feelings. You feel what you feel.'

'I miss her. That's what I feel,' she said, tears rolling freely now. 'I miss everything about her. I miss her laugh. I miss how impulsive she was. I miss the version of myself I was when I was with her. I miss the way she'd walk into a room and the energy would change. I miss smoking together. I miss her drama and light and lust for life. I miss her *so* much!' She covered her face with her hands as her body was wracked with sobs. 'And if it hadn't been for me, she'd still be here.'

'You're right about one thing,' Helena said. 'Joni died for us. And that's why we're not going to stand here and beat ourselves up or waste time feeling guilty. I could kick myself for all the awful things I said to Joni on that hike – holding her to account over my mother's funeral. Sharing that video. Grilling her over the cocaine – but where is the good in that? I've wrestled with those demons – turns out there's a lot of time for that when you're up half the night feeding – and you know what I've realised? Joni wouldn't want that. She'd want us to start living. Like she did. In the moment. Fast and hard and bright and fully.'

Liz wiped her face, nodding through her tears. Helena was right.

Freddie, strapped in the backpack, started to whine.

'We're trying to have a moment down here,' Helena said, reaching back to gently squeeze his toes.

Undeterred, Freddie continued to grizzle, little fists pumping in agitation.

'Looks like it's time to move,' Maggie said.

'Start walking. I'll catch you up,' Liz said, who was still barefoot.

She pulled on her socks, then pushed her sand-dusted feet into her hiking boots, thumbs brushing over the worn leather.

She paused for a moment, noticing how the heels were beginning to wear down and one of the eyelets was coming loose. Her boots were tired, sun-faded, and dusted with fragments of soil and sand and mountain dust. She'd walked in rain and mist and sunshine. She'd walked in pain and in happiness. She'd walked to get somewhere, and to leave another place. But she would always walk.

If the mountains had taught Liz anything, it was that the journey was never about reaching the peak. You climbed – and kept climbing – to push through the struggle and experience the glimpses of beauty along the way. For how the climb made you *feel*.

Before leaving the beach, Liz repaired the pattern of shells, so that Joni's name remained by the sea. She stole a final look at it, then turned and jogged after the others.

Maggie was walking at Helena's side, the two of them humming a light tune to soothe Freddie. The path was wide enough for Liz to join them. The lullaby they were humming was familiar and calming. Freddie's murmurs quietened, his fingers softening.

Then Liz realised: the song was familiar not because it was a lullaby, but because it was one of Joni's.

The corners of her lips turned up as she began to hum too, the vibration of the notes sending a ripple of pleasure through her body. She could feel the music inside her, easing her muscles, releasing tension in her shoulders.

She looked ahead to where their path flowed across a clifftop gilded by lowering sun, and she felt Joni's presence somewhere in that light, watching: the three of them, her music on their lips, taking one step after the other, and continuing to walk.

Author's Note

In *The Hike*, I chose to fictionalise the location of the Svelle trail and Blafjell mountain as I wanted to give Liz, Joni, Maggie, and Helena full artistic licence to lace up their hiking boots and make the adventure their own.

Acknowledgements

Thank you to my agent Judith Murray, my editor Charlotte Brabbin, and my publisher Kim Young – three brilliant, strong women, who've supported and championed me on every step of this writing journey. Thank you for encouraging me to ride forward in my career in a way that is important to me, striving to find balance with writing, adventuring, and family life.

Thank you to the wider team in the UK, which includes Kate Rizzo at Greene & Heaton, who does an incredible job of handling my foreign rights, and Jane Villiers at Sayle Screen, who has brought my TV and film dreams to life.

Thank you to the whole publishing team at HarperCollins in the UK, particularly Susanna Peden in publicity; Hannah O'Brien, Sarah Shea and Maddy Marshall in marketing; Sarah Munro and Izzy Coburn in UK sales; Alice Gomer in international sales; and Claire Ward in cover design.

Thank you to my US team, in particular my agent Grainne Fox at Fletcher & Co, and editor Danielle Dietrich at Putnam Books for your insightful editorial input, and for making it feel like there's not an ocean between us.

Thank you to Mimi Hall for walking shoulder to shoulder

with me through every draft of this book. Our daily voice-note habit and beach-side writing retreats are the gold in all of this.

Thank you to my early readers, who include Faye Buchanan, Laura Crossley and Becki Hunter.

Thank you to Alan James of UKClimbing.com for his expertise on all manner of things mountains and climbing. I'm so grateful for your help in navigating the technical areas. All mistakes are my own.

Thank you to Jorid Matthiessen at Strawberry Publishing for helping with the Norwegian language elements. It was wonderful to have your input.

Thank you to the booksellers, bookstagrammers, librarians, bloggers, and festival organisers who share and champion our books with such passion. It is so appreciated.

Thank you to my friends – beach and beyond – who stay at the bar longer than me on my book launches and cheer me along when the going gets tough. A big shout out to Alice Flynn, the original wild hike buddy!

Thank you to my family, Jane Clarke, Tony Clarke, Matt Clarke, Audrey Smith, Theresa Allan, and Philip Allan – all of whom support my writing in every form.

Thank you to my husband, James, for joining me on a research mission to Norway, where we hiked and hiked, discovering empty mountain cabins, wave-bounded coastline, streaming waterfalls, and the first snows. We dined on camp stove noodles, and no food has ever tasted better. Thanks for being an easy-going travel buddy, and for always carrying more than your share of the gear.

Thank you to my children, Tommy and Darcy, for putting the *wild* in wild hiking. Well done for walking ten miles a day on the South West Coast Path, carrying your own packs, and not complaining when the overnight temperature dropped to five degrees and all you had was a summer sleeping bag with a broken zip! You are my heroes.